A MODEST PROPOSAL
AND OTHER SATIRES

JONATHAN SWIFT

A MODEST PROPOSAL

AND OTHER SATIRES

🔖 Notes (on pp. 233 to 251)
are keyed thus in the margin

© 1997 for this edition
Könemann Verlagsgesellschaft mbH
Bonner Straße 126, D–50968 Köln

Series and volume editor: Michael Hulse
Cover design: Peter Feierabend
Layout and typesetting: Birgit Beyer
Printed in Hungary
ISBN 3-89508-688-6

CONTENTS

A
TALE
OF A
TUB.

Written for the Univerſal Improve
ment of Mankind.

Diu multumque deſideratum

To which is added,

An ACCOUNT of a
BATTEL
BETWEEN THE
Antient and Modern BOOKS
in St. *James's* Library.

Baſima eacabaſa eanaa irrauriſta, diarba da caeo-
taba fobor camelanthi. *Iren. Lib* 1 *C.* 18.

———— *Juvatque novos decerpere flores,*
Inſignemque meo capiti petere inde coronam,
Unde prius nulli velarunt tempora Muſæ Lucret.

LONDON.
Printed for *John Nutt,* near *Stationers-Hall.*
MDCCIV.

A TALE OF A TUB

Treatises written by the same author, most of them mentioned in the following Discourses; which will be speedily published.

A Character of the present Set of Wits in this Island.

A panegyrical Essay upon the Number Three.

A Dissertation upon the principal Productions of Grub-street.

Lectures upon a Dissection of Human Nature.

A Panegyric upon the World.

An analytical Discourse upon Zeal, *histori-theophysiologically* considered.

A general History of Ears.

A modest Defence of the Proceedings of the Rabble in all ages.

A Description of the Kingdom of Absurdities.

A Voyage into England, by a Person of Quality in *terra australis incognita*, translated from the Original.

A critical Essay upon the Art of Canting philosophically, physically, and musically considered.

AN APOLOGY FOR THE, &c.

If good and ill nature equally operated upon mankind, I might have saved myself the trouble of this apology; for it is manifest by the reception the following discourse has met with, that those who approve it are a great majority among the men of taste; yet there have been two or three treatises written expressly against it, beside many others that have flirted at it occasionally, without one syllable having been ever published in its defence, or even quotation to its advantage that I can remember, except by the polite author of a late discourse between a Deist and a Socinian.

Therefore, since the book seems calculated to live, at least as long as our language and our taste admit no great alterations, I am content to convey some apology along with it.

The greatest part of that book was finished about thirteen years since, 1696, which is eight years before it was published. The author was then young, his invention at the height, and his reading fresh in his head. By the assistance of some thinking, and much conversation, he had endeavoured to strip himself of as many real prejudices as he could; I say real ones, because under the notion of prejudices, he knew to what dangerous heights some men have proceeded. Thus prepared, he thought the numerous and gross corruptions in religion and learning might furnish matter for a satire that would be useful and diverting. He resolved to proceed in a manner that should be altogether new, the world having been already too long nauseated with endless repetitions upon every subject. The abuses in religion, he proposed to set forth in the allegory of the coats and the three brothers, which was to make up the body of the discourse: those in learning he chose to introduce by way of digressions. He was then a young gentleman much in the world, and wrote to the taste of those who were like himself; therefore, in order to allure them, he gave a liberty to his pen which might not suit with maturer years or graver characters, and which he could have easily corrected with a very few blots, had he been master of his papers for a year or two before their publication.

Not that he would have governed his judgment by the illplaced cavils of the sour, the envious, the stupid, and the tasteless, which he mentions with disdain. He acknowledges there are several youthful sallies, which from the grave and the wise may deserve a rebuke. But he desires to be answerable no further than he is guilty, and that his faults may not be multiplied by the ignorant, the unnatural, and uncharitable applications of those who have neither candour to suppose good meanings, nor palate to distinguish true ones. After which, he will forfeit his life if any one opinion can be fairly deduced from that book which is contrary to religion or morality.

Why should any clergyman of our church be angry to see the follies of fanaticism and superstition exposed, though in the most ridiculous manner; since that is perhaps the most probable way to cure them, or at least to hinder them from further spreading? Besides, though it was not intended for their perusal, it rallies nothing but what they preach against. It contains nothing to provoke them, by the least scurrility upon their persons or their functions. It celebrates the Church of England, as the most perfect of all others in discipline and doctrine; it advances no opinion they reject, nor condemns any they receive. If the clergy's resentment lay upon their hands, in my humble opinion they might have found more proper objects to employ them on; *nondum tibi defuit hostis:* I mean those heavy, illiterate scribblers, prostitute in their reputations, vicious in their lives, and ruined in their fortunes, who, to the shame of good sense as well as piety, are greedily read, merely upon the strength of bold, false, impious assertions, mixed with unmannerly reflections upon the priesthood, and openly intended against all religion: in short, full of such principles as are kindly received, because they are levelled to remove those terrors that religion tells men will be the consequence of immoral lives. Nothing like which is to be met with in this discourse, though some of them are pleased so freely to censure it. And I wish there were no other instance of what I have too frequently observed, that many of that reverend body are not always very nice in distinguishing between their enemies and their friends.

Had the author's intentions met with a more candid interpretation from some, whom out of respect he forbears to name, he might have been encouraged to an examination of books written by some of those authors above described, whose errors, ignorance, dulness and villainy, he thinks he could have detected and exposed in such a manner, that the persons who are most conceived to be affected by them would soon lay them aside and be ashamed; but he has now given over those thoughts, since the weightiest men in the weightiest stations are pleased to think it a more dangerous point to laugh at those corruptions in religion, which they themselves must disapprove, than to endeavour pulling up those very foundations wherein all Christians have agreed.

He thinks it no fair proceeding, that any person should offer determinately to fix a name upon the author of this discourse, who hath all along concealed himself from most of his nearest friends: yet several have gone a step farther, and pronounced another book* to have been the work of the same hand with this, which the author directly affirms to be a thorough mistake; he having as yet never so much as read that discourse: a plain instance how little truth there often is in general surmises, or in conjectures drawn from a similitude of style or way of thinking.

* Letter of Enthusiasm

Had the author written a book to expose the abuses in law or in physic, he believes the learned professors in either faculty would have been so far from resenting it as to have given him thanks for his pains; especially if he had made an honourable reservation for the true practice of either science: but religion, they tell us, ought not to be ridiculed, and they tell us truth: yet surely the corruptions in it may; for we are taught by the tritest maxim in the world, that Religion being the best of things, its corruptions are likely to be the worst.

There is one thing which the judicious reader cannot but have observed, that some of those passages in this discourse which appear most liable to objection, are what they call parodies, where the author personates the style and manner of other writers, whom he has a mind to expose. I shall produce one instance of a passage in which Dryden, L'Estrange, and some others I shall not name, are levelled at, who, having spent their lives in faction and apostacies, and all manner of vice, pretended to be sufferers for loyalty and religion. So Dryden tells us, in one of his prefaces, of *his merits and sufferings*, and thanks God that he *possesses his soul in patience*; in other places he talks at the same rate; and L'Estrange often uses the like style; and I believe the reader may find more persons to give that passage an application: but this is enough to direct those who may have overlooked the author's intention.

There are three or four other passages which prejudiced or ignorant readers have drawn by great force to hint at ill meanings; as if they glanced at some tenets in religion. In answer to all which, the author solemnly protests he is entirely innocent; and never had it once in his thoughts, that anything he said, would in the least be capable of such interpretations, which he will engage to deduce full as fairly from the most innocent book in the world. And it will be obvious to every reader, that this was not any part of his scheme or design, the abuses he notes being such as all church-of-England men agree in; nor was it proper for his subject to meddle with other points, than such as have been perpetually controverted since the Reformation.

To instance only in that passage about the three wooden machines mentioned in the introduction; in the original manuscript there was a description of a fourth, which those who had the papers in their power, blotted out, as having something in it of satire, that I suppose they thought was too particular; and therefore they were forced to change it to the number three, whence some have endeavoured to squeeze out a dangerous meaning, that was never thought on. And, indeed, the conceit was half spoiled by changing the numbers; that of four being much more cabalistic, and, therefore, better exposing the pretended virtue of numbers, a superstition there intended to be ridiculed.

Another thing to be observed is, that there generally runs an irony through the thread of the whole book, which the man of taste will observe and distinguish; and which will render some objections that have been made very weak and insignificant.

This Apology being chiefly intended for the satisfaction of future readers, it may be thought unnecessary to take any notice of such treatises as have been written against the ensuing discourse, which are already sunk into waste paper and oblivion, after the usual fate of common answerers to books which are allowed to have any merit: they are indeed like annuals, that grow about a young tree, and seem to vie with it for a summer, but fall and die with the leaves in autumn, and are never heard of more. When Dr. Eachard wrote his book about the contempt of the clergy, numbers of these answerers immediately started up, whose memory, if he had not kept alive by his replies, it would now be utterly unknown that he was ever answered at all. There is indeed an exception, when any great genius thinks it worth his while to expose a foolish piece; so we still read Marvell's answer to Parker with pleasure, though the book it answers be sunk long ago: so the Earl of Orrery's remarks will be read with delight, when the dissertation he exposes will neither be sought nor found: but these are no enterprises for common hands, nor to be hoped for above once or twice in an age. Men would be more cautious of losing their time in such an undertaking, if they did but consider that to answer a book effectually requires more pains and skill, more wit, learning, and judgment, than were employed in the writing of it. And the author assures those gentlemen who have given themselves that trouble with him, that his discourse is the product of the study, the observation, and the invention of several years; that he often blotted out much more than he left, and if his papers had not been a long time out of his possession, they must have still undergone more severe corrections: and do they think such a building is to be battered with dirt-pellets, however envenomed the mouths may be that discharge them? He has seen the productions but of two answerers, one of which at first appeared as from an unknown hand, but since avowed by a person who, upon some occasions, has discovered no ill vein of humour. It is a pity any occasion should put him under a necessity of being so hasty in his productions, which, otherwise, might be entertaining. But there were other reasons obvious enough for his miscarriage in this; he wrote against the conviction of his talent, and entered upon one of the wrongest attempts in nature to turn into ridicule, by a week's labour, a work which had cost so much time and met with so much success in ridiculing others: the manner how he handled his subject I have now forgot, having just looked it over, when it first came out, as others did, merely for the sake of the title.

The other answer is from a person of a graver character, and is made up of half invective, and half annotation, in the latter of which he has generally succeeded well enough. And the project at that time was not amiss to draw in readers to his pamphlet, several having appeared desirous that there might be some explication of the more difficult passages. Neither can he be altogether blamed for offering at the invective part, because it is agreed on all hands, that the author had given him sufficient provocation. The great objection is against his manner of treating it, very unsuitable to one of his function. It was determined by a fair majority that this answerer had, in a way not to be pardoned, drawn his pen against a certain great man then alive, and universally reverenced for every good quality that could possibly enter into the composition of the most accomplished person; it was observed how he was pleased, and affected to have that noble writer called his adversary; and it was a point of satire well directed; for I have been told Sir William Temple was sufficiently mortified at the term. All the men of wit and politeness were immediately up in arms through indignation, which prevailed over their contempt, by the consequences they apprehended from such an example; and it grew Porsenna's case *idem trecenti juravimus.* In short, things were ripe for a general insurrection, till my Lord Orrery had a little laid the spirit, and settled the ferment. But his lordship being principally engaged with another antagonist, it was thought necessary, in order to quiet the minds of men, that this opposer should receive a reprimand, which partly occasioned that discourse of the Battle of the Books; and the author was further at the pains to insert one or two remarks on him in the body of the book.

This answerer has been pleased to find fault with about a dozen passages, which the author will not be at the trouble of defending, further than by assuring the reader, that for the greater part, the reflector is entirely mistaken, and forces interpretations which never once entered into the writer's head, nor will (he is sure) into that of any reader of taste and candour; he allows two or three at most, there produced, to have been delivered unwarily; for which he desires to plead the excuse offered already, of his youth, and frankness of speech, and his papers being out of his power at the time they were published.

But this answerer insists, and says, what he chiefly dislikes, is the design: what that was, I have already told, and I believe there is not a person in England who can understand that book, that ever imagined it to be anything else, but to expose the abuses and corruptions in learning and religion.

But it would be good to know what design this reflector was serving, when he concludes his pamphlet with a caution to the reader to beware of thinking the author's wit was entirely his own: surely this must have had some allay of personal animosity at least, mixed with the design of serving the public, by so useful a discovery; and it indeed touches the author in a tender point; who insists upon it, that through the whole book he has not borrowed one single hint from any writer in the world; and he thought, of all criticisms, that would never have been one. He conceived, it was never disputed to be an original, whatever faults it might have. However, this answerer produces three instances to prove this author's wit is not his own in many places. The first is, that the names of Peter, Martin, and Jack, are borrowed from a letter of the late Duke of Buckingham. Whatever wit is contained in those three names, the author is content to give it up, and desires his readers will subtract as much as they placed upon that account; at the same time protesting solemnly, that he never once heard of that letter, except in this passage of the answerer: so that the names were not borrowed, as he affirms, though they should happen to be the same; which, however, is odd enough, and what he hardly believes: that of Jack being not quite so obvious as the other two. The second instance to show the author's wit is not his own is Peter's banter (as he calls it in his Alsatia phrase) upon transubstantiation, which is taken from the same duke's conference with an Irish priest, where a cork is turned into a horse. This the author confesses to have seen about ten years after his book was written, and a year or two after it was published. Nay the answerer overthrows this himself; for he allows the Tale was written in 1697; and I think that pamphlet was not printed in many years after. It was necessary that corruption should have some allegory as well as the rest; and the author invented the properest he could, without inquiring what other people had written; and the commonest reader will find, there is not the least resemblance between the two stories.—The third instance is in these words: "I have been assured, that the battle in St. James's Library is *mutatis mutandis*, taken out of a French book entitled, *Combat des Livres*, if I misremember not." In which passage there are two clauses observable; "I have been assured;" and, "if I misremember not." I desire first to know whether, if that conjecture proves an utter falsehood, those two clauses will be a sufficient excuse for this worthy critic? The matter is a trifle; but, would he venture to pronounce at this rate upon one of greater moment? I know nothing more contemptible in a writer than the character of a plagiary, which he here fixes at a venture; and this not for a passage, but a whole discourse, taken out from another book, only *mutatis mutandis*. The author is as much in the dark about this as the answerer; and will imitate him by an affirmation at random; that if there be a word of truth in this reflection, he is a paltry, imitating pendant; and the answerer is a person of wit, manners, and truth. He takes his boldness, from never having seen any such treatise in his life, nor heard of it before; and he is sure it is impossible for two writers, of different times and countries, to agree in their thoughts after such a manner, that two continued discourses shall be the same, only *mutatis mutandis*. Neither will he insist upon the mistake in the title; but let the answerer and his friend produce any book they please, he defies them to show one single particular where the judicious reader will affirm he has been obliged for the smallest hint; giving only allowance for the accidental encountering of a single thought, which he knows may sometimes happen; though he has never yet found it in that discourse, nor has heard it objected by anybody else.

So that if ever any design was unfortunately executed it must be that of this answerer, who, when he would have it observed that the author's wit is none of his own, is able to produce but three instances—two of them mere trifles, and all three manifestly false. If this be the way these gentlemen deal with the world in those criticisms, where we have not leisure to defeat them, their readers had need be cautious how they rely upon their credit; and whether this proceeding can be reconciled to humanity or truth, let those who think it worth their while determine.

It is agreed this answerer would have succeeded much better if he had stuck wholly to his business as a commentator upon the Tale of a Tub, wherein it cannot be denied that he hath been of some service to the public, and hath given very fair conjectures towards clearing up some difficult passages; but it is the frequent error of those men (otherwise very commendable for their labours), to make excursions beyond their talent and their office by pretending to point out the beauties and the faults, which is no part of their trade—which they always fail in—which the world never expected from them, nor gave them any thanks for endeavouring at. The part of Minellius, or Farnaby, would have fallen in with his genius, and might have been serviceable to many readers, who cannot enter into the abstruser parts of that discourse; but *optat ephippia bos piger*; the dull, unwieldly, ill-shaped ox, would needs put on the furniture of a horse, not considering he was born to labour, to plough the ground for the sake of superior beings, and that he has neither the shape, mettle, nor speed, of the noble animal he would affect to personate.

It is another pattern of this answerer's fair dealing to give us hints that the author is dead, and yet to lay the suspicion upon somebody, I know not who, in the country; to which can only be returned, that he is absolutely mistaken in all his conjectures; and surely conjectures are, at best, too light a pretence to allow a man to assign a name in public. He condemns a book, and consequently the author, of whom he is utterly ignorant; yet at the same time he fixes in print what he thinks a disadvantageous character upon those who never deserved it. A man who receives a buffet in the dark may be allowed to be vexed; but it is an odd kind of revenge to go to cuffs in broad day with the first he meets and lay the last night's injury at his door. And thus much for the discreet, candid, pious, and ingenious answerer.

How the author came to be without his papers is a story not proper to be told, and of very little use, being a private fact; of which the reader would believe as little, or as much, as he thought good. He had, however, a blotted copy by him, which he intended to have written over with many alterations; and this the publishers were well aware of, having put it into the bookseller's preface that they apprehended a surreptitious copy, which was to be altered, etc. This, though not regarded by readers, was a real truth, only the surreptitious copy was rather that which was printed; and they made all the haste they could, which, indeed, was needless, the author not being at all prepared; but he has been told the bookseller was in much pain, having given a good sum of money for the copy.

In the author's original copy there were not so many chasms as appear in the book, and why some of them were left he knows not. Had the publication been trusted to him, he would have made several corrections of passages, against which nothing has been ever objected: he would likewise have altered a few of those that seem with any reason to be excepted against; but, to deal freely, the greatest number he should have left untouched, as never suspecting it possible any wrong interpretations could be made of them.

The author observes, at the end of the book, there is a discourse called a *Fragment*, which he more wondered to see in print than all the rest, having been a most imperfect sketch, with the addition of a few loose hints, which he once lent a gentleman who had designed a discourse on somewhat the same subject; he never thought of it afterwards, and it was a sufficient surprise to see it pieced up together wholly out of the method and scheme he had intended, for it was the groundwork of a much larger discourse, and he was sorry to observe the materials so foolishly employed.

There is one further objection made by those who have answered this book, as well as by some others, that Peter is frequently made to repeat oaths and curses. Every reader observes, it was necessary to know that Peter did swear and curse. The oaths are not printed out, but only supposed: and the idea of an oath is not immoral, like the idea of a profane or immodest speech. A man may laugh at the Popish folly of cursing people to hell, and imagine them swearing, without any crime; but lewd words, or dangerous opinions, though printed by halves, fill the reader's mind with ill ideas; and of these the author cannot be accused. For the judicious reader will find that the severest strokes of satire in his book are levelled against the modern custom of employing wit upon those topics; of which there is a remarkable instance in the 153d. page, as well as in several others, though perhaps once or twice expressed in too free a manner, excusable only for the reasons already alleged. Some overtures have been made by a third hand to the bookseller for the author's altering those pages which he thought might require it; but it seems the bookseller will not hear of any such thing, being apprehensive it might spoil the sale of the book.

The author cannot conclude this apology without making this one reflection: that, as wit is the noblest and most useful gift of human nature, so humour is the most agreeable; and where these two enter far into the composition of any work, they will render it always acceptable to the world. Now, the great part of those who have no share or taste of either, but by their pride, pedantry, and ill manners, lay themselves bare to the lashes of both, think the blow is weak, because they are insensible; and, where wit has any mixture of raillery, it is but calling it banter, and the work is done. This polite word of theirs was first borrowed from the bullies in Whitefriars, then fell among the footmen, and at last retired to the pedants; by whom it is applied as properly to the production of wit as if I should apply it to Sir Isaac Newton's mathematics. But, if this bantering, as they call it, be so despisable a thing, whence comes it to pass they have such a perpetual itch toward it themselves? To instance only in the answerer already mentioned: it is grievous to see him, in some of his writings, at every turn going out of his way to be waggish, to tell us of a cow that pricked up her tail; and in his answer to this discourse, he says, it is all a farce and a ladle; with other passages equally shining. One may say of these *impedimenta literarum*, that wit owes them a shame; and they cannot take wiser counsel than to keep out of harm's way, or, at least, not to come till they are sure they are called.

To conclude: with those allowances above required this book should be read; after which, the author conceives few things will remain which may not be excused in a young writer.

He wrote only to the men of wit and taste; and he thinks he is not mistaken in his accounts when he says they have been all of his side enough to give him the vanity of telling his name; wherein the world, with all its wise conjectures, is yet very much in the dark; which circumstance is no disagreeable amusement either to the public or himself.

The author is informed that the bookseller has prevailed on several gentlemen to write some explanatory notes, for the goodness of which he is not to answer, having never seen any of them, nor intending it, till they appear in print; when it is not unlikely he may have the pleasure to find twenty meanings which never entered into his imagination.

June 3, 1709.

Postscript.—Since the writing of this, which was about a year ago, a prostitute bookseller has published a foolish paper, under the name of *Notes on the Tale of a Tub*, with some account of the author: and, with an insolence which I suppose is punishable by law, has presumed to assign certain names. It will be enough for the author to assure the world, that the writer of that paper is utterly wrong in all his conjectures upon that affair. The author further asserts that the whole work is entirely of one hand, which every reader of judgment will easily discover; the gentleman who gave the copy to the bookseller, being a friend of the author, and using no other liberties besides that of expunging certain passages, where now the chasms appear under the name of *desiderata*. But, if any person will prove his claim to three lines in the whole book, let him step forth and tell his name and titles; upon which, the bookseller shall have orders to prefix them to the next edition, and the claimant shall from henceforward be acknowledged the undisputed author.

TO THE RIGHT HONOURABLE
JOHN LORD SOMMERS

My Lord,

—Although the author has written a large dedication, yet that being addressed to a prince, whom I am never likely to have the honour of being known to; a person besides, as far as I can observe, not at all regarded, or thought on by any of our present writers; and being wholly free from that slavery which booksellers usually lie under, to the caprice of authors, I think it a wise piece of presumption to inscribe these papers to your lordship and to implore your lordship's protection of them. God and your lordship know their faults and their merits; for, as to my own particular, I am altogether a stranger to the matter; and though everybody else should be equally ignorant, I do not fear the sale of the book, at all the worse, upon that score. Your lordship's name on the front in capital letters will at any time get off one edition: neither would I desire any other help to grow an alderman, than a patent for the sole privilege of dedicating to your lordship.

I should now, in right of a dedicator, give your lordship a list of your own virtues, and at the same time, be very unwilling to offend your modesty; but chiefly, I should celebrate your liberality towards men of great parts and small fortunes, and give you broad hints that I mean myself. And I was just going on, in the usual method, to peruse a hundred or two of dedications, and transcribe an abstract to be applied to your lordship; but I was diverted by a certain accident: for upon the covers of these papers I casually observed written in large letters the two following words, DETUR DIGNISSIMO; which, for aught I knew, might contain some important meaning. But it unluckily fell out, that none of the authors I employ understood Latin; (though I have them often in pay to translate out of that language); I was therefore compelled to have recourse to the curate of our parish, who englished it thus, "Let it be given to the worthiest:" and his comment was, that the author meant his work should be dedicated to the sublimest genius of the age for wit, learning, judgment, eloquence, and wisdom. I called at a poet's chamber (who works for my shop) in an alley hard by, showed him the translation, and desired his opinion who it was that the author could mean: he told me, after some consideration, that vanity was a thing he abhorred; but by the description, he thought himself to be the person aimed at; and at the same time, he very kindly offered his own assistance gratis towards penning a dedication to himself. I desired him, however, to give a second guess; Why then, said he, it must be I, or my Lord Somers. From thence I went to several other wits of my acquaintance, with no small hazard and weariness to my person, from a prodigious number of dark, winding stairs; but found them all in the same story, both of your lordship and themselves. Now, your lordship is to understand, that this proceeding was not of my own invention; for I have somewhere heard it as a maxim, that those to whom everybody allows the second place, have an undoubted title to the first.

This infallibly convinced me that your lordship was the person intended by the author. But being very unacquainted in the style and form of dedications, I employed those wits aforesaid to furnish me with hints and materials, towards a panegyric upon your lordship's virtues.

In two days they brought me ten sheets of paper, filled up on every side. They swore to me, that they had ransacked whatever could be found in the characters of Socrates, Aristides, Epaminondas, Cato, Tully, Atticus, and other hard names, which I cannot now recollect. However, I have reason to believe, they imposed upon my ignorance; because, when I came to read over their collections, there was not a syllable there but what I and everybody else knew as well as themselves; therefore I grievously suspect a cheat; and that these authors of mine stole and transcribed every word, from the universal report of mankind. So that I look upon myself as fifty shillings out of pocket, to no manner of purpose.

If by altering the title I could make the same materials serve for another dedication (as my betters have done), it would help to make up my loss; but I have made several persons dip here and there in those papers, and before they read three lines, they have all assured me plainly, that they cannot possibly be applied to any person besides your lordship.

I expected, indeed, to have heard of your lordship's bravery at the head of an army; of your undaunted courage in mounting a breach, or scaling a wall; or to have had your pedigree traced in a lineal descent from the house of *Austria*; or, of your wonderful talent at dress and dancing; or, your profound knowledge in *algebra, metapyhsics*, and the *oriental* tongues. But to ply the world with an old beaten story of your wit, and eloquence, and learning, and wisdom, and justice, and politeness, and candour, and evenness of temper in all scenes of life; of that great discernment in discovering, and readiness in favouring deserving men; with forty other common topics; I confess, I have neither conscience nor countenance to do it. Because there is no virtue, either of a public or a private life, which some circumstances of your own have not often produced upon the stage of the world; and those few, which, for want of occasions to exert them, might otherwise have passed unseen, or unobserved, by your friends, your enemies have at length brought to light.

It is true, I should be very loth the bright example of your lordship's virtues should be lost to after-ages, both for their sake and your own; but chiefly because they will be so very necessary to adorn the history of a late reign; and that is another reason why I would forbear to make a recital of them here; because I have been told by wise men, that as dedications have run for some years past, a good historian will not be apt to have recourse thither in search of characters.

There is one point, wherein I think we dedicators would do well to change our measures; I mean, instead of running on so far upon the praise of our patrons' liberality, to spend a word or two in admiring their patience. I can put no greater compliment on your lordship's, than by giving you so ample an occasion to exercise it at present.—Though perhaps I shall not be apt to reckon much merit to your lordship upon that score, who having been formerly used to tedious harangues and sometimes to as little purpose, will be the readier to pardon this; especially when it is offered by one, who is, with all respect and veneration,

My lord,
Your lordship's most obedient
and most faithful servant,
The Bookseller.

THE BOOKSELLER TO THE READER

It is now six years since these papers came first to my hand, which seems to have been about a twelvemonth after they were written; for the author tells us in his preface to the first treatise, that he has calculated it for the year 1697, and in several passages of that discourse, as well as the second, it appears they were written about that time.

As to the author, I can give no manner of satisfaction; however I am credibly informed, that this publication is without his knowledge; for he concludes the copy is lost, having lent it to a person, since dead, and being never in possession of it after: so that, whether the work received his last hand, or whether he intended to fill up the defective places, is likely to remain a secret.

If I should go about to tell the reader, by what accident I became master of these papers, it would, in this unbelieving age, pass for little more than the cant or jargon of the trade. I therefore gladly spare both him and myself so unnecessary a trouble. There yet remains a difficult question, why I published them no sooner. I forbore upon two accounts; first, because I thought I had better work upon my own hands; and secondly, because I was not without some hope of hearing from the author, and receiving his directions. But I have been lately alarmed with intelligence of a surreptitious copy, which a certain great wit had new polished and refined, or, as our present writers express themselves, fitted to the humour of the age; as they have already done, with great felicity to, Don Quixote, Boccalini, La Bruyere, and other authors. However, I thought it fairer dealing to offer the whole work in its naturals. If any gentleman will please to furnish me with a key, in order to explain the more difficult parts, I shall very gratefully acknowledge the favour, and print it by itself.

THE EPISTLE DEDICATORY
TO HIS ROYAL HIGHNESS PRINCE POSTERITY[1]

Sir,

—I here present your highness with the fruits of a very few leisure hours, stolen from the short intervals of a world of business, and of an employment quite alien from such amusements as this the poor production of that refuse of time, which has laid heavy upon my hands during a long prorogation of parliament, a great dearth of foreign news, and a tedious fit of rainy weather; for which, and other reasons, it cannot choose extremely to deserve such a patronage as that of your highness, whose numberless virtues, in so few years, make the world look upon you as the future example to all princes; for although your highness is hardly got clear of infancy, yet has the universal learned world already resolved upon appealing to your future dictates, with the lowest and most resigned submission; fate having decreed you sole arbiter of the productions of human wit, in this polite and most accomplished age. Methinks the number of appellants were enough to shock and startle any judge, of a genius less unlimited than yours; but in order to prevent such glorious trials, the person, it seems, to whose care the education of your highness is committed, has resolved (as I am told) to keep you in almost a universal ignorance of our studies, which it is your inherent birth-right to inspect.

It is amazing to me that this person should have the assurance, in the face of the sun, to go about persuading your highness that our age is almost wholly illiterate, and has hardly produced one writer upon any subject. I know very well, that when your highness shall come to riper years, and have gone through the learning of antiquity, you will be too curious to neglect inquiring

1 The citation out of Irenæus in the title-page, which seems to be all gibberish, is a form of initiation used anciently by the Marcosian heretics. W. Wotton.

It is the usual style of decry'd writers to appeal to Posterity, who is here represented as a prince in his nonage, and Time as his governor, and the author begins in a way very frequent with him, by personating other writers, who sometimes offer such reasons and excuses for publishing their works as they ought chiefly to conceal and be asham'd of.

into the authors of the very age before you: and to think that this insolent, in the account he is preparing for your view, designs to reduce them to a number so insignificant as I am ashamed to mention; it moves my zeal and my spleen for the honour and interest of our vast flourishing body, as well as of myself, for whom, I know by long experience, he has professed, and still continues, a peculiar malice.

It is not unlikely that, when your highness will one day peruse what I am now writing, you may be ready to expostulate with your governor upon the credit of what I here affirm, and command him to show you some of our productions. To which he will answer (for I am well informed of his designs), by asking your highness where they are? and what is become of them? and pretend it a demonstration that there never were any, because they are not then to be found. Not to be found! who has mislaid them? are they sunk in the abyss of things? it is certain, that in their own nature, they were light enough to swim upon the surface for all eternity. Therefore the fault is in him, who tied weights so heavy to their heels as to depress them to the centre. Is their very essence destroyed? who has annihilated them? were they drowned by purges, or martyred by pipes? who administered them to the posteriors of ——? But, that it may no longer be a doubt with your highness, who is to be the author of this universal ruin, I beseech you to observe that large and terrible scythe which your governor affects to bear continually about him. Be pleased to remark the length and strength, the sharpness and hardness of his nails and teeth: consider his baneful, abominable breath, enemy to life and matter, infectious and corrupting: and then reflect whether it be possible for any mortal ink and paper of this generation to make a suitable resistance. O! that your highness would one day resolve to disarm this usurping *maître du palais*[1] of his furious engines, and bring your empire *hors de page*[2].

---

1 Comptroller.
2 Out of guardianship.

It were needless to recount the several methods of tyranny and destruction which your governor is pleased to practise upon this occasion. His inveterate malice is such to the writings of our age, that of several thousands produced yearly from this renowned city, before the next revolution of the sun, there is not one to be heard of: Unhappy infants! many of them barbarously destroyed, before they have so much as learnt their mother tongue to beg for pity. Some he stifles in their cradles; others he frights into convulsions, whereof they suddenly die; some he flays alive; others he tears limb from limb. Great numbers are offered to Moloch; and the rest, tainted by his breath, die of a languishing consumption.

But the concern I have most at heart, is for our corporation of poets; from whom I am preparing a petition to your highness, to be subscribed with the names of one hundred and thirty-six of the first rate; but whose immortal productions are never likely to reach your eyes, though each of them is now an humble and earnest appellant for the laurel, and has large comely volumes ready to show, for a support to his pretensions. The never-dying works of these illustrious persons, your governor, sir, has devoted to unavoidable death; and your highness is to be made believe, that our age has never arrived at the honour to produce one single poet.

We confess Immortality to be a great and powerful goddess; but in vain we offer up to her our devotions and our sacrifices, if your highness's governor, who has usurped the priesthood, must, by an unparalleled ambition and avarice, wholly intercept and devour them.

To affirm that our age is altogether unlearned, and devoid of writers in any kind, seems to be an assertion so bold and so false, that I have been some time thinking the contrary may almost be proved by uncontrollable demonstration. It is true, indeed, that although their numbers be vast, and their productions numerous in proportion, yet are they hurried so hastily off the scene, that they escape our memory, and elude our sight. When I first thought of this address, I had prepared a copious list of titles to present your highness, as an undisputed argument for what I affirm. The originals were posted fresh upon all gates and corners of streets; but, returning in a very few hours to take a review, they were all torn down, and fresh ones in their places. I inquired after them among readers and booksellers; but I inquired in vain; the memorial of them was lost among men; their places were no more to be found; and I was laughed to scorn for a clown and a pedant, without all taste and refinement, little versed in the course of present affairs, and that knew nothing of what had passed in the best companies of court and town. So that I can only avow in general to your highness, that we do abound in learning and wit; but to fix upon particulars, is a task too slippery for my slender abilities. If I should venture in a windy day to affirm to your highness, that there is a large cloud near the horizon, in the form of a bear, another in the zenith, with the head of an ass; a third to the westward, with claws like a dragon; and your highness should in a few minutes think fit to examine the truth, it is certain they would all be changed in figure and position; new ones would arise, and all we could agree upon would be, that clouds there were, but that I was grossly mistaken in the zoography and topography of them.

But your governor perhaps may still insist, and put the question—What is then become of those immense bales of paper, which must needs have been employed in such numbers of books? can these also be wholly annihilate, and so of a sudden, as I pretend? What shall I say in return of so invidious an objection? it ill befits the distance between your highness and me, to send you for ocular conviction to a jakes, or an oven; to the windows of a bawdy-house, or to a sordid lantern. Books, like men their authors, have no more than one way of coming into the world, but there are ten thousand to go out of it, and return no more.

I profess to your highness, in the integrity of my heart, that what I am going to say is literally true this minute I am writing: what revolutions may happen before it shall be ready for your perusal, I can by no means warrant; however, I beg you to accept it as a specimen of our learning, our politeness, and our wit. I do therefore affirm, upon the word of a sincere man, that there is now actually in being a certain poet, called John Dryden, whose translation of Virgil was lately printed in a large folio, well bound, and, if diligent search were made, for aught I know, is yet to be seen. There is another, called Nahum Tate, who is ready to make oath that he has caused many reams of verse to be published, whereof both himself and his bookseller (if lawfully required) can still produce authentic copies, and therefore wonders why the world is pleased to make such a secret of it. There is a third, known by the name of Tom Durfey, a poet of vast comprehension, a universal genius, and most profound learning. There are also one Mr. Rymer, and one Mr. Dennis, most profound critics. There is a person styled Dr. Bentley, who has written near a thousand pages of immense erudition, giving a full and true account of a certain squabble, of wonderful importance, between himself and a bookseller: he is a writer of infinite wit and humour; no man rallies with a better grace, and in more sprightly turns. Further, I avow to your highness, that with these eyes I have beheld the person of William Wotton, B.D., who has written a good sizeable volume against a friend of your governor, (from whom, alas! he must therefore look for little favour), in a most gentlemanly style, adorned with the utmost politeness and civility; replete with discoveries equally valuable for their novelty and use; and embellished with traits of wit, so poignant and so apposite, that he is a worthy yokemate to his forementioned friend.

Why should I go upon further particulars, which might fill a volume with the true eulogies of my contemporary brethren? I shall bequeath this piece of justice to a larger work, wherein I intend to write a character of the present set of wits in our nation: their persons I shall describe particularly and at length, their genius and understandings in miniature.

In the meantime I do here make bold to present your highness with a faithful abstract, drawn from the universal body of all arts and sciences, intended wholly for your service and instruction: nor do I doubt in the least, but your highness will peruse it as carefully, and make as considerable improvements, as other young princes have already done, by the many volumes of late years written for a help to their studies.

That your highness may advance in wisdom and virtue, as well as years, and at last outshine all your royal ancestors, shall be the daily prayer of,

Sir,

December,
1697.

Your highness's

Most devoted, etc.

THE PREFACE

The wits of the present age being so very numerous and penetrating, it seems the grandees of church and state begin to fall under horrible apprehensions, lest these gentlemen, during the intervals of a long peace, should find leisure to pick holes in the weak sides of religion and government. To prevent which, there has been much thought employed of late, upon certain projects for taking off the force and edge of those formidable inquirers, from canvassing and reasoning upon such delicate points. They have at length fixed upon one, which will require some time as well as cost to perfect. Meanwhile, the danger hourly increasing, by new levies of wits, all appointed (as there is reason to fear) with pen, ink, and paper, which may, at an hour's warning, be drawn out into pamphlets, and other offensive weapons, ready for immediate execution, it was judged of absolute necessity, that some present expedient be thought on, till the main design can be brought to maturity. To this end, at a grand committee some days ago, this important discovery was made by a certain curious and refined observer—that seamen have a custom, when they meet a whale, to fling him out an empty tub by way of amusement, to divert him from laying violent hands upon the ship. This parable was immediately mythologised; the whale was interpreted to be Hobbes's Leviathan, which tosses and plays with all schemes of religion and government, whereof a great many are hollow, and dry, and empty, and noisy, and wooden, and given to rotation: this is the leviathan, whence the terrible wits of our age are said to borrow their weapons. The ship in danger is easily understood to be its old antitype, the commonwealth. But how to analyse the tub, was a matter of difficulty; when, after long inquiry and debate, the literal meaning was preserved; and it was decreed that, in order to prevent these leviathans from tossing and sporting with the commonwealth, which of itself is too apt to fluctuate, they should be diverted from that game by a Tale of a Tub. And, my genius being conceived to lie not unhappily that way, I had the honour done me to be engaged in the performance.

This is the sole design in publishing the following treatise, which I hope will serve for an *interim* of some months to employ those unquiet spirits, till the perfecting of that great work; into the secret of which, it is reasonable the courteous reader should have some little light.

It is intended, that a large academy be erected, capable of containing nine thousand seven hundred forty and three persons; which, by modest computation, is reckoned to be pretty near the current number of wits in this island. These are to be disposed into the several schools of this academy, and there pursue those studies to which their genius most inclines them. The undertaker himself will publish his proposals with all convenient speed; to which I shall refer the curious reader for a more particular account, mentioning at present only a few of the principal schools. There is, first, a large pæderastic school, with French and Italian masters. There is also the spelling school, a very spacious building: the school of looking-glasses: the school of swearing: the school of critics: the school of salivation: the school of hobby-horses: the school of poetry: the school of tops[1]: the school of spleen: the school of gaming: and many others, too tedious to recount. No person to be admitted member into any of these schools without an attestation under two sufficient person's hands certifying him to be a wit.

But, to return: I am sufficiently instructed in the principal duty of a preface, if my genius were capable of arriving at it. Thrice have I forced my imagination to make the tour of my invention, and thrice has it returned empty; the latter having been wholly drained by the following treatise. Not so my more successful brethren the moderns; who will by no means let slip a preface or dedication, without some notable distinguishing

---

1 This I think the author should have omitted, it being of the very same nature with the school of hobby-horses, if one may venture to censure one who is so severe a censurer of others, perhaps with too little distinction.

stroke to surprise the reader at the entry, and kindle a wonderful expectation of what is to ensue. Such was that of a most ingenious poet, who, soliciting his brain for something new, compared himself to the hangman, and his patron to the patient: this was *insigne, recens, indictum ore alio*[1]*. When I went through that necessary * Hor.
and noble course of study, I had the happiness to observe many such egregious touches, which I shall not injure the authors by transplanting: because I have remarked, that nothing is so very tender as a modern piece of wit, and which is apt to suffer so much in the carriage. Some things are extremely witty today, or fasting, or in this place, or at eight o'clock, or over a bottle, or spoke by Mr. What'd'y-call'm, or in a summer's morning: any of the which, by the smallest transposal or misapplication, is utterly annihilate. Thus wit has its walks and purlieus, out of which it may not stray the breadth of a hair, upon peril of being lost. The moderns have artfully fixed this mercury, and reduced it to the circumstances of time, place, and person. Such a jest there is, that will not pass out of Covent Garden; and such a one that is nowhere intelligible but at Hyde Park Corner. Now, though it sometimes tenderly affects me to consider, that all the towardly passages I shall deliver in the following treatise, will grow quite out of date and relish with the first shifting of the present scene, yet I must needs subscribe to the justice of this proceeding: because, I cannot imagine why we should be at the expense to furnish wit for succeeding ages, when the former have made no sort of provision for ours: wherein I speak the sentiment of the very newest, and consequently the most orthodox refiners, as well as my own. However, being extremely solicitous that every accomplished person, who has got into the taste of wit calculated for this present month of August, 1679, should descend to the very bottom of all the sublime, throughout this treatise; I hold fit to lay down this general maxim: whatever

1 Something extraordinary, new and never hit upon before.

reader desires to have a thorough comprehension of an author's thoughts, cannot take a better method than by putting himself into the circumstances and postures of life, that the writer was in upon every important passage, as it flowed from his pen: for this will introduce a parity, and strict correspondence of ideas, between the reader and the author. Now, to assist the diligent reader in so delicate an affair, as far as brevity will permit, I have recollected, that the shrewdest pieces of this treatise were conceived in bed in a garret; at other times, for a reason best known to myself, I thought fit to sharpen my invention with hunger; and, in general, the whole work was begun, continued, and ended, under a long course of physic, and a great want of money. Now, I do affirm, it will be absolutely impossible for the candid peruser to go along with me in a great many bright passages, unless, upon the several difficulties emergent, he will please to capacitate and prepare himself by these directions. And this I lay down as my principal *postulatum*.

Because I have professed to be a most devoted servant of all modern forms, I apprehend some curious wit may object against me, for proceeding thus far in a preface, without declaiming, according to the custom, against the multitude of writers, whereof the whole multitude of writers most reasonably complain. I am just come from perusing some hundreds of prefaces, wherein the authors do, at the very beginning, address the gentle reader concerning this enormous grievance. Of these I have preserved a few examples, and shall set them down as near as my memory has been able to retain them.

One begins thus:—For a man to set up for a writer, when the press swarms with, etc.

Another:—The tax upon paper does not lessen the number of scribblers, who daily pester, etc.

Another:—When every little would-be wit takes pen in hand, 'tis in vain to enter the lists, etc.

Another:—To observe what trash the press swarms with, etc.

Another:—Sir, It is merely in obedience to your commands that I venture into the public; for who upon a less consideration would be of a party with such a rabble of scribblers, etc.

Now, I have two words in my own defence against this objection. First, I am far from granting the number of writers a nuisance to our nation, having strenuously maintained the contrary, in several parts of the following discourse. Secondly, I do not well understand the justice of this proceeding; because I observe many of these polite prefaces to be not only from the same hand, but from those who are most voluminous in their several productions. Upon which I shall tell the reader a short tale.

A mountebank, in Leicester Fields, had drawn a huge assembly about him. Among the rest, a fat unwieldly fellow, half stifled in the press, would be every fit crying out, "Lord! what a filthy crowd is here! pray, good people, give way a little. Bless me! what a devil has raked this rabble together! z—ds? what squeezing is this! honest friend, remove your elbow." At last a weaver, that stood next him, could hold no longer. "A plague confound you (said he) for an overgrown sloven; and who, in the devil's name, I wonder, helps to make up the crowd half so much as yourself? Don't you consider, with a pox, that you take up more room with that carcass than any five here? Is not the place as free for us as for you? bring your own guts to a reasonable compass, and be d—n'd, and then I'll engage we shall have room enough for us all."

There are certain common privileges of a writer, the benefit whereof, I hope, there will be no reason to doubt; particularly, that where I am not understood, it shall be concluded, that something very useful and profound is couched underneath: and again, that whatever word or sentence is printed in a different character, shall be judged to contain something extraordinary either of wit or sublime.

As for the liberty I have thought fit to take of praising myself, upon some occasions or none, I am sure it will need no excuse, if a multitude of great examples be allowed sufficient authority: for it is here to be noted, that praise was originally a pension paid by the world; but the moderns, finding the trouble and charge too great in collecting it, have lately bought out the fee-simple; since which time the right of presentation is wholly in ourselves. For this reason it is, that when an author makes his own eulogy, he uses a certain form to declare and insist upon his title, which is commonly in these or the like words, "I speak without vanity;" which I think plainly shows it to be a matter of right and justice. Now I do here once for all declare, that in every encounter of this nature through the following treatise, the form aforesaid is implied; which I mention, to save the trouble of repeating it on so many occasions.

It is a great ease to my conscience, that I have written so elaborate and useful a discourse, without one grain of satire intermixed; which is the sole point wherein I have taken leave to dissent from the famous originals of our age and country. I have observed some satirists to use the public much at the rate that pedants do a naughty boy, ready horsed for discipline: first, expostulate the case, then plead the necessity of the rod from great provocations, and conclude every period with a lash. Now, if I know anything of mankind, these gentlemen might very well spare their reproof and correction: for there is not, through all nature, another so callous and insensible a member as the world's posteriors, whether you apply to it the toe or the birch. Besides, most of our late satirists seem to lie under a sort of mistake; that because nettles have the prerogative to sting, therefore all other weeds must do so too. I make not this comparison out of the least design to detract from these worthy writers; for it is well known among mythologists, that weeds have the pre-eminence over all other vegetables; and therefore the first monarch of this island, whose taste and judgment were so acute and refined, did very wisely root out the roses from the collar of the order, and plant the thistles in their stead, as the nobler flower of the two. For which reason it is conjectured by profounder antiquaries, that the satirical itch, so prevalent in this part of our island, was first brought among us from beyond the Tweed. Here may it long flourish and abound: may it survive and neglect the scorn of the world, with as much ease and contempt as the world is insensible to the lashes of it. May their own dullness, or that of their party, be no discouragement for the authors to proceed; but let them remember, it is with wits as with razors, which are never so apt to cut those they are employed on as when they have lost their edge. Besides, those whose teeth are too rotten to bite, are best, of all others, qualified to revenge that defect with their breath.

I am not like other men, to envy or undervalue the talents I cannot reach; for which reason I must needs bear a true honour to this large eminent sect of our British writers. And I hope this little panegyric will not be offensive to their ears, since it has the advantage of being only designed for themselves. Indeed, nature herself has taken order, that fame and honour should be purchased at a better pennyworth by satire than by any other productions of the brain; the world being soonest provoked to praise by lashes, as men are to love. There is a problem in an ancient author, why dedications and other bundles of flattery, run all upon stale musty topics, without the smallest tincture of anything new; not only to the torment and nauseating of the Christian reader; but, if not suddenly prevented, to the universal spreading of that pestilential disease, the lethargy, in this island: whereas there is very little satire, which has not something in it untouched before. The defects of the former are usually imputed to the want of invention among those who are dealers in that kind; but, I think, with a great deal of injustice; the solution being easy and natural; for the materials of panegyric, being very few in number, have been long since exhausted. For, as health is but one thing and has been always the same, whereas diseases are by thousands, beside new and daily additions; so, all the virtues that have been ever in mankind, are to be counted upon a few fingers; but their follies and vices are innumerable, and time adds hourly to the heap. Now the utmost a poor poet can do, is to get by heart a list of the cardinal virtues, and deal them with his utmost liberality to his hero or his patron: he may ring the changes as far as it will go, and very his phrase till he has talked round; but the reader quickly finds it is all pork*, with a little variety of sauce. For there is no inventing terms of art beyond our ideas; and, when our ideas are exhausted terms of art must be so too.

* Plutarch.

But though the matter for panegyric were as fruitful as the topics of satire, yet would it not be hard to find out a sufficient reason why the latter will be always better received than the first. For, this being bestowed only upon one, or a few persons at a time, is sure to raise envy, and consequently ill words from the rest, who have no share in the blessing; but satire, being levelled at all, is never resented for an offence by any, since every individual person makes bold to understand it of others, and very wisely removes his particular part of the burden upon the shoulders of the world, which are broad enough, and able to bear it. To this purpose, I have sometimes reflected upon the difference between Athens and England, with respect to the point before us. In the Attic common-wealth*, it was the privilege and birth-right of every citizen and poet to rail aloud, and in public, or to expose upon the stage, by name, any person they pleased, though of the greatest figure, whether a Creon, an Hyperbolus, an Alcibiades, or a Demosthenes; but on the other side, the least reflecting word let fall against the people, in general, was immediately caught up, and revenged upon the authors, however considerable for their quality or their merits. Whereas in England it is just the reverse of all this. Here, you may securely display your utmost rhetoric against mankind, in the face of the world; tell them, "That all are gone astray; that there is none that doth good, no not one; that we live in the very dregs of time; that knavery and atheism are epidemic as the pox; that honesty is fled with Astræa;" with any other

* Vid. Xenoph.

commonplaces, equally new and eloquent, which are furnished by the *splendida bilis*[1]*. And when you have done, the whole audience, far from being offended, shall return you thanks as a deliverer of precious and useful truths. Nay, further; it is but to venture your lungs, and you may preach in Covent Garden against foppery and fornication, and something else: against pride and dissimulation and bribery, at Whitehall: you may expose rapine and injustice in the inns of court chapel: and in a city pulpit, be as fierce as you please against avarice, hypocrisy, and extortion. 'Tis but a ball banded to and fro, and every man carries a racket about him, to strike it from himself, among the rest of the company. But, on the other side, whoever should mistake the nature of things so far as to drop but a single hint in public, how such a one starved half the fleet, and half poisoned the rest: how such a one, from a true principle of love and honour, pays no debts but for wenches and play: how such a one has got a clap, and runs out of his estate: how Paris, bribed by Juno and Venus[2], loth to offend either party, slept out the whole cause on the bench: or, how such an orator makes long speeches in the senate, with much thought, little sense, and to no purpose; whoever, I say, should venture to be thus particular, must expect to be imprisoned for *scandalum magnatum*; to have challenges sent him; to be sued for defamation; and to be brought before the bar of the house.

But I forget that I am expatiating on a subject wherein I have no concern, having neither a talent nor an inclination for satire. On the other side, I am so entirely satisfied with the whole present procedure of human things, that I have been some years preparing materials towards "A panegyric upon the World;" to which I intended to add a second part, entitled, "A modest defence of the Proceedings of the Rabble in all Ages."

* Hor.

1 Spleen.
2 Juno and Venus are money and a mistress, very powerful bribes to a judge, if scandal says true. I remember such reflexions were cast about that time, but I cannot fix the person intended here.

Both these I had thoughts to publish, by way of appendix to the following treatise; but finding my commonplace book fill much slower than I had reason to expect, I have chosen to defer them to another occasion. Besides, I have been unhappily prevented in that design by a certain domestic misfortune; in the particulars whereof, though it would be very seasonable, and much in the modern way, to inform the gentle reader, and would also be of great assistance towards extending this preface into the size now in vogue, which by rule ought to be large in proportion as the subsequent volume is small; yet I shall now dismiss our impatient reader from any further attendance at the porch, and, having duly prepared his mind by a preliminary discourse, shall gladly introduce him to the sublime mysteries that ensue.

A TALE OF A TUB, &c

SECT. I

The Introduction

Whoever has an ambition to be heard in a crowd, must press, and squeeze, and thrust, and climb, with indefatigable pains, till he has exalted himself to a certain degree of altitude above them. Now in all assemblies, though you wedge them ever so close, we may observe this peculiar property, that over their heads there is room enough, but how to reach it is the difficult point; it being as hard to get quit of number as of hell;

> "——evadere ad auras,
> Hoc opus, hic labor est."
> —Virgil[1]

To this end, the philosopher's way, in all ages, has been by erecting certain edifices in the air: but, whatever practice and reputation these kind of structures have formerly possessed, or may still continue in, not excepting even that of Socrates, when he was suspended in a basket to help contemplation, I think, with due submission, they seem to labour under two inconveniences. First, That the foundations being laid too high, they have been often out of sight, and ever out of hearing. Secondly, That the materials, being very transitory, have suffered much from inclemencies of air, especially in these north-west regions.

Therefore, towards the just performance of this great work, there remain but three methods that I can think of; whereof the wisdom of our ancestors being highly sensible, has, to encourage all aspiring adventurers, thought fit to erect three

---

1 But to return, and view the cheerful skies;
  In this the task and mighty labour lies.

wooden machines for the use of those orators who desire to talk much without interruption. These are, the pulpit, the ladder, and the stage itinerant. For as to the bar, though it be compounded of the same matter, and designed for the same use, it cannot, however, be well allowed the honour of a fourth, by reason of its level or inferior situation exposing it to perpetual interruption from collaterals. Neither can the bench itself, though raised to a prominency, put in a better claim, whatever its advocates insist on. For, if they please to look into the original design of its erection, and the circumstances or adjuncts subservient to that design, they will soon acknowledge the present practice exactly correspondent to the primitive institution, and both to answer the etymology of the name, which in the Phœnician tongue is a word of great signification, importing, if literally interpreted, the place of sleep; but in common acceptation, a seat well bolstered and cushioned, for the repose of old and gouty limbs: *senes ut in otia tuta recedant.* Fortune being indebted to them this part of retaliation, that, as formerly they have long talked while others slept; so now they may sleep as long while others talk.

But if no other argument could occur to exclude the bench and the bar from the list of oratorial machines, it were sufficient that the admission of them would overthrow a number, which I was resolved to establish, whatever argument it might cost me; in imitation of that prudent method observed by many other philosophers and great clerks, whose chief art in division has been to grow fond of some proper mystical number, which their imaginations have rendered sacred, to a degree, that they force common reason to find room for it, in every part of nature; reducing, including, and adjusting every genus and species within that compass, by coupling some against their wills, and banishing others at any rate. Now, among all the rest, the profound number THREE is that which has most employed my sublimest speculations, nor ever without wonderful delight. There is now in the press, and will be published next term, a panegyrical essay of mine upon this number; wherein I have, by most convincing proofs, not only reduced the senses and the elements under its banner, but brought over several deserters from its two great rivals, SEVEN and NINE.

Now, the first of these oratorial machines, in place as well as dignity, is the pulpit. Of pulpits there are in this island several sorts; but I esteem only that made of timber from the *sylva Caledonia*, which agrees very well with our climate. If it be upon its decay, it is the better both for conveyance of sound, and for other reasons to be mentioned by-and-by. The degree of perfection in shape and size I take to consist in being extremely narrow, with little ornament; and, best of all, without cover (for, by ancient rule, it ought to be the only uncovered vessel in every assembly, where it is rightfully used), by which means, from its near resemblance to a pillory, it will ever have a mighty influence on human ears.

Of ladders I need say nothing: it is observed by foreigners themselves, to the honour of our country, that we excel all nations in our practice and understanding of this machine. The ascending orators do not only oblige their audience in the agreeable delivery, but the whole world in the early publication of their speeches; which I look upon as the choicest treasury of our British eloquence, and whereof, I am informed, that worthy citizen and bookseller, Mr. John Dunton, hath made a faithful and painful collection, which he shortly designs to publish, in twelve volumes in folio, illustrated with copper-plates. A work highly useful and curious, and altogether worthy of such a hand.

The last engine of orators is the stage itinerant[1], erected with much sagacity, *sub Jove pluvio, in triviis et quadriviis*[2]. It is the great seminary of the two former, and its orators are sometimes preferred to the one, and sometimes to the other, in proportion to their deservings; there being a strict and perpetual intercourse between all three.

---

1 Is the mountebank's stage, whose orators the author determines either to the gallows or a conventicle.
2 In the open air, and in streets where the greatest resort is.

From this accurate deduction it is manifest, that for obtaining attention in public there is of necessity required a superior position of place. But, although this point be generally granted, yet the cause is little agreed in; and it seems to me that very few philosophers have fallen into a true, natural solution of this phenomenon. The deepest account, and the most fairly digested of any I have yet met with, is this; that air being a heavy body, and therefore, according to the system of Epicurus*, continually descending, must needs be more so when loaded and pressed down by words; which are also bodies of much weight and gravity, as it is manifest from those deep impressions they make and leave upon us; and therefore must be delivered from a due altitude, or else they will neither carry a good aim, nor fall down with a sufficient force.

* Lucret. Lib. 2.

"Corpoream quoque enim vocem constare fatendum est,
Et sonitum, quoniam possunt impellere sensus[1]."
—Lucr. Lib. 4.

And I am the readier to favour this conjecture, from a common observation, that in the several assemblies of these orators nature itself has instructed the hearers to stand with their mouths open, and erected parallel to the horizon, so as they may be intersected by a perpendicular line from the zenith to the centre of the earth. In which position, if the audience be well compact, every one carries home a share, and little or nothing is lost.

I confess there is something yet more refined, in the contrivance and structure of our modern theatres. For, first, the pit is sunk below the stage, with due regard to the institution above deduced; that, whatever weighty matter shall be delivered thence, whether it be lead or gold, may fall plump into the jaws of certain critics, as I think they are called, which stand ready opened to devour them. Then, the boxes are built

---

1 'Tis certain then, that voice that thus can wound
  Is all material; body every sound.

round, and raised to a level with the scene, in deference to the ladies; because, that large portion of wit, laid out in raising pruriences and protuberances, is observed to run much upon a line, and ever in a circle. The whining passions, and little starved conceits, are gently wafted up by their own extreme levity, to the middle region, and there fix and are frozen by the frigid understandings of the inhabitants. Bombastry and buffoonery, by nature lofty and light, soar highest of all, and would be lost in the roof, if the prudent architect had not, with much foresight, contrived for them a fourth place, called the twelve-penny gallery, and there planted a suitable colony, who greedily intercept them in their passage.

Now this physico-logical scheme of oratorial receptacles or machines contains a great mystery; being a type, a sign, an emblem, a shadow, a symbol, bearing analogy to the spacious commonwealth of writers, and to those methods by which they must exalt themselves to a certain eminency above the inferior world. By the pulpit are adumbrated the writings of our modern saints in Great Britain, as they have spiritualised and refined them, from the dross and grossness of sense and human reason. The matter, as we have said, is of rotten wood; and that upon two considerations; because it is the quality of rotten wood to give light in the dark: and secondly, because its cavities are full of worms; which is a type[1] with a pair of handles, having a respect to the two principal qualifications of the orator, and the two different fates attending upon his works.

The ladder is an adequate symbol of *faction* and of poetry, to both of which so noble a number of authors are indebted for their fame. Of faction, because[2] * * * * * * * * * * * * * *
* *

Hiatus in MS *
* *

---

1 The two principal qualifications of a fanatic preacher are, his inward light, and his head full of maggots, and the two different fates of his writings are, to be burnt or worm eaten.
2 Here is pretended a defect in the manuscript, and this is very frequent with our author, either when he thinks he cannot say any thing worth reading, or when he has no mind to enter

Of *poetry*, because its orators do *perorare* with a song; and because, climbing up by slow degrees, fate is sure to turn them off before they can reach within many steps of the top: and because it is a preferment attained by transferring of propriety, and a confounding of *meum* and *tuum*.

Under the stage itinerant are couched those productions designed for the pleasure and delight of mortal man; such as, Six-penny-worth of Wit, Westminster Drolleries, Delightful Tales, Complete Jesters, and the like; by which the writers of and for *Grub Street* have in these latter ages so nobly triumphed over Time; have clipped his wings, pared his nails, filed his teeth, turned back his hour-glass, blunted his scythe, and drawn the hobnails out of his shoes. It is under this class I have presumed to list my present treatise, being just come from having the honour conferred upon me to be adopted a member of that illustrious fraternity.

Now, I am not unaware how the productions of the Grub Street brotherhood have of late years fallen under many prejudices, nor how it has been the perpetual employment of two junior start-up societies to ridicule them and their authors, as unworthy their established post in the commonwealth of wit and learning. Their own consciences will easily inform them whom I mean; nor has the world been so negligent a looker-on as not to observe the continual efforts made by the societies of Gresham and of Will's[1] to edify a name and reputation upon the ruin of OURS. And this is yet a more feeling grief to us, upon the regards of tenderness as well as of justice, when we reflect on their proceedings not only as unjust, but as ungrateful, undutiful, and unnatural. For how can it be forgot by the world or themselves, to say nothing of onge us to a comparison of books, both as to weight and number. In return to which, with license from our president, I humbly

on the subject, or when it is a matter of little moment, or perhaps to amuse his reader (whereof he is frequently very fond) or lastly, with some satirical intention.
1 Will's coffee-house was formerly the place where the poets usually met, which tho it be yet fresh in memory, yet in some years may be forgot, and want this explanation.

offer two answers: first, we say, the proposal is like that which
Archimedes made upon a smaller affair*,
including an impossibility in the practice; for
where can they find scales of capacity enough for the first; or
an arithmetician of capacity enough for the second? Secondly,
we are ready to accept the challenge; but with this condition,
that a third indifferent person be assigned, to whose impartial
judgment it should be left to decide which society each book,
treatise, or pamphlet do most properly belong to. This point,
God knows, is very far from being fixed at present; for we are
ready to produce a catalogue of some thousands, which in all
common justice ought to be entitled to our fraternity, but by
the revolted and new-fangled writers, most prefidiously
ascribed to the others. Upon all which, we think it very
unbecoming our prudence that the determination should be
remitted to the authors themselves; when our adversaries, by
briguing and caballing, have caused so universal a defection
from us, that the greatest part of our society has already
deserted to them, and our nearest friends begin to stand aloof,
as if they were half ashamed to own us.

* Viz. About moving the Earth.

This is the utmost I am authorised to say upon so ungrateful
and melancholy a subject; because we are extremely unwilling
to inflame a controversy whose continuance may be so fatal to
the interests of us all, desiring much rather that things be
amicably composed; and we shall so far advance on our side as
to be ready to receive the two prodigals with open arms
whenever they shall think fit to return from their husks and their
harlots; which, I think, from the present
course* of their studies, they most
properly may be said to be engaged in; and, like an indulgent
parent, continue to them our affection and our blessing.

* Virtuoso experiments, and modern comedies.

But the greatest maim given to that general reception which
the writings of our society have formerly received (next to the
transitory state of all sublunary things) has been a superficial
vein among many readers of the present age, who will by no
means be persuaded to inspect beyond the surface and the

rind of things; whereas, wisdom is a fox, who, after long hunting, will at last cost you the pains to dig out; it is a cheese, which, by how much the richer, has the thicker, the homelier, and the coarser coat; and whereof, to a judicious palate, the maggots are the best: it is a sack-posset, wherein the deeper you go, you will find it the sweeter. Wisdom is a hen, whose cackling we must value and consider, because it is attended with an egg; but then lastly, it is a nut, which, unless you choose with judgment, may cost you a tooth, and pay you with nothing but a worm. In consequence of these momentous truths, the Grubæan sages have always chosen to convey their precepts and their arts shut up within the vehicles of types and fables; which having been perhaps more careful and curious in adorning than was altogether necessary, it has fared with these vehicles, after the usual fate of coaches over-finely painted and gilt, that the transitory gazers have so dazzled their eyes and filled their imaginations with the outward lustre, as neither to regard or consider the person or the parts of the owner within. A misfortune we undergo with somewhat less reluctancy, because it has been common to us with Pythagoras, Æsop, Socrates, and other of our predecessors.

However, that neither the world nor ourselves may any longer suffer by such misunderstandings, I have been prevailed on, after much importunity from my friends, to travel in a complete and laborious dissertation upon the prime productions of our society; which, beside their beautiful externals, for the gratification of superficial readers, have darkly and deeply couched under them the most finished and refined systems of all sciences and arts; as I do not doubt to lay open, by untwisting or unwinding, and either to draw up by exantlation, or display by incision.

This great work was entered upon some years ago, by one of our most eminent members; he began with the *History of Reynard the Fox*[1], but neither lived to publish his essay nor to proceed farther in so useful an attempt; which is very much to be lamented, because the discovery he made and communicated with his friends is now universally received; nor do I think any of the learned will dispute that famous treatise to be a complete body of civil knowledge, and the revelation, or rather the apocalypse, of all state arcana. But the progress I have made is much greater, having finished my annotations upon several dozens; from some of which I shall impart a few hints to the candid reader, as far as will be necessary to the conclusion at which I aim.

The first piece I have handled is that of *Tom Thumb*, whose author was a Pythagorean philosopher. This dark treatise contains the whole scheme of the Metempsychosis, deducing the progress of the soul through all her stages.

The next is *Dr. Faustus*, penned by Artephius, an author *bonœ notœ*, and an *adeptus*; he published it in the nine-hundred-eighty-fourth* year of his age; this

* He lived a thousand.

writer proceeds wholly by reincrudation, or in the *via humida*; and the marriage between Faustus and Helen does most conspicuously dilucidate the fermenting of the male and female dragon.

Whittington and his Cat is the work of that mysterious rabbi, Jehuda Hannasi, containing a defence of the gemara of the Jerusalem misna, and its just preference to that of Babylon, contrary to the vulgar opinion.

The Hind and Panther. This is the masterpiece of a famous writer* now living, intended for a complete

* Viz in the year 1698.

abstract of sixteen thousand schoolmen, from Scotus to Bellarmin.

Tommy Potts. Another piece, supposed by the same hand, by way of supplement to the former.

The Wise Men of Gotham, cum appendice. This is a treatise of immense erudition, being the great original and fountain of those arguments bandied about both in France and England

---

1 The author seems here to be mistaken, for I have seen a Latin edition of Reynard the Fox, above an hundred years old, which I take to be the original; for the rest it has been thought by many people to contain some satirical design in it.

for a just defence of the moderns' learning and wit, against the presumption, the pride, and ignorance of the ancients. This unknown author has so exhausted the subject, that a penetrating reader will easily discover whatever has been written since upon that dispute to be little more than repetition. An abstract of this treatise[1] has been lately published by a worthy member of our society.

These notices may serve to give the learned reader an idea, as well as a taste, of what the whole work is likely to produce; wherein I have now altogether circumscribed my thoughts and my studies; and, if I can bring it to a perfection before I die, shall reckon I have well employed the poor remains of an unfortunate life[2]. This, indeed, is more than I can justly expect, from a quill worn to the pith in the service of the state, in *pros* and *cons* upon Popish plots, and meal-tubs[3], and exclusion bills, and passive obedience, and addresses of lives and fortunes, and prerogative, and property, and liberty of conscience, and letters to a friend; from an understanding and a conscience threadbare and ragged with perpetual turning; from a head broken in a hundred places by the malignants of the opposite factions; and from a body spent with poxes ill cured, by trusting to bawds and surgeons, who, as it afterwards appeared, were professed enemies to me and the government, and revenged their party's quarrel upon my nose and shins. Fourscore and eleven pamphlets have I written under three reigns, and for the service of six-and-thirty factions. But, finding the state has no farther occasion for me and my ink, I retire willingly to draw it out into speculations more becoming a philosopher; having, to my unspeakable comfort, passed a long life with a conscience void of offence.

---

1 This I suppose to be understood of Mr. W-tt-n's discourse of ancient and modern learning.
2 Here the author seems to personate L'Estrange, Dryden, and some others, who after having past their lives in vices, faction and falsehood, have the impudence to talk of merit and innocence and sufferings.
3 In King Charles the II. time, there was an account of a Presbyterian plot, found in a tub, which then made much noise.

But to return. I am assured, from the reader's candour, that the brief specimen I have given will easily clear all the rest of our society's productions from an aspersion grown, as it is manifest, out of envy and ignorance: that they are of little farther use or value to mankind beyond the common entertainments of their wit and their style; for these I am sure have never yet been disputed by our keenest adversaries; in both which, as well as the more profound and mystical part, I have, throughout this treatise, closely followed the most applauded originals. And to render all complete, I have, with much thought and application of mind, so ordered, that the chief title prefixed to it, I mean that under which I design it shall pass in the common conversations of court and town, is modelled exactly after the manner peculiar to our society.

I confess to have been somewhat liberal in the business of titles*, having observed the humour of multiplying them to bear great vogue among certain writers, whom I exceedingly reverence. And indeed it seems not unreasonable that books, the children of the brain, should have the honour to be christened with variety of names as well as other infants of quality. Our famous Dryden has ventured to proceed a point farther, endeavouring to introduce also a multiplicity of godfathers*; which is an improvement of much more advantage upon a very obvious account. It is a pity this admirable invention has not been better cultivated, so as to grow by this time into general imitation, when such an authority serves it for a precedent. Nor have my endeavours been wanting to second so useful an example; but it seems there is an unhappy expense usually annexed to the calling of a godfather, which was clearly out of my head, as it is very reasonable to believe. Where the pinch lay I cannot certainly affirm; but having employed a world of thoughts

* The title page in the original was so torn, that it was not possible to recover several titles which the author here speaks of.

* See Virgil translated, &c.

and pains to split my treatise into forty sections, and having entreated forty lords of my acquaintance that they would do me the honour to stand, they all made it a matter of conscience, and sent me their excuses.

SECTION II

꿈 Once upon a time there was a man who had three sons[1] by one wife, and all at a birth, neither could the midwife tell certainly which was the eldest. Their father died while they were young; and upon his death-bed, calling the lads to him, spoke thus:

꿈 "Sons, because I have purchased no estate, nor was born to any, I have long considered of some good legacies to bequeath you; and at last, with much care, as well as expense, have provided each of you (here they are) a new coat[2]. Now, you are to understand that these coats have two virtues contained in them; one is, that with good wearing they will last you fresh and sound as long as you live; the other is, that they will grow in the same proportion with your bodies, lengthening and widening of themselves, so as to be always fit. Here; let me see them on you before I die. So; very well; pray, children, wear them clean, and brush them often. You will find in my will[3] (here it is) full instructions in every particular concerning the wearing and management of your coats; wherein you must be very exact, to avoid the penalties I have appointed for every trangression or neglect, upon which your future fortunes will entirely depend. I have also commanded in my will that you should live together in one house like brethren and friends, for then you will be sure to thrive, and not otherwise."

Here the story says, this good father died, and the three sons went all together to seek their fortunes.

I shall not trouble you with recounting what adventures they met for the first seven years, any farther than by taking notice

---

1 By these three sons, Peter, Martin and Jack; Popery, the Church of England, and our Ptotestant dissenters are designed. W. Wotton.
2 By his coats which he gave his sons, the garments of the Israelites. W. Wotton.
    An error (with submission) of the learned commentator; for by the coats are meant the doctrine and faith of Christianity, by the wisdom of the divine founder fitted to all times, places and circumstances. Lambin.
3 The New Testament.

that they carefully observed their father's will, and kept their coats in very good order: that they travelled through several countries, encountered a reasonable quantity of giants, and slew certain dragons.

Being now arrived at the proper age for producing themselves, they came up to town, and fell in love with the ladies, but especially three, who about that time were in chief reputation: the Duchess d'Argent, Madame de Grands Titres, and the Countess d'Orgueil[1]. On their first appearance our three adventurers met with a very bad reception; and soon with great sagacity guessing out the reason, they quickly began to improve in the good qualities of the town; they wrote, and rallied, and rhymed, and sung, and said, and said nothing; they drank, and fought, and whored, and slept, and swore, and took snuff; they went to new plays on the first night, haunted the chocolate-houses, beat the watch, lay on bulks, and got claps they bilked hackney-coachmen, ran in debt with shopkeepers, and lay with their wives; they killed bailiffs, kicked fiddlers downstairs, eat at Locket's, loitered at Will's; they talked of the drawing-room, and never came there; dined with lords they never saw; whispered a duchess, and spoke never a word; exposed the scrawls of their laundress for billets-doux of quality; came over just from court, and were never seen in it; attended the levee *sub dio*; got a list of peers by heart in one company, and with great familiarity retailed them in another. Above all, they constantly attended those committees of senators who are silent in the house and loud in the coffee-house; where they nightly adjourn to chew the cud of politics, and are encompassed with a ring of disciples, who lie in wait to catch up their droppings. The three brothers had acquired forty other qualifications of the like stamp, too tedious to recount, and by consequence were justly reckoned the most

1 Their mistresses are the Duchess d'Argent, Mademoiselle de Grands Titres, and the Countess d'Orgueil, i.e. Covetousness, Ambition and Pride, which were the three great vices that the ancient fathers inveighed against as the first corruptions of Christianity. W. Wotton.

accomplished persons in the town; but all would not suffice, and the ladies aforesaid continued still inflexible. To clear up which difficulty I must, with the reader's good leave and patience, have recourse to some points of weight, which the authors of that age have not sufficiently illustrated.

For about this time[1] it happened a sect arose whose tenets obtained and spread very far, especially in the *grand monde*, and among everybody of good fashion. They worshipped a sort of idol, who, as their doctrine delivered, did daily create men by a kind of manufactory operation. This idol[2] they placed in the highest part of the house, on an altar erected about three foot; he was shown in the posture of a Persian emperor, sitting on a superficies, with his legs interwoven under him. This god had a goose for his ensign; whence it is that some learned men pretend to deduce his original from Jupiter Capitolinus. At his left hand, beneath the altar, hell seemed to open and catch at the animals the idol was creating; to prevent which, certain of his priests hourly flung in pieces of the uninformed mass, or substance, and sometimes whole limbs already enlivened, which that horrid gulf insatiably swallowed, terrible to behold. The goose was also held a subaltern divinity or *deus minorum gentium*, before whose shrine was sacrificed that creature whose hourly food is human gore, and who is in so great renown abroad for being the delight and favourite of the Ægyptian Cercopithecus[3]. Millions of these animal were cruelly slaughtered every day to appease the hunger of that consuming deity. The chief idol was also worshipped as the inventor of the yard and needle; whether as the god of seamen, or on account of certain other mystical attributes, has not been sufficiently cleared.

The worshippers of this deity had also a system of their belief, which seemed to turn upon the following funda-

---

1 This is an occasional satire upon dress and fashion, in order to introduce what follows.
2 By this idol is meant a tailor.
3 The Ægyptians worship'd a monkey, which animal is very fond of eating lice, styled here creatures that feed on human gore.

mentals. They held the universe to be a large suit of clothes, which invests everything; that the earth is invested by the air; the air is invested by the stars; and the stars are invested by the *primum mobile*. Look on this globe of earth, you will find it to be a very complete and fashionable dress. What is that which some call land but a fine coat faced with green? or the sea, but a waistcoat of water-tabby? Proceed to the particular works of the creation, you will find how curious journeyman Nature has been to trim up the vegetable beaux; observe how sparkish a periwig adorns the head of a beech, and what a fine doublet of white satin is worn by the birch. To conclude from all, what is man himself but a microcoat[1], or rather a complete suit of clothes with all its trimmings? As to his body there can be no dispute; but examine even the acquirements of his mind, you will find them all contribute in their order towards furnishing out an exact dress: to instance no more; is not religion a cloak, honesty a pair of shoes worn out in the dirt, self-love a surtout, vanity a shirt, and conscience a pair of breeches, which, though a cover for lewdness as well as nastiness, is easily slipt down for the service of both?

These postulata being admitted, it will follow in due course of reasoning that those beings, which the world calls improperly suits of clothes, are in reality the most refined species of animals; or, to proceed higher, that they are rational creatures or men. For, is it not manifest that they live, and move, and talk, and perform all other offices of human life? are not beauty, and wit, and mien, and breeding, their inseparable proprieties? in short, we see nothing but them, hear nothing but them. Is it not they who walk the streets, fill up parliament-, coffee-, play-, bawdy-houses? It is true, indeed, that these animals, which are vulgarly called suits of clothes, or dresses, do, according to certain compositions, receive different appellations. If one of them be trimmed up with a gold chain,

---

1 Alluding to the word microcosm, or a little world, as Man hath been called by philosophers.

and a red gown, and white rod, and a great horse, it is called a lord-mayor: if certain ermines and furs be placed in a certain position, we style them a judge; and so an apt conjunction of lawn and black satin we entitle a bishop.

Others of these professors, though agreeing in the main system, were yet more refined upon certain branches of it; and held that man was an animal compounded of two dresses, the natural and celestial suit, which were the body and the soul: that the soul was the outward, and the body the inward clothing; that the latter was *ex traduce*; but the former of daily creation and circumfusion; this last they proved by scripture, because in them we live, and move, and have our being; as likewise by philosophy, because they are all in all, and all in every part. Besides, said they, separate these two and you will find the body to be only a senseless unsavoury carcase; by all which it is manifest that the outward dress must needs be the soul.

To this system of religion were tagged several subaltern doctrines, which were entertained with great vogue: as particularly the faculties of the mind were deduced by the learned among them in this manner; embroidery was sheer wit, gold fringe was agreeable conversation, gold lace was repartee, a huge long periwig was humour, and a coat full of powder was very good raillery—all which required abundance of *finesse* and *delicatesse* to manage with advantage, as well as a strict observance after times and fashions.

I have, with much pains and reading, collected out of ancient authors this short summary of a body of philosophy and divinity, which seems to have been composed by a vein and race of thinking very different from any other systems either ancient or modern. And it was not merely to entertain or satisfy the reader's curiosity, but rather to give him light into several circumstances of the following story; that, knowing the state of dispositions and opinions in an age so remote, he may better comprehend those great events which were the issue of them. I advise, therefore, the courteous reader to peruse with a world of application, again and again, whatever I have written upon this matter. And so leaving these broken ends, I carefully gather up the chief thread of my story and proceed.

These opinions, therefore, were so universal, as well as the practices of them, among the refined part of court and town, that our three brother adventurers, as their circumstances then stood, were strangely at a loss. For, on the one side[1], the three ladies they addressed themselves to, whom we have named already, were ever at the very top of the fashion, and abhorred all that were below it but the breadth of a hair. On the other side, their father's will was very precise; and it was the main precept in it, with the greatest penalties annexed, not to add to or diminish from their coats one thread, without a positive command in the will. Now, the coats their father had left them were, it is true, of very good cloth, and besides so neatly sewn, you would swear they were all of a piece; but at the same time very plain, and with little or no ornament: and it happened that before they were a month in town great shoulder-knots[2] came up—straight all the world was shoulder-knots—no approaching the ladies' *ruelles* without the *quota* of shoulder-knots. That fellow, cries one, has no soul; where is his shoulder-knot? Our three brethren soon discovered their want by sad experience, meeting in their walks with forty mortifications and indignities. If they went to the playhouse the door-keeper showed them into the twelvepenny gallery; if they called a boat, says a waterman, "I am first sculler;" if they

---

1 The first part of the Tale is the history of Peter; thereby Popery is exposed, every body knows the Papists have made great additions to Christianity, that indeed is the great exception which the Church of England makes against them, accordingly Peter begins his pranks, with adding a shoulder-knot to his coat. W. Wotton.

His description of the cloth of which the coat was made, has a farther meaning than the words may seem to import. "The coats their father had left them, were of very good cloth, and besides so neatly sown, you would swear it had been all of a piece, but at the same time very plain with little or no ornament." This is the distinguishing character of the Christian religion. Christiana religio absoluta & simplex, was Ammianus Marcellinus's description of it, who was himself a heathen. W. Wotton.

2 By this is understood the first introducing of pageantry, and unnecessary ornaments in the Church, such as were neither for convenience nor edification, as a shoulder-knot, in which there is neither symmetry nor use.

stepped to the Rose to take a bottle, the drawer would cry, "Friend, we sell no ale;" if they went to visit a lady, a footman met them at the door with "Pray send up your message." In this unhappy case they went immediately to consult their father's will, read it over and over, but not a word of the shoulder-knot. What should they do?—what temper should they find?—obedience was absolutely necessary, and yet shoulder-knots appeared extremely requisite. After much thought one of the brothers, who happened to be more book-learned than the other two, said he had found an expedient. It is true, said he, there is nothing here in this will, *totidem verbis*[1], making mention of shoulder-knots: but I dare conjecture we may find them *inclusive*, or *totidem syllabis*. This distinction was immediately approved by all, and so they fell again to examine; but their evil star had so directed the matter that the first syllable was not to be found in the whole writings. Upon which disappointment, he who found the former evasion took heart, and said, "Brothers, there are yet hopes; for though we cannot find them *totidem verbis*, nor *totidem syllabis*, I dare engage we shall make them out *tertio modo* or *totidem literis*. This discovery was also highly commended, upon which they fell once more to the scrutiny, and soon picked out S, H, O, U, L, D, E, R; when the same planet, enemy to their repose, had wonderfully contrived that a K was not to be found. Here was a weighty difficulty! but the distinguishing brother, for whom we shall hereafter find a name, now his hand was in, proved by a very good argument that K was a modern, illegitimate letter, unknown to the learned ages, nor anywhere to be found in ancient manuscripts. It is true, said he, the word Calendæ hath in Q. V. C.*[2] been sometimes

* Quibusdam Veteribus Codicibus.

---

1 When the Papists cannot find any thing which they want in Scripture, they go to oral tradition: thus Peter is introduced satisfy'd with the tedious way of looking for all the letters of any word, which he has occasion for in the will, when neither the constituent syllables, nor much less the whole word, were there in terminis. W. Wotton.
2 Some ancient manuscripts.

written with a K, but erroneously; for in the best copies it has been ever spelt with a C. And, by consequence, it was a gross mistake in our language to spell knot with a K; but that from henceforward he would take care it should be written with a C. Upon this all farther difficulty vanished—shoulder-knots were made clearly out to be *jure paterno*, and our three gentlemen swaggered with as large and as flaunting ones as the best. But, as human happiness is of a very short duration, so in those days were human fashions, upon which it entirely depends. Shoulder-knots had their time, and we must now imagine them in their decline; for a certain lord came just from Paris, with fifty yards of gold lace upon his coat, exactly trimmed after the court fashion of that month. In two days all mankind appeared closed up in bars of gold lace[1]: whoever durst peep abroad without his complement of gold lace was as scandalous as a —, and as ill received among the women: what should our three knights do in this momentous affair? they had sufficiently strained a point already in the affair of shoulder-knots: upon recourse to the will, nothing appeared there but *altum silentium*. That of the shoulder-knots was a loose, flying, circumstantial point; but this of gold lace seemed too considerable an alteration without better warrant; it did *aliquo modo essentiæ adhærere*, and therefore required a positive precept. But about this time it fell out that the learned brother aforesaid had read *Aristotelis dialectica*, and especially that wonderful piece *de interpretatione*, which has the faculty of teaching its readers to find out a meaning in everything but itself; like commentators on the Revelations, who proceed prophets without understanding a syllable of the text. Brothers, said he, you are to be informed[2] that of wills

---

1 I cannot tell whether the author means any new innovation by this word, or whether it be only to introduce the new methods of forcing and perverting Scripture.
2 The next subject of our author's wit, is the glosses and interpretations of Scripture, very many absurd ones of which are allow'd in the most authentic books of the Church of Rome. W. Wotton.

duo sunt genera, nuncupatory[1] and scriptory: that in the scriptory will here before us there is no precept or mention about gold lace, *conceditur*: but *si idem affirmetur de nuncupatorio, negatur*. For, brothers, if you remember, we heard a fellow say when we were boys that he heard my father's man say that he would advise his sons to get gold lace on their coats as soon as ever they could procure money to buy it. By G——! that is very true, cries the other; I remember it perfectly well, said the third. And so without more ado they got the largest gold lace in the parish, and walked about as fine as lords.

A while after there came up all in fashion a pretty sort of flame-coloured satin[2] for linings; and the mercer brought a pattern of it immediately to our three gentlemen, An please your worships, said he, my lord Conway[3] and Sir John Walters had linings out of this very piece last night: it takes wonderfully, and I shall not have a remnant left enough to make my wife a pincushion by tomorrow morning at ten o'clock. Upon this they fell again to rummage the will, because the present case also required a positive precept—the lining being held by orthodox writers to be of the essence of the coat. After a long search they could fix upon nothing to the matter in hand, except a short advice of their father in the will to take care of fire[4] and put out their candles before they went

---

1 By this is meant tradition, allowed to have an equal authority with the Scripture, or rather greater.

2 This is purgatory, whereof he speaks more particularly hereafter, but here only to shew how Scripture was perverted to prove it, which was done by giving equal authority with the Canon to Apocrypha, called here a codicil annex'd.

   It is likely the author, in every one of these changes in the brother's dresses, refers to some particular error in the Church of Rome; tho' it is not easy I think to apply them all, but by this of flame colour'd satin is manifestly intended purgatory; by gold lace may perhaps be understood, the lofty ornaments and plate in the churches. The shoulder-knots and silver fringe, are not so obvious, at least to me; but the Indian figures of men, women and children plainly relate to the pictures in the Romish churches, of God like an old man, of the Virgin Mary and our Saviour as a child.

3 This shews the time the author writ, it being about fourteen years since those two persons were reckoned the fine gentlemen of the town.

4 That is, to take care of hell, and, in order to do that, to subdue and extinguish their lusts.

to sleep. This, though a good deal for the purpose, and helping very far towards self-conviction, yet not seeming wholly of force to establish a command (being resolved to avoid further scruple as well as future occasion for scandal), says he that was the scholar, I remember to have read in wills of a codicil annexed, which is indeed a part of the will, and what it contains has equal authority with the rest. Now, I have been considering of this same will here before us, and I cannot reckon it to be complete for want of such a codicil: I will therefore fasten one in its proper place very dexterously—I have had it by me some time—it was written by a dog-keeper[1] of my grandfather's, and talks a great deal, as good luck would have it, of this very flame-coloured satin. The project was immediately approved by the other two; an old parchment scroll was tagged on according to art in the form of a codicil annexed, and the satin bought and worn.

Next winter a player, hired for the purpose by the corporation of fringe-makers, acted his part in a new comedy, all covered with silver fringe[2], and, according to the laudable custom, gave rise to that fashion. Upon which the brothers, consulting their father's will, to their great astonishment found these words; *item*, I charge and command my said three sons to wear no sort of silver fringe upon or about their said coats, etc., with a penalty, in case of disobedience, too long here to insert. However, after some pause, the brother so often mentioned for his erudition, who was well skilled in criticisms, had found in a certain author, which he said should be nameless, that the same word which in the will is called fringe does also signify a broomstick: and doubtless ought to have the same interpretation in this paragraph. This another of the brothers disliked, because of that epithet silver, which could not, he humbly conceived, in propriety of speech be reason-

1 I believe this refers to that part of the Apocrypha where mention is made of Tobit and his dog.
2 This is certainly the farther introducing the pomps of habit and ornament.

ably applied to a broomstick: but it was replied upon him that this epithet was understood in a mythological and allegorical sense. However, he objected again why their father should forbid them to wear a broomstick on their coats—a caution that seemed unnatural and impertinent; upon which he was taken up short, as one that spoke irreverently of a mystery, which doubtless was very useful and significant, but ought not to be over-curiously pried into or nicely reasoned upon. And, in short, their father's authority being now considerably sunk, this expedient was allowed to serve as a lawful dispensation for wearing their full proportion of silver fringe.

A while after was revived an old fashion, long antiquated, of embroidery with Indian figures[1] of men, women, and children. Here they remembered but too well how their father had always abhorred this fashion; that he made several paragraphs on purpose, importing his utter detestation of it, and bestowing his everlasting curse to his sons whenever they should wear it. For all this, in a few days they appeared higher in the fashion than anybody else in the town. But they solved the matter by saying that these figures were not at all the same with those that were formerly worn and were meant in the will. Besides, they did not wear them in the sense as forbidden by their father; but as they were a commendable custom, and of great use to the public. That these rigorous clauses in the will did therefore require some allowance and a favourable interpretation, and ought to be understood *cum grano salis*.

But fashions perpetually altering in that age, the scholastic brother grew weary of searching farther evasions, and solving everlasting contradictions. Resolved, therefore, at all hazards, to comply with the modes of the world, they concerted matters together, and agreed unanimously to lock

---

1 The images of saints, the Blessed Virgin, and our Saviour as an infant.
  Ibid. Images in the Church of Rome give him but too fair a handle. The brothers remembered, &c. The allegory here is direct. W. Wotton.

up their father's will[1] in a strong box, brought out of Greece or Italy, I have forgotten which, and trouble themselves no farther to examine it, but only refer to its authority whenever they thought fit. In consequence whereof, a while after it grew a general mode to wear an infinite number of points, most of them tagged with silver: upon which the scholar pronounced, *ex cathedra*[2], that points were absolutely *jure paterno*, as they might very well remember. It is true, indeed, the fashion prescribed somewhat more than were directly named in the will; however, that they, as heirs-general of their father, had power to make and add certain clauses for public emolument, though not deducible, *totidem verbis*, from the letter of the will, or else *multa absurda sequerentur*. This was understood for canonical, and therefore, on the following Sunday, they came to church all covered with points.

The learned brother, so often mentioned, was reckoned the best scholar in all that or the next street to it, insomuch as, having run something behindhand in the world, he obtained the favour of a certain lord[3] to receive him into his house, and to teach his children. A while after the lord died, and he, by long practice upon his father's will, found the way of contriving a deed of conveyance of that house to himself and his heirs; upon which he took possession, turned the young squires out, and received his brothers in their stead.

---

1 The Papists formerly forbad the people the use of Scripture in a vulgar tongue, Peter therefore locks up his father's will in a strong box, brought out of Greece or Italy. Those countries are named because the New Testament is written in Greek; and the Vulgar Latin, which is the authentic edition of the Bible in the Church of Rome, is in the language of old Italy. W. Wotton.

2 The Popes in their decretals and bulls, have given their sanction to very many gainful doctrines which are now received in the Church of Rome that are not mention'd in Scriptures, and are unknown to the Primitive Church. Peter accordingly pronounces ex cathedra, that points tagged with silver were absolutely jure paterno, and so they wore them in great numbers. W. Wotton.

3 This was Constantine the Great, from whom the Popes pretend a donation of St. Peter's patrimony, which they have been never able to produce.

A Digression Concerning Critics

Although I have been hitherto as cautious as I could, upon all occasions, most nicely to follow the rules and methods of writing laid down by the example of our illustrious moderns; yet has the unhappy shortness of my memory led me into an error from which I must immediately extricate myself, before I can decently pursue my principal subject. I confess with shame it was an unpardonable omission to proceed so far as I have already done before I had performed the due discourses, expostulatory, supplicatory, or deprecatory, with my good lords the critics. Towards some atonement for this grievous neglect, I do here make bold humbly to present them with a short account of themselves and their art, by looking into the original and pedigree of the word, as it is generally understood among us; and very briefly considering the ancient and present state thereof.

By the word critic, at this day so frequent in all conversations, there have sometimes been distinguished three very different species of mortal men, according as I have read in ancient books and pamphlets. For first, by this term were understood such persons as invented or drew up rules for themselves and the world, by observing which a careful reader might be able to pronounce upon the productions of the learned, form his taste to a true relish of the sublime and the admirable, and divide every beauty of matter or of style from the corruption that apes it: in their common perusal of books singling out the errors and defects, the nauseous, the fulsome, the dull, and the impertinent, with the caution of a man that walks through Edinburgh streets in a morning, who is indeed as careful as he can to watch diligently and spy out the filth in his way; not that he is curious to observe the colour and complexion of the ordure, or take its dimensions, much less to be paddling in or tasting it; but only with a design to come out as cleanly as he may. These men seem, though very erroneously, to have understood the appellation of critic in a literal sense; that one principal part of his office was to praise and acquit; and that a critic who sets up to read only for an occasion of censure and reproof is a creature as barbarous as a judge who should take up a resolution to hang all men that came before him upon a trial.

Again, by the word critic have been meant the restorers of ancient learning from the worms, and graves, and dust of manuscripts.

Now the races of those two have been for some ages utterly extinct; and besides, to discourse any farther of them would not be at all to my purpose.

The third and noblest sort is that of the TRUE CRITIC, whose original is the most ancient of all. Every true critic is a hero born, descending in a direct line from a celestial stem by Momus and Hybris, who begat Zoilus, who begat Tigellius, who begat Etcætera the elder; who begat Bentley, and Rymer, and Wotton, and Perrault, and Dennis; who begat Etcætera the younger.

And these are the critics from whom the commonwealth of learning has in all ages received such immense benefits, that the gratitude of their admirers placed their origin in Heaven, among those of Hercules, Theseus, Perseus, and other great deservers of mankind. But heroic virtue itself has not been exempt from the obloquy of evil tongues. For it has been objected that those ancient heroes, famous for their combating so many giants, and dragons, and robbers, were in their own persons a greater nuisance to mankind than any of those monsters they subdued; and therefore, to render their obligations more complete, when all other vermin were destroyed, should, in conscience, have concluded with the same justice upon themselves. As Hercules most generously did, and upon that score procured to himself more temples and votaries than the best of his fellows. For these reasons I suppose it is why some have conceived it would be very expedient for the public good of learning that every true critic, as soon as he had finished his task assigned, should immediately deliver himself up to ratsbane, or hemp, or leap from some convenient altitude; and that no man's pretensions to so illustrious a character should by any means be received before that operation were performed.

Now, from this heavenly descent of criticism, and the close analogy it bears to heroic virtue, it is easy to assign the proper employment of a true ancient genuine critic, which is, to travel through this vast world of writings; to pursue and hunt those monstrous faults bred within them; to drag out the lurking errors, like Cacus from his den; to multiply them like Hydra's heads; and rake them together like Augeas's dung: or else drive away a sort of dangerous fowl, who have a perverse inclination to plunder the best branches of the tree of knowledge, like those Stymphalian birds that eat up the fruit.

These reasonings will furnish us with an adequate definition of a true critic: that he is discoverer and collector of writers' faults; which may be farther put beyond dispute by the following demonstration; that whoever will examine the writings in all kinds, wherewith this ancient sect has honoured the world, shall immediately find, from the whole thread and tenor of them, that the ideas of the authors have been altogether conversant and taken up with the faults, and blemishes, and oversights, and mistakes of other writers: and, let the subject treated on be whatever it will, their imaginations are so entirely possessed and replete with the defects of other pens, that the very quintessence of what is bad does of necessity distil into their own; by which means the whole appears to be nothing else but an abstract of the criticisms themselves have made.

Having thus briefly considered the original and office of a critic, as the word is understood in its most noble and universal acceptation, I proceed to refute the objections of those who argue from the silence and pretermission of authors; by which they pretend to prove that the very art of criticism, as now exercised, and by me explained, is wholly modern; and consequently that the critics of Great Britain and France have no title to an original so ancient and illustrious as I have deduced. Now, if I can clearly make out, on the contrary, that the ancient writers have particularly described both the person and the office of a true critic, agreeably to the definition laid down by me, their grand objection, from the silence of authors, will fall to the ground.

I confess to have, for a long time, borne a part in this general error: from which I should never have acquitted myself, but through the assistance of our noble moderns! whose most edifying volumes I turn undefatigably over night and day for the improvement of my mind and the good of my country: these have, with unwearied pains, made many useful searches into the weak sides of the ancients, and given us a comprehensive list of them. Besides*, they * See Wotton, Of Ancient and Modern Learning. have proved beyond contradiction that the very finest things delivered of old have been long since invented and brought to light by much later pens; and that the noblest discoveries those ancients ever made, of art or of nature, have all been produced by the transcending genius of the present age. Which clearly shows how little merit those ancients can justly pretend to, and takes off that blind admiration paid them by men in a corner who have the unhappiness of conversing too little with present things. Reflecting maturely upon all this, and taking in the whole compass of human nature, I easily concluded that these ancients, highly sensible of their many imperfections, must needs have endeavoured, from some passages in their works, to obviate, soften, or divert the censorious reader, by satire or panegyric upon the true critics, in imitation of their masters, the moderns. Now, in the commonplaces of * Satire, and panegyric upon critics. both these* I was plentifully instructed by a long course of useful study in prefaces and prologues; and therefore immediately resolved to try what I could discover of either by a diligent perusal of the most ancient writers, and especially those who treated of the earliest times. Here I found to my great surprise, that although they all entered, upon occasion, into particular descriptions of the true critic, according as they were governed by their fears or their hopes, yet whatever they touched of that kind was with abundance of caution, adventuring no further than mythology and hieroglyphic. This, I suppose, gave ground to superficial readers for urging the silence of authors against the antiquity of the true critic, though the types are so opposite, and the applications so necessary and natural, that it is not easy to conceive how any reader of a modern eye and taste could overlook them. I shall venture from a great number to produce a few, which, I am very confident, will put this question beyond dispute.

It well deserves considering that these ancient writers, in treating enigmatically upon this subject, have generally fixed upon the very same hieroglyph, varying only the story, according to their affections or their wit. For first; Pausanias is of opinion that the perfection of writing correct was entirely owing to the institution of critics; and that he can possibly mean no other than the true critic is, I think, manifest enough from the following description. He says, they were a race of men who delighted to nibble at the superfluities and excrescencies of books, which the learned at length observing, took warning, of their own accord, to lop the luxuriant, the rotten, the dead, the sapless, and the overgrown branches from their works. But now all this he cunningly shades under the following allegory; that the Nauplians* in * Lib – Argos learned the art of pruning their vines, by observing, that when an ASS had browsed upon one of them, it thrived the better and bore fairer * Lib. 4. fruit. But Herodotus*, holding the very same hieroglyph, speaks much plainer, and almost *in terminis*. He has been so bold as to tax the true critics of ignorance and malice; telling us openly, for I think nothing can be plainer, that in the western part of Libya there were ASSES with horns:

Vide excerpta ex eo apud Photium. upon which relation Ctesias* yet refines, mentioning the very same animal about India, adding that, whereas all other ASSES wanted a gall, these horned ones were so redundant in that part, that their flesh was not to be eaten, because of its extreme bitterness.

Now, the reason why those ancient writers treated this subject only by types and figures was, because they durst not make open attacks against a party so potent and so terrible as the critics of those ages were; whose very voice was so dreadful that a legion of authors would tremble and drop their pens at the sound; for so Herodotus* tells us *Lib. 4.* expressly in another place, how a vast army of Scythians was put to flight in a panic terror by the braying of an ASS. From hence it is conjectured by certain profound philologers that the great awe and reverence paid to a true critic by the writers of Britain have been derived to us from those our Scythian ancestors. In short, this dread was so universal, that in process of time those authors who had a mind to publish their sentiments more freely, in describing the true critics of their several ages, were forced to leave off the use of the former hieroglyph, as too nearly approaching the prototype, and invented other terms instead thereof, that were more cautious and mystical: so, Diodorus*, *Lib.* speaking to the same purpose, ventures no farther than to say that in the mountains of Helicon there grows a certain weed which bears a flower of so damned a scent as to poison those who offer to smell it. Lucretius gives exactly the same relation:—

"Est etiam in magnis Heliconis montibus arbos,
Floris odore hominem tetro consueta necare."
—*Lib.* 6[1].

But Ctesias, whom we recently quoted, has been a great deal bolder; he had been used with much severity by the true critics

---

1 Near Helicon, and round the learned hill,
  Grow trees, whose blossoms with their odour kill.

of his own age, and therefore could not forbear to leave behind him at least one deep mark of his vengeance against the whole tribe. His meaning is so near the surface, that I wonder how it possibly came to be overlooked by those who deny the antiquity of the true critics. For, pretending to make a description of many strange animals about India, he has set down these remarkable words: Among the rest, says he, there is a serpent that wants teeth, and consequently cannot bite; but if its vomit, to which it is much addicted, happens to fall upon anything, a certain rottenness or corruption ensues: these serpents are generally found among the mountains where jewels grow, and they frequently emit a poisonous juice: whereof whoever drinks, that person's brains fly out of his nostrils.

There was also among the ancients a sort of critics, not distinguished in species from the former, but in growth or degree, who seem to have been only the tyros or junior scholars; yet, because of their differing employments, they are frequently mentioned as a sect by themselves. The usual exercise of these younger students was to attend constantly at theatres, and learn to spy out the worst parts of the play, whereof they were obliged carefully to take note and render a rational account to their tutors. Fleshed at these smaller sports, like young wolves, they grew up in time to be nimble and strong enough for hunting down large game. For it has been observed, both among ancients and moderns, that a true critic has one quality in common with a whore and an alderman, never to change his title or his nature; that a grey critic has been certainly a green one, the perfections and acquirements of his age being only the improved talents of his youth; like hemp, which some naturalists inform us is bad for suffocations, though taken but in the seed. I esteem the invention, or at least the refinement of prologues, to have been owing to these younger proficients, of whom Terence makes frequent and honourable mention, under the name of *malevoli*.

Now, it is certain the institution of the true critics was of absolute necessity to the commonwealth of learning. For all human actions seem to be divided, like Themistocles and his company; one man can fiddle, and another can make a small town a great city; and he that cannot do either one or the other deserves to be kicked out of the creation. The avoiding of which penalty has doubtless given the first birth to the nation of critics; and withal, an occasion for their secret detractors to report that a true critic is a sort of mechanic, set up with a stock and tools for his trade at as little expense as a tailor; and that there is much analogy between the utensils and abilities of both: that the tailor's hell is the type of a critic's commonplace book, and his wit and learning held forth by the goose; that it requires at least as many of these to the making up of one scholar, as of the others to the composition of a man; that the valour of both is equal, and their weapons nearly of a size. Much may be said in answer to those invidious reflections; and I can positively affirm the first to be a falsehood: for, on the contrary, nothing is more certain than that it requires greater layings out to be free of the critic's company than of any other you can name. For as, to be a true beggar, it will cost the richest candidate every groat he is worth; so, before one can commence a true critic, it will cost a man all the good qualities of his mind; which, perhaps for a less purchase, would be thought but an indifferent bargain.

Having thus amply proved the antiquity of criticism, and described the primitive state of it, I shall now examine the present condition of this empire, and show how well it agrees with its ancient self. A certain author*, whose works have

* A quotation after the manner of a great author. Vide Bentley's Dissertation, &c.

many ages since been entirely lost, does, in his fifth book and eighth chapter, say of critics that their writings are the mirrors of learning. This I understand in a literal sense, and suppose our author must mean, that whoever designs to be a perfect writer must inspect into the books of critics, and correct his invention there, as in a mirror. Now, whoever considers that the mirrors of the ancients were made of brass, and the *sine mercurio*, may presently apply the two principal qualifications of a true modern critic, and consequently must needs conclude that these have always been, and must be for ever, the same. For brass is an emblem of duration, and, when it is skilfully burnished, will cast reflection from its own superficies, without any assistance of mercury from behind. All the other talents of a critic will not require a particular mention, being included or easily deducible to these. However, I shall conclude with three maxims, which may serve both as characteristics to distinguish a true modern critic from a pretender, and will be also of admirable use to those worthy spirits who engage in so useful and honourable an art.

The first is, that criticism, contrary to all other faculties of the intellect, is ever held the truest and best when it is the very first result of the critic's mind; as fowlers reckon the first aim for the surest, and seldom fail of missing the mark if they stay for a second.

Secondly, the true critics are known by their talent of swarming about the noblest writers, to which they are carried merely by instinct, as a rat to the best cheese, or as a wasp to the fairest fruit. So when the king is on horseback, he is sure to be the dirtiest person of the company; and they that make their court best are such as bespatter him most.

Lastly, a true critic, in the perusal of a book, is like a dog at a feast, whose thoughts and stomach are wholly set upon what the guests fling away, and consequently is apt to snarl most when there are the fewest bones.

Thus much, I think, is sufficient to serve by way of address to my patrons, the true modern critics; and may very well atone for my past silence, as well as that which I am likely to observe for the future. I hope I have deserved so well of their whole body as to meet with generous and tender usage at their hands. Supported by which expectation, I go on boldly to pursue those adventures already so happily begun.

SECTION IV

A Tale of a Tub

I have now, with much pains and study, conducted the reader to a period where he must expect to hear of great revolutions. For no sooner had our learned brother, so often mentioned, got a warm house of his own over his head than he began to look big and to take mightily upon him; insomuch that, unless the gentle reader, out of his great candour, will please a little to exalt his idea, I am afraid he will henceforth hardly know the hero of the play when he happens to meet him; his part, his dress, and his mien being so much altered.

He told his brothers he would have them to know that he was their elder, and consequently his father's sole heir; nay, a while after, he would not allow them to call him brother, but *Mr.* PETER, and then he must be styled *Father* PETER; and sometimes, *My Lord* PETER. To support this grandeur, which he soon began to consider could not be maintained without a better *fonde* than what he was born to, after much thought, he cast about at last to turn projector and virtuoso, wherein he so well succeeded, that many famous discoveries, projects, and machines, which bear great vogue and practice at present in the world, are owing entirely to lord PETER'S invention. I will deduce the best account I have been able to collect of the chief among them, without considering much the order they came out in; because I think authors are not well agreed as to that point.

I hope, when this treatise of mine shall be translated into foreign languages (as I may without vanity affirm that the labour of collecting, the faithfulness in recounting, and the great usefulness of the matter to the public, will amply deserve that justice), that the worthy members of the several academies abroad, especially those of France and Italy, will favourably accept these humble offers for the advancement of universal knowledge. I do also advertise the most reverend fathers, the

Eastern missionaries, that I have, purely for their sakes, made use of such words and phrases as will best admit an easy turn into any of the oriental languages, especially the Chinese. And so I proceed with great content of mind, upon reflecting how much emolument this whole globe of the earth is likely to reap by my labours.

The first undertaking of lord Peter was, to purchase a large continent[1], lately said to have been discovered in *terra australis incognita*. This tract of land he bought at a very great pennyworth from the discoverers themselves (though some pretended to doubt whether they had ever been there), and then retailed it into several cantons to certain dealers, who carried over colonies, but were all shipwrecked in the voyage. Upon which lord Peter sold the said continent to other customers again, and again, and again, and again, with the same success.

The second project I shall mention was his sovereign remedy for the worms[2], especially those in the spleen[3]. The patient was to eat nothing after supper for three nights: as soon as he went to bed he was carefully to lie on one side, and when he grew weary to turn upon the other; he must also duly confine his two eyes to the same object; and by no means break wind at both ends together without manifest occasion. These prescriptions diligently observed, the worms would void insensibly by perspiration, ascending through the brain.

A third invention was the erecting of a whispering-office[4] for the public good and ease of all such as are hypochondriacal or troubled with the colic; as likewise of all eavesdroppers, physicians, midwives, small politicians, friends fallen out,

---

1 That is purgatory.

2 Penance and absolution are plaid upon under the notion of a sovereign remedy for the worms, especially in the spleen, which by observing Peter's prescription would void sensibly by perspiration ascending thro' the brain, &c. W. Wotton.

3 Here the author ridicules the penances of the Church of Rome, which may be made as easy to the sinner as he pleases, provided he will pay for them accordingly.

4 By his whispering-office, for the relief of eaves-droppers, physicians, bawds, and privy counsellors, he ridicules auricular confession, and the priest who takes it, is described by the ass's head. W. Wotton.

repeating poets, lovers happy or in despair, bawds, privy-counsellors, pages, parasites, and buffoons; in short, of all such as are in danger of bursting with too much wind. An ass's head was placed so conveniently that the party affected might easily with his mouth accost either of the animal's ears; to which he was to apply close for a certain space, and by a fugitive faculty, peculiar to the ears of that animal, receive immediate benefit, either by eructation, or expiration, or evomitation.

Another very beneficial project of lord Peter's was, an office of insurance[1] for tobacco-pipes, martyrs of the modern zeal, volumes of poetry, shadows, ——, and rivers; that these, nor any of these, shall receive damage by fire. Whence our friendly societies may plainly find themselves to be only transcribers from this original; though the one and the other have been of great benefit to the undertakers, as well as of equal to the public.

Lord Peter was also held the original author of puppets and raree-shows[2]; the great usefulness whereof being so generally known, I shall not enlarge farther upon this particular.

But another discovery, for which he was much renowned, was his famous universal pickle[3]. For, having remarked how your common pickle[4] in use among housewives was of no farther benefit than to preserve dead flesh and certain kinds of vegetables, Peter, with great cost as well as art, had contrived a pickle proper for houses, gardens, towns, men, women, children, and cattle; wherein he could preserve them as sound as insects in amber. Now, this pickle, to the taste, the smell, and the sight, appeared exactly the same with what is in common service for beef, and butter, and herrings, and has been often

---

1 This I take to be the office of indulgences, the gross abuses whereof first gave occasions for the Reformation.
2 I believe are the monkeries and ridiculous processions, &c. among the Papists.
3 Holy water, he calls an universal pickle to preserve houses, gardens, towns, men, women, children and cattle, wherein he could preserve them as sound as insects in amber. W. Wotton.
4 This is easily understood to be holy water, composed of the same ingredients with many other pickles.

that way applied with great success; but, for its many sovereign virtues, was a quite different thing. For Peter would put in a certain quantity of his powder pimperlim pimp[1], after which it never failed of success. The operation was performed by spargefaction, in a proper time of the moon. The patient who was to be pickled, if it were a house, would infallibly be preserved from all spiders, rats, and weasels; if the party affected were a dog, he should be exempt from mange, and madness, and hunger. It also infallibly took away all scabs, and lice, and scalled heads from children, never hindering the patient from any duty, either at bed or board.

But of all Peter's rarities he most valued a certain set of bulls[2], whose race was by great fortune preserved in a lineal descent from those that guarded the golden fleece. Though some, who pretended to observe them curiously, doubted the breed had not been kept entirely chaste, because they had degenerated from their ancestors in some qualities, and had acquired others very extraordinary, by a foreign mixture. The bulls of Colchis are recorded to have brazen feet; but whether it happened by ill pasture and running, by an allay from intervention of other parents, from stolen intrigues; whether a weakness in their progenitors had impaired the seminal virtue, or by a decline necessary through a long course of time, the originals of nature being depraved in these latter sinful ages of the world; whatever was the cause, it is certain that lord Peter's bulls were extremely vitiated by the rust of time in the metal of their feet, which was now sunk into common lead. However, the terrible roaring peculiar to their lineage was preserved; as likewise that faculty of breathing out fire from their nostrils, which,

1 And because holy water differs only in consecration from common water, therefore he tells us that his pickle by the powder of pimperlim pimp receives new virtues though it differs not in sight nor smell from the common pickle, which preserves beef, and butter, and herrings. W. Wotton.

2 The Papal bulls are ridicul'd by name, so that here we are at no loss for the author's meaning. W. Wotton.

Ibid. Here the author has kept the name, and means the Pope's bulls, or rather his fulminations and excommunications, of heretical princes, all sign'd with lead and the seal of the Fisherman.

notwithstanding, many of their detractors took to be a feat of art, to be nothing so terrible as it appeared, proceeding only from their usual course of diet, which was of squibs and crackers[1]. However, they had two peculiar marks, which extremely distinguished them from the bulls of Jason, and which I have not met together in the description of any other monster beside that in Horace:

"Varias inducere plumas;"

and

"Atrum desinat in piscem."

For these had fishes' tails, yet upon occasion could outfly any bird in the air. Peter put these bulls upon several employs. Sometimes he would set them a-roaring to fright naughty boys[2], and make them quiet. Sometimes he would send them out upon errands of great importance; where, it is wonderful to recount (and perhaps the cautious reader may think much to believe it), an *appetitus sensibilis* deriving itself through the whole family from their noble ancestors, guardians of the golden fleece, they continued so extremely fond of gold, that if Peter sent them abroad, though it were only upon a compliment, they would roar, and spit, and belch, and piss, and fart, and snivel out fire, and keep a perpetual coil, till you flung them a bit of gold; but then, *pulveris exigui jactu*, they would grow calm and quiet as lambs. In short, whether by secret connivance or encouragement from their master, or out of their own liquorish affection to gold, or both, it is certain they were no better than a sort of sturdy, swaggering beggars; and where they could not prevail to get an alms, would make women miscarry, and children fall into fits, who to this very day usually call sprights and hobgoblins by the name of bull-beggars. They grew at last so very troublesome to the neighbourhood, that some gentlemen of the north-west got a parcel of right English bull-dogs, and baited them so terribly that they felt it ever after.

1 These are the fulminations of the Pope threatening hell and damnation to those princes who offend him.
2 That is kings who incur his displeasure.

I must needs mention one more of lord Peter's projects, which was very extraordinary, and discovered him to be master of a high reach and profound invention. Whenever it happened that any rogue of Newgate was condemned to be hanged, Peter would offer him a pardon for a certain sum of money; which, when the poor caitiff had made all shifts to scrape up and send, his lordship would return a piece of paper[1] in this form:—

"To all mayors, sheriffs, jailors, constables, bailiffs, hangmen, etc. Whereas we are informed that A. B. remains in the hands of you, or some of you, under the sentence of death. We will and command you, upon sight hereof, to let the said prisoner depart to his own habitation, whether he stands condemned for murder, sodomy, rape, sacrilege, incest, treason, blasphemy, etc., for which this shall be your sufficient warrant; and if you fail hereof, G— d—mn you and yours to all eternity. And so we bid you heartily farewell.

Your most humble

Man's man,

EMPEROR PETER."

The wretches, trusting to this, lost their lives and money too.

I desire of those whom the learned among posterity will appoint for commentators upon this elaborate treatise, that they will proceed with great caution upon certain dark points, wherein all who are not *verè adepti* may be in danger to form rash and hasty conclusions, especially in some mysterious paragraphs, where certain *arcana* are joined for brevity sake, which in the operation must be divided. And I am certain that future sons of art will return large thanks to my memory for so grateful, so useful an *innuendo*.

It will be no difficult part to persuade the reader that so many worthy discoveries met with great success in the world; though I may justly assure him that I have related much the smallest number; my design having been only to single out

---

1 This is a copy of a general pardon sign'd Servus Servorum.

such as will be of most benefit for public imitation, or which best served to give some idea of the reach and wit of the inventor. And therefore it need not be wondered at if by this time lord Peter was become exceeding rich: but, alas! he had kept his brain so long and so violently upon the rack, that at last it shook itself, and began to turn round for a little ease. In short, what with pride, projects, and knavery, poor Peter was grown distracted, and conceived the strangest imaginations in the world. In the height of his fits, as it is usual with those who run mad out of pride, he would call himself God Almighty[1], and sometimes monarch of the universe. I have seen him (says my author) take three old high-crowned hats[2], and clap them all on his head three storey high, with a huge bunch of keys[3] at this girdle, and an angling-rod in his hand. In which guise, whoever went to take him by the hand in the way of salutation, Peter with much grace, like a well-educated spaniel, would present them with his foot[4], and if they refused his civility, then he would raise it as high as their chaps, and give them a damned kick on the mouth, which has ever since been called a salute. Whoever walked by without paying him their compliments, having a wonderful strong breath, he would blow their hats off into the dirt. Meantime his affairs at home went upside down, and his two brothers had a wretched time; where his first *boutade*[5] was to kick both their wives[6] one morning out of doors, and his own too; and in their stead gave orders to pick up the first three strollers that could be met with in the streets. A while after he nailed up the cellar-door, and

---

1 The Pope is not only allow'd to be the Vicar of Christ, but by several divines is call'd God upon earth, and other blasphemous titles.
2 The triple crown.
3 The keys of the Church.
  Ibid. The Pope's universal monarchy, and his triple crown, and keys, and fisher's ring. W. Wotton.
4 Neither does his arrogant way of requiring men to kiss his slipper, escape reflexion. Wotton.
5 This word properly signifies a sudden jerk, or lash of an horse, when you do not expect it.
6 The celibacy of the Romish clergy is struck at in Peter's beating his own and brothers' wives out of doors. W. Wotton.

would not allow his brothers a drop of drink[1] to their victuals. Dining one day at an alderman's in the city, Peter observed him expatiating, after the manner of his brethren, in the praises of his sirloin of beef. "Beef," said the sage magistrate, "is the king of meat; beef comprehends in it the quintessence of partridge, and quail, and venison, and pheasant, and plum-pudding, and custard." When Peter came home he would needs take the fancy of cooking up this doctrine into use, and apply the precept, in default of a sirloin, to his brown loaf. "Bread," says he, "dear brothers, is the staff of life; in which bread is contained, inclusive, the quintessence of beef, mutton, veal, venison, partridge, plum-pudding, and custard; and, to render all complete, there is intermingled a due quantity of water, whose crudities are also corrected by yeast or barm, through which means it becomes a wholesome fermented liquor, diffused through the mass of the bread." Upon the strength of these conclusions, next day at dinner was the brown loaf served up in all the formality of a city feast. "Come, brothers," said Peter, "fall to, and spare not; here is excellent good mutton[2]; or hold, now my hand is in, I will help you." At which word, in much ceremony, with fork and knife, he carves out two good slices of a loaf, and presents each on a plate to his brothers. The elder of the two, not suddenly entering into lord Peter's conceit, began with very civil language to examine the mystery. "My lord," said he, "I doubt, with great submission, there may be some mistake."—"What," says Peter, "you are pleasant; come then, let us hear this jest your head is so big with."—"None in the world, my lord; but, unless I am very much deceived, your lordship was pleased a while ago to let fall a word about mutton, and I would be glad to see it with all my heart."—"How," said Peter, appearing in great surprise, "I do not

---

1 The Pope's refusing the cup to the laity, persuading them that the blood is contain'd in the bread, and that the bread is the real and entire body of Christ.

2 Transubstantiation. Peter turns his bread into mutton, and according to the Popish doctrine of concomitants, his wine too, which in his way he calls, pauming his damn'd crusts upon the brothers for mutton. W. Wotton.

comprehend this at all." Upon which the younger interposing to set the business aright, "My lord," said he, "my brother, I suppose, is hungry, and longs for the mutton your lordship has promised us to dinner."—"Pray," said Peter, "take me along with you; either you are both mad, or disposed to be merrier than I approve of; if you there do not like your piece I will carve you another; though I should take that to be the choice bit of the whole shoulder."—"What then, my lord," replied the first, "it seems this is a shoulder of mutton all this while?"—"Pray, sir," says Peter, "eat your victuals, and leave off your impertinence, if you please, for I am not disposed to relish it at present:" but the other could not forbear, being over-provoked at the affected seriousness of Peter's countenance: "By G—, my lord," said he, "I can only say, that to my eyes, and fingers, and teeth, and nose, it seems to be nothing but a crust of bread." Upon which the second put in his word: "I never saw a piece of mutton in my life so nearly resembling a slice from a twelvepenny loaf."—"Look ye, gentlemen," cries Peter, in a rage; "to convince you what a couple of blind, positive, ignorant, wilful puppies you are, I will use but this plain argument: by G—, it is true, good, natural mutton as any in Leadenhall Market; and G— confound you both eternally if you offer to believe otherwise." Such a thundering proof as this left no farther room for objection; the two unbelievers began to gather and pocket up their mistake as hastily as they could. "Why, truly," said the first, "upon more mature consideration——" —"Ay," says the other, interrupting him, "now I have thought better on the thing, your lordship seems to have a great deal of reason."—"Very well," said Peter; "here, boy, fill me a beer-glass of claret; here's to you both with all my heart." The two brethren, much delighted to see him so readily appeased, returned their most humble thanks, and said they would be glad to pledge his lordship. "That you shall," said Peter; "I am not a person to refuse you anything that is reasonable: wine, moderately taken, is a cordial; here is a glass a-piece for you; it is true natural juice from the grape, none of your damned vintner's brewings."

Having spoke thus, he presented to each of them another large dry crust, bidding them drink it off, and not be bashful, for it would do them no hurt. The two brothers, after having performed the usual office in such delicate conjunctures, of staring a sufficient period at lord Peter and each other, and finding how matters were likely to go, resolved not to enter on a new dispute, but let him carry the point as he pleased; for he was now got into one of his mad fits, and to argue or expostulate farther would only serve to render him a hundred times more untractable.

I have chosen to relate this worthy matter in all its circumstances, because it gave a principal occasion to that great and famous rupture[1] which happened about the same time among these brethren, and was never afterwards made up. But of that I shall treat at large in another section.

However, it is certain that lord Peter, even in his lucid intervals, was very lewdly given in his common conversation, extremely wilful and positive, and would at any time rather argue to the death than allow himself once to be in an error. Besides, he had an abominable faculty of telling huge palpable lies upon all occasions; and not only swearing to the truth, but cursing the whole company to hell if they pretended to make the least scruple of believing him. One time he swore he had a cow[2] at home which gave as much milk at a meal as would fill three thousand churches; and, what was yet more extra-ordinary, would never turn sour. Another time he was telling of an old sign-post[3], that belonged to his father, with nails and timber enough in it to build sixteen large men of war. Talking one day of Chinese waggons, which were made so light as to sail over mountains, "Z—ds," said Peter, "where's the wonder of

---

1 By this rupture is meant the Reformation.
2 The ridiculous multiplying of the Virgin Mary's milk among the Papists, under the allegory of a cow, which gave as much milk at a meal, as would fill three thousand churches. W. Wotton.
3 By this sign-post is meant the cross of our blessed Saviour.

that? By G—, I saw a large house[1] of lime and stone travel over sea and land (granting that it stopped sometimes to bait) above two thousand German leagues." And that which was the good of it, he would swear desperately all the while that he never told a lie in his life; and at every word, "By G—, gentlemen, I tell you nothing but the truth; and the d—l broil them eternally that will not believe me."

In short, Peter grew so scandalous, that all the neighbourhood began in plain words to say he was no better than a knave. And his two brothers, long weary of his ill-usage, resolved at last to leave him; but first they humbly desired a copy of their father's will, which had now lain by neglected time out of mind. Instead of granting this request he called them damned sons of whores, rogues, traitors, and the rest of the vile names he could muster up. However, while he was abroad one day upon his projects, the youngsters watched their opportunity, made a shift to come at the will, and took a *copia vera*[2] by which they presently saw how grossly they had been abused; their father having left them equal heirs, and strictly commanded that whatever they got should lie in common among them all. Pursuant to which their next enterprise was to break open the cellar-door, and get a little good drink[3], to spirit and comfort their hearts. In copying the will they had met another precept against whoring, divorce, and separate maintenance; upon which their next work[4] was to discard their concubines, and send for their wives. While all this was in agitation there enters a solicitor from Newgate, desiring lord Peter would please procure a pardon for a thief that was to be hanged tomorrow. But the two brothers told him

---

1 The chapel of Loretto. He falls here only upon the ridiculous inventions of Popery: the Church of Rome intended by these things, to gall silly, superstitious people, and rook them of their money; that the world had been too long in slavery, our ancestors gloriously redeem'd us from that yoke. The Church of Rome therefore ought to be expos'd, and he deserves well of mankind that does expose it. W. Wotton.

Ibid. The chapel of Loretto, which travell'd from the Holy Land to Italy.

2 Translated the Scriptures into the vulgar tongues.

3 Administred the cup to the laity at the communion.

4 Allowed the marriages of priests.

he was a coxcomb to seek pardons from a fellow who deserved to be hanged much better than his client; and discovered all the method of that imposture in the same form I delivered it a while ago, advising the solicitor to put his friend upon obtaining a pardon[1] from the king. In the midst of all this clutter and revolution, in comes Peter with a file of dragoons[2] at his heels, and gathering from all hands what was in the wind, he and his gang, after several millions of scurrilities and curses, not very important here to repeat, by main force very fairly kicked[3] them both out of doors, and would never let them come under his roof from that day to this.

---

1 Directed penitents not to trust to pardons and absolutions procur'd for money, but sent them to implore the mercy of God, from whence alone remission is to be obtain'd.
2 By Peter's dragoons, is meant the civil power which those princes, who were bigotted to the Romish superstition, employ'd against the reformers.
3 The Pope shuts all who dissent from him out of the Church.

SECTION V

A Digression in the Modern Kind

We, whom the world is pleased to honour with the title of modern authors, should never have been able to compass our great design of an everlasting remembrance and never-dying fame, if our endeavours had not been so highly serviceable to the general good of mankind. This, O universe! is the adventurous attempt of me thy secretary;

"——Quemvis perferre laborem
Suadet, et inducit noctes vigilare serenas."

To this end I have some time since, with a world of pains and art, dissected the carcase of human nature, and read many useful lectures upon the several parts, both containing and contained: till at last it smelt so strong I could preserve it no longer. Upon which I have been at a great expense to fit up all the bones with exact contexture and in due symmetry; so that I am ready to show a very complete anatomy thereof to all curious gentlemen and others. But not to digress farther in the midst of a digression, as I have known some authors enclose digressions in one another like a nest of boxes, I do affirm that, having carefully cut up human nature, I have found a very strange, new, and important discovery, that the public good of mankind is performed by two ways, instruction and diversion. And I have farther proved, in my said several readings (which perhaps the world may one day see, if I can prevail on any friend to steal a copy, or on certain gentlemen of my admirers to be very importunate), that as mankind is now disposed, he receives much greater advantage by being diverted than instructed: his epidemical diseases being fastidiosity, amorphy, and oscitation; whereas in the present universal empire of wit and learning, there seems but little matter left for instruction. However, in compliance with a lesson of great age and authority, I have attempted carrying the point in all its heights; and accordingly, throughout this divine treatise, have skilfully

91

kneaded up both together, with a layer of *utile* and a layer of *dulce*.

When I consider how exceedingly our illustrious moderns have eclipsed the weak glimmering lights of the ancients, and turned them out of the road of all fashionable commerce, to a degree that our choice town wits[1], of most refined accomplishments, are in grave dispute whether there have been ever any ancients or not; in which point we are likely to receive wonderful satisfaction from the most useful labours and lucubrations of that worthy modern, Dr. Bentley: I say, when I consider all this, I cannot but bewail that no famous modern has ever yet attempted a universal system, in a small portable volume, of all things that are to be known, or believed, or imagined, or practised in life. I am, however, forced to acknowledge, that such an enterprise was thought on some time ago by a great philosopher of O. Brazile[2]. The method he proposed was, by a certain curious receipt, a nostrum, which, after his untimely death, I found among his papers; and do here, out of my great affection to the modern learned, present them with it, not doubting it may one day encourage some worthy undertaker.

You take fair correct copies, well bound in calf-skin and lettered at the back, of all modern bodies of arts and sciences whatsoever, and in what language you please. These you distil *in balneo Mariæ*, infusing quintessence of poppy Q. S., together with three pints of Lethe, to be had from the apothecaries. You cleanse away carefully the *sordes* and *caput mortuum*, letting all that is volatile evaporate. You preserve only the first running, which is again to be distilled seventeen times, till what remains will amount to about two drachms. This you keep in a glass phial, hermetically sealed, for one-and-twenty days. Then you begin your catholic treatise, taking

---

1 The learned person here meant by our author, hath been endeavouring to annihilate so many ancient writers, that until he is pleas'd to stop his hand it will be dangerous to affirm, whether there have been ever any ancients in the world.
2 This is an imaginary island, of kin to that which is call'd the Painters' Wives' Island, placed in some unknown part of the ocean, merely at the fancy of the map-maker.

every morning fasting, first shaking the phial, three drops of this elixir, snuffing it strongly up your nose. It will dilate itself about the brain (where there is any) in fourteen minutes, and you immediately perceive in your head an infinite number of abstracts, summaries, compendiums, extracts, collections, medullas, *excerpta quœdams*, *florilegias*, and the like, all disposed into great order, and reducible upon paper.

I must needs own it was by the assistance of this arcanum that I, though otherwise *impar*, have adventured upon so daring an attempt, never achieved or undertaken before, but by a certain author called Homer; in whom, though otherwise a person not without some abilities, and, for an ancient, of a tolerable genius, I have discovered many gross errors which are not to be forgiven his very ashes, if by chance any of them are left. For whereas we are assured he designed his work for a complete body* of all knowledge, human, divine, political, and mechanic, it is manifest he has wholly neglected some, and been very imperfect in the rest. For first of all, as eminent a cabalist as his disciples would represent him, his account of the *opus magnum* is extremely poor and deficient; he seems to have read but very superficially either Sendivogus, Behmen or Anthroposophia Theomagica[1]. He is also quite mistaken about the *sphœra pyroplastica*, a neglect not to be atoned for; and if the reader will admit so severe a censure, *vix crederem autorem hunc unquam audivisse ignis vocem*. His failings are not less prominent in several parts of the mechanics. For, having read his writings with the utmost application usual among modern wits, I could never yet discover the least direction about the structure of that useful instrument, a save-all; for want of which, if the moderns had not lent their assistance, we might yet have wandered in the dark. But I have still behind a fault far more notorious to tax this

* Homerus omnes res humanas poematis complexus est. Xenoph. in conviv.

---

1 A treatise written about fifty years ago, by a Welsh gentleman of Cambridge, his name, as I remember, was Vaughan, as appears by the answer to it, writ by the learned Dr. Henry Moor, it is a piece of the most unintelligible fustian, that, perhaps, was ever publish'd in any language.

author with; I mean his gross ignorance[1] in the common laws of this realm, and in the doctrine as well as discipline of the church of England. A defect indeed, for which both he and all the ancients stand most justly censured by my worthy and ingenious friend Mr. Wotton, Bachelor of Divinity, in his incomparable Treatise of Ancient and Modern Learning: a book never to be sufficiently valued, whether we consider the happy turns and flowings of the author's wit, the great usefulness of his sublime discoveries upon the subject of flies and spittle, or the laborious eloquence of his style. And I cannot forbear doing that author the justice of my public acknowledgments for the great helps and liftings I had out of his incomparable piece, while I was penning this treatise.

But beside these omissions in Homer already mentioned, the curious reader will also observe several defects in that author's writings, for which he is not altogether so accountable. For whereas every branch of knowledge has received such wonderful acquirements since his age, especially within these last three years, or thereabouts, it is almost impossible he could be so very perfect in modern discoveries as his advocates pretend. We freely acknowledge him to be the inventor of the compass, of gunpowder, and the circulation of the blood: but I challenge any of his admirers to show me in all his writings a complete account of the spleen: does he not also leave us wholly to seek in the art of political wagering? What can be more defective and unsatisfactory than his long dissertation upon tea? And as to his method of salivation without mercury so much celebrated of late, it is, to my own knowledge and experience, a thing very little to be relied on.

It was to supply such momentous defects that I have been prevailed on, after long solicitation, to take pen in hand; and I dare venture to promise, the judicious reader shall find

---

1 Mr. W-tt-n (to whom our author never gives any quarter) in hias comparison of ancient and modern learning, numbers divinity, law, &c. among those parts of knowledge wherein we excel the ancients.

nothing neglected here that can be of use upon any emergency of life. I am confident to have included and exhausted all that human imagination can rise or fall to. Particularly, I recommend to the perusal of the learned certain discoveries that are wholly untouched by others; whereof I shall only mention, among a great many more, my new help for smatterers, or the art of being deep-learned and shallow-read. A curious invention about mouse-traps. A universal rule of reason, or every man his own carver; together with a most useful engine for catching of owls. All which, the judicious reader will find largely treated on in the several parts of this discourse.

I hold myself obliged to give as much light as is possible into the beauties and excellencies of what I am writing; because it is become the fashion and humour most applauded among the authors of this polite and learned age, when they would correct the ill-nature of critical, or inform the ignorance of courteous readers. Besides, there have been several famous pieces lately published, both in verse and prose, wherein, if the writers had not been pleased, out of their great humanity and affection to the public, to give us a nice detail of the sublime and the admirable they contain, it is a thousand to one whether we should ever have discovered one grain of either. For my own particular, I cannot deny that whatever I have said upon this occasion had been more proper in a preface, and more agreeable to the mode which usually directs it thither. But I here think fit to lay hold on that great and honourable privilege of being the last writer: I claim an absolute authority in right, as the freshest modern, which gives me a despotic power over all authors before me. In the strength of which title I do utterly disapprove and declare against that pernicious custom of making the preface a bill of fare to the book. For I have always looked upon it as a high point of indiscretion in monster-mongers, and other retailers of strange sights, to hang out a fair large picture over the door, drawn after the life, with a most eloquent description underneath: this has saved me many a threepence; for my curiosity was fully satisfied, and I never offered to go in, though often invited by the urging and attending orator, with his last moving and standing piece of rhetoric:—Sir, upon my word we are just going to begin. Such is exactly the fate at this time of prefaces, epistles, advertisements, introduction, prolegomenas, apparatuses, to the readers. This expedient was admirable at first; our great Dryden has long carried it as far as it would go, and with incredible success. He has often said to me in confidence, that the world would have never suspected him to be so great a poet, if he had not assured them so frequently in his prefaces that it was impossible they could either doubt or forget it. Perhaps it may be so; however, I much fear his instructions have edified out of their place, and taught men to grow wiser in certain points where he never intended they should; for it is lamentable to behold with what a lazy scorn many of the yearning readers of our age do now a-days twirl over forty or fifty pages of preface and dedication (which is the usual modern stint), as if it were so much Latin. Though it must be also allowed, on the other hand, that a very considerable number is known to proceed critics and wits by reading nothing else. Into which two factions I think all present readers may justly be divided. Now, for myself, I profess to be of the former sort; and therefore, having the modern inclination to expatiate upon the beauty of my own productions, and display the bright parts of my discourse, I thought best to do it in the body of the work; where, as it now lies, it makes a very considerable addition to the bulk of the volume; a circumstance by no means to be neglected by a skilful writer.

Having thus paid my due deference and acknowledgment to an established custom of our newest authors, by a long digression unsought for, and a universal censure unprovoked; by forcing into the light, with much pains and dexterity, my own excellencies and other men's defaults, with great justice to myself and candour to them, I now happily resume my subject, to the infinite satisfaction both of the reader and the author.

SECTION VI

A Tale of a Tub

We left lord Peter in open rupture with his two brethren; both for ever discarded from his house, and resigned to the wide world, with little or nothing to trust to. Which are circumstances that render them proper subjects for the charity of a writer's pen to work on; scenes of misery ever affording the fairest harvest for great adventures. And in this the world may perceive the difference between the integrity of a generous author and that of a common friend. The latter is observed to adhere closely in prosperity, but on the decline of fortune to drop suddenly off. Whereas the generous author, just on the contrary, finds his hero on the dunghill, from thence by gradual steps raises him to a throne, and then immediately withdraws, expecting not so much as thanks for his pains; in imitation of which example, I have placed lord Peter in a noble house, given him a title to wear and money to spend. There I shall leave him for some time; returning where common charity directs me, to the assistance of his two brothers at their lowest ebb. However, I shall by no means forget my character of a historian to follow the truth step by step, whatever happens, or wherever it may lead me.

The two exiles, so nearly united in fortune and interest, took a lodging together; where, at their first leisure, they began to reflect on the numberless misfortunes and vexations of their life past, and could not tell on the sudden to what failure in their conduct they ought to impute them; when, after some recollection, they called to mind the copy of their father's will, which they had so happily recovered. This was immediately produced, and a firm resolution taken between them to alter whatever was already amiss, and reduce all their future measures to the strictest obedience prescribed therein. The main body of the will (as the reader cannot easily have forgot) consisted in certain admirable rules about the wearing of their coats; in the perusal whereof, the two brothers at every period duly comparing the doctrine with the practice, there was never seen a wider difference between two things; horrible downright transgressions of every point. Upon which they both resolved, without farther delay, to fall immediately upon reducing the whole exactly after their father's model.

But here it is good to stop the hasty reader, ever impatient to see the end of an adventure before we writers can duly prepare him for it. I am to record that these two brothers began to be distinguished at this time by certain names. One of them desired to be called MARTIN[1], and the other took the appellation of JACK[2]. These two had lived in much friendship and agreement under the tyranny of their brother Peter, as it is the talent of fellow-sufferers to do; men in misfortune being like men in the dark, to whom all colours are the same: but when they came forward into the world, and began to display themselves to each other and to the light, their complexions appeared extremely different; which the present posture of their affairs gave them sudden opportunity to discover.

But here the severe reader may justly tax me as a writer of short memory, a deficiency to which a true modern cannot but of necessity be a little subject. Because memory, being an employment of the mind upon things past, is a faculty for which the learned in our illustrious age have no manner of occasion, who deal entirely with invention, and strike all things out of themselves, or at least by collision from each other: upon which account we think it highly reasonable to produce our great forgetfulness as an argument unanswerable for our great wit. I ought in method to have informed the reader, about fifty pages ago, of a fancy lord Peter took, and infused into his brothers, to wear on their coats whatever trimmings came up in fashion; never pulling off any as they went out of the mode, but keeping on all together, which amounted in time to a

1 Martin Luther.
2 John Calvin.

medley the most antic you can possibly conceive; and this to a
degree, that upon the time of their falling out there was hardly
a thread of the original coat to be seen: but an infinite quantity
of lace, and ribbons, and fringe, and embroidery, and points; I
mean only those tagged with silver[1], for the rest fell off. Now
this material circumstance, having been forgot in due place, as
good fortune has ordered, comes in very properly here when
the two brothers are just going to reform their vestures into the
primitive state prescribed by their father's will.

They both unanimously entered upon this great work,
looking sometimes on their coats; and sometimes on the will.
Martin laid the first hand; at one twitch brought off a large
handful of points; and, with a second pull, stripped away ten
dozen yards of fringe. But when he had gone thus far he
demurred a while: he knew very well there yet remained a
great deal more to be done; however, the first heat being over,
his violence began to cool, and he resolved to proceed more
moderately in the rest of the work, having already narrowly
escaped a swinging rent, in pulling of the points, which, being
tagged with silver (as we have observed before), the judicious
workman had, with much sagacity, double sewn, to preserve
them from falling. Resolving, therefore, to rid his coat of a huge
quantity of gold-lace, he picked up the stitches with much
caution, and diligently gleaned out all the loose threads as he
went, which proved to be a work of time. Then he fell about the
embroidered Indian figures of men, women, and children;
against which, as you have heard in its due place, their father's
testament was extremely exact and severe; these, with much
dexterity and application, were, after a while, quite eradicated
or utterly defaced. For the rest, where he observed the
embroidery to be worked so close as not to be got away
without damaging the cloth, or where it served to hide or

---

1 Points tagg'd with silver, are those doctrines that promote the greatness and wealth of the
church, which have been therefore woven deepest in the body of Popery.

strengthen any flaw in the body of the coat, contracted by the perpetual tampering of workmen upon it, he concluded the wisest course was to let it remain, resolving in no case whatsoever that the substance of the stuff should suffer injury; which he thought the best method for serving the true intent and meaning of his father's will. And this is the nearest account I have been able to collect of Martin's proceedings upon this great revolution.

But his brother Jack, whose adventures will be so extra-ordinary as to furnish a great part in the remainder of this discourse, entered upon the matter with other thoughts and a quite different spirit. For the memory of lord Peter's injuries produced a degree of hatred and spite which had a much greater share of inciting him than any regards after his father's commands; since these appeared, at best, only secondary and subservient to the other. However, for this medley of humour he made a shift to find a plausible name, honouring it with the title of zeal; which is perhaps the most significant word that has been ever yet produced in any language: as I think I have fully proved in my excellent analytical discourse upon that subject; wherein I have deduced a histori-theo-physilogical account of zeal, showing how it first proceeded from a notion into a word, and thence, in a hot summer, ripened into a tangible substance. This work, containing three large volumes in folio, I design very shortly to publish by the modern way of subscription, not doubting but the nobility and gentry of the land will give me all possible encouragement; having had already such a taste of what I am able to perform.

I record, therefore, that brother Jack, brimful of this miraculous compound, reflecting with indignation upon Peter's tyranny, and, farther provoked by the despondency of Martin, prefaced his resolutions to this purpose. "What," said he, "a rogue that locked up his drink, turned away our wives, cheated us of our fortunes; palmed his damned crusts upon us for mutton; and at last kicked us out of doors; must we be in his fashions, with a pox! a rascal, besides, that all the street cries out against." Having thus kindled and inflamed himself as high as possible, and by consequence in a delicate temper for beginning a reformation, he set about the work immediately; and in three minutes made more despatch than Martin had done in as many hours. For, courteous reader, you are given to understand that zeal is never so highly obliged as when you set it a-tearing; and Jack, who doted on that quality in himself, allowed it at this time its full swing. Thus it happened that, stripping down a parcel of gold lace a little too hastily, he rent the main body of his coat from top to bottom; and whereas his talent was not of the happiest in taking up a stitch, he knew no better way than to darn it again with packthread and a skewer. But the matter was yet infinitely worse (I record it with tears) when he proceeded to the embroidery: for, being clumsy by nature, and of temper impatient; withal, beholding millions of stitches that required the nicest hand and sedatest constitution to extricate; in a great rage he tore off the whole piece, cloth and all, and flung it into the kennel, and furiously thus continued his career: "Ah, good brother Martin," said he, "do as I do, for the love of God; strip, tear, pull, rend, flay off all, that we may appear as unlike that rogue Peter as it is possible; I would not for a hundred pounds carry the least mark about me that might give occasion to the neighbours of suspecting that I was related to such a rascal." But Martin, who at this time happened to be extremely phlegmatic and sedate, begged his brother, of all love, not to damage his coat by any means; for he never would get such another: desired him to consider that it was not their business to form their actions by any reflection upon Peter, but by observing the rules prescribed in their father's will. That he should remember Peter was still their brother, whatever faults or injuries he had committed; and therefore they should by all means avoid such a thought as that of taking measures for good and evil from no other rule than of opposition to him. That it was true, the testament of their good father was very exact in what related to the wearing of their coats: yet it was no less penal and strict in prescribing agreement, and friendship, and affection between them. And therefore, if straining a point were at all dispensable, it would certainly be so rather to the advance of unity than increase of contradiction.

MARTIN had still proceeded as gravely as he began, and doubtless would have delivered an admirable lecture of morality, which might have exceedingly contributed to my reader's repose both of body and mind, the true ultimate end of ethics; but Jack was already gone a flight-shot beyond his patience. And as in scholastic disputes nothing serves to rouse the spleen of him that opposes so much as a kind of pedantic affected calmness in the respondent; disputants being for the most part like unequal scales, where the gravity of one side advances the lightness of the other, and causes it to fly up and kick the beam; so it happened here that the weight of Martin's argument exalted Jack's levity, and made him fly out, and spurn against his brother's moderation. In short, Martin's patience put Jack in a rage; but that which most afflicted him was, to observe his brother's coat so well reduced into the state of innocence; while his own was either wholly rent to his shirt, or those places which had escaped his cruel clutches were still in Peter's livery. So that he looked like a drunken beau, half rifled by bullies; or like a fresh tenant of Newgate, when he has refused the payment of garnish; or like a discovered shoplifter, left to the mercy of Exchange women; or like a bawd in her old velvet petticoat, resigned into the secular hands of the mobile. Like any, or like all of these, a medley of rags, and lace, and rents, and fringes, unfortunate Jack did now appear: he would have been extremely glad to see his coat in the condition of Martin's, but infinitely gladder to find that of Martin in the same predicament with his. However, since neither of these was likely to come to pass, he thought fit to lend the whole business another turn, and to dress up necessity into a virtue. Therefore, after as many of the fox's arguments as he could muster up, for bringing Martin to reason, as he called it; or, as he meant it, into his own ragged, bobtailed condition; and observing he said all to little purpose; what, alas! was left for the forlorn Jack to do, but, after a million of scurrilities against his brother, to run mad with spleen, and spite, and contradiction. To be short, here began a mortal breach between these two. Jack went immediately to new lodgings, and in a few days it was for certain reported that he had run out of his wits. In a short time after he appeared abroad, and confirmed the report by falling into the oddest whimseys that ever a sick brain conceived.

And now the little boys in the streets began to salute him with several names. Sometimes they would call him Jack the bald[1], sometimes, Jack with a lantern[2]; sometimes, Dutch Jack[3]; sometimes, French Hugh[4]; sometimes, Tom the beggar[5]; and sometimes, Knocking Jack of the North[6]. And it was under one, or some, or all of these appellations, which I leave the learned reader to determine, that he has given rise to the most illustrious and epidemic sect of Æolists; who, with honourable commemoration, do still acknowledge the renowned JACK for their author and founder. Of whose original, as well as principles, I am now advancing to gratify the world with a very particular account.

"—Melleo contingens cuncta lepore."

---

1 That is Calvin, from calvus, bald.
2 All those who pretend to inward light.
3 Jack of Leyden, who gave rise to the Anabaptists.
4 The Hugonots.
5 The Gueuses, by which name some Protestants in Flanders were call'd.
6 John Knox, the Reformer of Scotland.

SECTION VII

A Digression in Praise of Digressions

I have sometimes heard of an Iliad in a nutshell; but it has been my fortune to have much oftener seen a nutshell in an Iliad. There is no doubt that human life has received most wonderful advantages from both; but to which of the two the world is chiefly indebted I shall leave among the curious as a problem worthy of their utmost inquiry. For the invention of the latter I think the commonwealth of learning is chiefly obliged to the great modern improvement of digressions: the late refinements in knowledge running parallel to those of diet in our nation, which, among men of a judicious taste, are dressed up in various compounds, consisting in soups and olios, fricassees and ragouts.

It is true, there is a sort of morose, detracting, ill-bred people, who pretend utterly to disrelish these polite innovations; and as to the similitude from diet, they allow the parallel, but are so bold to pronounce the example itself a corruption and degeneracy of taste. They tell us that the fashion of jumbling fifty things together in a dish was at first introduced, in compliance to a depraved and debauched appetite, as well as to a crazy constitution: and to see a man hunting through an olio, after the head and brains of a goose, a widgeon, or a woodcock, is a sign he wants a stomach and digestion for more substantial victuals. Farther, they affirm that digressions in a book are like foreign troops in a state, which argue the nation to want a heart and hands of its own, and often either subdue the natives, or drive them into the most unfruitful corners.

But, after all that can be objected by these supercilious censors, it is manifest the society of writers would quickly be reduced to a very inconsiderable number if men were put upon making books with the fatal confinement of delivering nothing beyond what is to the purpose. It is acknowledged, that were the case the same among us as with the Greeks and

Romans, when learning was in its cradle, to be reared and fed, and clothed by invention, it would be an easy task to fill up volumes upon particular occasions, without farther expatiating from the subjects than by moderate excursions, helping to advance or clear the main design. But with knowledge it has fared as with a numerous army, encamped in a fruitful country, which, for a few days, maintains itself by the product of the soil it is on; till provisions being spent, they are sent to forage many a mile, among friends or enemies, it matters not. Meanwhile, the neighbouring fields, trampled and beaten down, become barren and dry, affording no sustenance but clouds of dust.

The whole course of things being thus entirely changed between us and the ancients, and the moderns wisely sensible of it, we of this age have discovered a shorter and more prudent method to become scholars and wits, without the fatigue of reading or of thinking. The most accomplished way of using books at present is two-fold; either, first, to serve them as some men do lords, learn their titles exactly, and then brag of their acquaintance. Or, secondly, which is indeed the choicer, the profounder, and politer method, to get a thorough insight into the index, by which the whole book is governed and turned, like fishes by the tail. For to enter the palace of learning at the great gate requires an expense of time and forms; therefore men of much haste and little ceremony are content to get in by the back door. For the arts are all in flying march, and therefore more easily subdued by attacking them in the rear. Thus physicians discover the state of the whole body by consulting only what comes from behind. Thus men catch knowledge by throwing their wit into the posteriors of a book, as boys do sparrows with flinging salt upon their tails. Thus human life is best understood by the wise man's rule of regarding the end. Thus are the sciences found, like Hercules's oxen, by tracing them backwards. Thus are old sciences unravelled, like old stockings, by beginning at the foot.

Beside all this, the army of the sciences has been of late, with a world of martial discipline, drawn into its close order, so that a view or a muster may be taken of it with abundance of expedition. For this great blessing we are wholly indebted to systems and abstracts, in which the modern fathers of learning, like prudent usurers, spent their sweat for the ease of us their children. For labour is the seed of idleness, and it is the peculiar happiness of our noble age to gather the fruit.

Now, the method of growing wise, learned, and sublime, having become so regular an affair, and so established in all its forms, the number of writers must needs have increased accordingly, and to a pitch that has made it of absolute necessity for them to interfere continually with each other. Besides, it is reckoned that there is not at this present a sufficient quantity of new matter left in nature to furnish and adorn any one particular subject to the extent of a volume. This I am told by a very skilful computer, who has given a full demonstration of it from rules of arithmetic.

This perhaps may be objected against by those who maintain the infinity of matter, and therefore will not allow that any species of it can be exhausted. For answer to which, let us examine the noblest branch of modern wit or invention, planted and cultivated by the present age, and which, of all others, has borne the most and the fairest fruit. For, though some remains of it were left us by the ancients, yet have not any of those, as I remember, been translated or compiled into systems for modern use. Therefore we may affirm, to our own honour, that it has, in some sort, been both invented and brought to perfection by the same hands. What I mean is, that highly celebrated talent among the modern wits of deducing similitudes, allusions, and applications, very surprising, agreeable, and apposite, from the *pudenda* of either sex, together with their proper uses. And truly, having observed how little invention bears any vogue, beside what is derived into these channels, I have sometimes had a thought that the happy genius of our age and country was prophetically held

forth by that ancient typical description* of *Ctesiæ fragm. apud
the Indian pigmies, whose stature did not Photium.
exceed above two foot; *sed quorum pudenda crassa, et ad*
talos usque pertingentia. Now I have been very curious to
inspect the late productions wherein the beauties of this kind
have most prominently appeared; and although this vein has
bled so freely, and all endeavours have been used in the power
of human breath to dilate, extend, and keep it open, like the
Scythians, who had a custom*, and an
instrument, to blow up the privities of their * Herodot. L. 4.
mares, that they might yield the more milk; yet I am under an
apprehension it is near growing dry and past all recovery; and
that either some new *fonde* of wit should, if possible, be
provided, or else that we must even be content with repetition
here, as well as upon all other occasions.

This will stand as an incontestable argument that our
modern wits are not to reckon upon the infinity of matter for a
constant supply. What remains, therefore, but that our last
recourse must be had to large indexes and little compendiums?
quotations must be plentifully gathered, and booked in
alphabet; to this end, though authors need be little consulted,
yet critics, and commentators, and lexicons, carefully must. But
above all, those judicious collectors of bright parts, and
flowers, and observandas, are to be nicely dwelt on by some
called the sieves and boulters of learning; though it is left
undetermined whether they dealt in pearls or meal; and,
consequently, whether we are more to value that which passed
through, or what staid behind.

By these methods, in a few weeks there starts up many a
writer capable of managing the profoundest and most
universal subjects. For what though his head be empty,
provided his commonplace-book be full? and if you will bate
him but the circumstances of method, and style, and grammar,
and invention; allow him but the common privileges of
transcribing from others, and digressing from himself, as often
as he shall see occasion; he will desire no more ingredients

towards fitting up a treatise that shall make a very comely figure on a bookseller's shelf; there to be preserved neat and clean for a long eternity, adorned with the heraldry of its title fairly inscribed on a label; never to be thumbed or greased by students, nor bound to everlasting chains of darkness in a library: but when the fulness of time is come, shall happily undergo the trial of purgatory, in order to ascend the sky.

Without these allowances, how is it possible we modern wits should ever have an opportunity to introduce our collections, listed under so many thousand heads of a different nature; for want of which the learned world would be deprived of infinite delight, as well as instruction, and we ourselves buried beyond redress in an inglorious and undistinguished oblivion?

From such elements as these I am alive to behold the day wherein the corporation of authors can outvie all its brethren in the guild. A happiness derived to us, with a great many others, from our Scythian ancestors; among whom the number of pens was so infinite, that the Grecian eloquence had no other way of expressing it than by saying that in the regions far to the north it was hardly possible for a man to travel, the very air was so replete with feathers.

The necessity of this digression will easily excuse the length; and I have chosen for it as proper a place as I could readily find. If the judicious reader can assign a fitter, I do here empower him to remove it into any other corner he pleases. And so I return with great alacrity, to pursue a more important concern.

SECTION VIII

A Tale of a Tub

The learned Æolists[1] maintain the original cause of all things to
be wind, from which principle this whole universe was at first
produced, and into which it must at last be resolved; that the
same breath which had kindled and blew up the flame of
nature should one day blow it out—

"Quod procul a nobis flectat Fortuna gubernans."

This is what the *adepti* understand by their *anima mundi*;
that is to say, the spirit, or breath, or wind of the world; for,
examine the whole system by the particulars of nature, and
you will find it not to be disputed. For whether you please to
call the *forma informans* of man by the name of *spiritus*,
animus, *afflatus*, or *anima*; what are all these but several
appellations for wind, which is the ruling element in every
compound, and into which they all resolve upon their
corruption? Farther, what is life itself but, as it is commonly
called, the breath of our nostrils? Whence it is very justly
observed by naturalists that wind still continues of great
emolument in certain mysteries not to be named, giving
occasion for those happy epithets of *turgidus* and *inflatus*,
applied either to the *emittent* or *recipient* organs.

By what I have gathered out of ancient records, I find the
compass of their doctrine took in two-and-thirty points,
wherein it would be tedious to be very particular. However, a
few of their most important precepts, deducible from it, are by
no means to be omitted; among which the following maxim
was of much weight; that since wind had the master share, as
well as operation, in every compound, by consequence, those
beings must be of chief excellence wherein that *primordium*
appears most prominently to abound; and therefore man is in
the highest perfection of all created things, as having, by the

---

1 All pretenders to inspiration whatsoever.

great bounty of philosophers, been endued with three distinct *animas* or winds, to which the sage Æolists, with much liberality, have added a fourth, of equal necessity as well as ornament with the other three; by this *quartum principium* taking in the four corners of the world; which gave occasion to that renowned *cabalist, Bumbastus*[1], of placing the body of a man in due position to the four cardinal points.

In consequence of this, their next principle was, that man brings with him into the world a peculiar portion or grain of wind, which may be called a *quinta essentia*, extracted from the other four. This quintessence is of a catholic use upon all emergencies of life, is improvable into all arts and sciences, and may be wonderfully refined, as well as enlarged, by certain methods in education. This, when blown up to its perfection, ought not to be covetously hoarded up, stifled, or hid under a bushel, but freely communicated to mankind. Upon these reasons, and others of equal weight, the wise Æolists affirm the gift of belching to be the noblest act of a rational creature. To cultivate which art, and render it more serviceable to mankind, they made use of several methods. At certain seasons of the year you might behold the priests among them, in vast numbers, with their mouths gaping wide[2] against a storm. At other times were to be seen several hundreds linked together in a circular chain, with every man a pair of bellows applied to his neighbour's breech, by which they blew up each other to the shape and size of a tun; and for that reason, with great propriety of speech, did usually call their bodies their vessels. When, by these and the like performances, they were grown sufficiently replete, they would immediately depart, and disembogue, for the public good, a plentiful share of their acquirements into their disciples' chaps. For we must here observe that all learning was esteemed among them to be

1 This is one of the names of Paracelsus; he was call'd Christophorus, Theophrastus, Paracelsus, Bumbastus.
2 This is meant of those seditious preachers who blow up the seeds of rebellion, &c.

compounded from the same principle. Because, first, it is generally affirmed, or confessed, that learning puffeth men up: and, secondly, they proved it by the following syllogism: Words are but wind; and learning is nothing but words; *ergo*, learning is nothing but wind. For this reason, the philosophers among them did, in their schools, deliver to their pupils all their doctrines and opinions by eructation, wherein they had acquired a wonderful eloquence, and of incredible variety. But the great characteristic by which their chief sages were best distinguished was a certain position of countenance, which gave undoubted intelligence to what degree or proportion the spirit agitated the inward mass. For, after certain gripings, the wind and vapours issuing forth, having first, by their turbulence and convulsions within, caused an earthquake in man's little world, distorted the mouth, bloated the cheeks, and given the eyes a terrible kind of relievo; at such junctures all their belches were received for sacred, the sourer the better, and swallowed with infinite consolation by their meagre devotees. And, to render these yet more complete, because the breath of man's life is in his nostrils, therefore the choicest, most edifying, and most enlivening belches, were very wisely conveyed through that vehicle, to give them a tincture as they passed.

Their gods were the four winds, whom they worshipped as the spirits that pervade and enliven the universe, and as those from whom alone all inspiration can properly be said to proceed. However, the chief of these, to whom they performed the adoration of *latria*, was the almighty North, an ancient deity, whom the inhabitants of Megalopolis, in Greece, had likewise in the highest reverence: *omnium deorum Boream maxime *celebrant.* This god, though endued with ubiquity, was yet supposed, by the profounder Æolists, to possess one peculiar habitation, or (to speak in form) a *cœlum empyrœum*, wherein he was more intimately present. This was situated in a certain region, well known to the ancient Greeks, by them called Σκοτία, or the land

* Pausan. L. 8.

113

of darkness. And although many controversies have arisen upon that matter, yet so much is undisputed, that from a region of the like denomination the most refined Æolists have borrowed their original; whence, in every age, the zealous among their priesthood have brought over their choicest inspiration, fetching it with their own hands from the fountain-head in certain bladders, and disploding it among the sectaries in all nations, who did, and do, and ever will, daily gasp and pant after it.

Now, their mysteries and rites were performed in this manner. It is well known among the learned that the virtuosoes of former ages had a contrivance for carrying and preserving winds in casks or barrels, which was of great assistance upon long sea-voyages: and the loss of so useful an art at present is very much to be lamented; although, I know not how, with great negligence omitted by Pancirolus[1]. It was an invention ascribed to Æolus himself, from whom this sect is denominated; and who, in honour of their founder's memory, have to this day preserved great numbers of those barrels, whereof they fix one in each of their temples, first beating out the top; into this barrel, upon solemn days, the priest enters; where, having before duly prepared himself by the methods already described, a secret funnel is also conveyed from his posteriors to the bottom of the barrel which admits new supplies of inspiration from a northern chink or cranny. Whereupon, you behold him swell immediately to the shape and size of his vessel. In this posture he disembogues whole tempests upon his auditory, as the spirit from beneath gives him utterance; which, issuing *ex adytis et penetralibus*, is not performed without much pain and gripings. And the wind, in breaking forth, deals with his face[2] as it does with that of the sea, first blackening, then wrinkling, and at last bursting it into a foam. It is in this guise the sacred Æolist delivers his oracular

---

1 An author who writ De Artibus Perditis, &c., of arts lost, and of arts invented.
2 This is an exact description of the changes made in the face by enthusiastic preachers.

belches to his panting disciples; of whom, some are greedily gaping after the sanctified breath; others are all the while hymning out the praises of the winds; and, gently wafted to and fro by their own humming, do thus represent the soft breezes of their deities appeased.

It is from this custom of the priests that some authors maintain these Æolists to have been very ancient in the world. Because the delivery of their mysteries, which I have just now mentioned, appears exactly the same with that of other ancient oracles, whose inspirations were owing to certain subterraneous effluviums of wind, delivered with the same pain to the priest, and much about the same influence on the people. It is true, indeed, that these were frequently managed and directed by female officers, whose organs were understood to be better disposed for the admission of those oracular gusts, as entering and passing up through a receptacle of greater capacity, and causing also a pruriency by the way, such as, with due management, hath been refined from carnal into a spiritual ecstasy. And, to strengthen this profound conjecture, it is farther insisted, that this custom of female priests[1] is kept up still in certain refined colleges of our modern Æolists, who are agreed to receive their inspiration, derived through the receptacle aforesaid, like their ancestors the sibyls.

And whereas the mind of a man, when he gives the spur and bridle to his thoughts, does never stop, but naturally sallies out into both extremes, of high and low, of good and evil; his first flight of fancy commonly transports him to ideas of what is most perfect, finished, and exalted; till, having soared out of his own reach and sight, not well perceiving how near the frontiers of height and depth border upon each other; with the same course and wing he falls down plumb into the lowest bottom of things; like one who travels the east into the west; or like a straight line drawn by its own length into a circle. Whether a

---

1 Quakers who suffer their women to preach and pray.

tincture of malice in our natures makes us fond of furnishing every bright idea with its reverse; or whether reason, reflecting upon the sum of things, can, like the sun, serve only to enlighten one-half of the globe, leaving the other half by necessity under shade and darkness; or whether fancy, flying up to the imagination of what is highest and best, becomes overshot, and spent, and weary, and suddenly falls, like a dead bird of paradise, to the ground; or whether, after all these metaphysical conjectures, I have not entirely missed the true reason; the proposition, however, which has stood me in so much circumstance, is altogether true; that as the most uncivilised parts of mankind have some way or other climbed up into the conception of a god or supreme power, so they have seldom forgot to provide their fears with certain ghastly notions, which, instead of better, have served them pretty tolerably for a devil. And this proceeding seems to be natural enough; for it is with men, whose imaginations are lifted up very high, after the same rate as with those whose bodies are so; that, as they are delighted with the advantage of a nearer contemplation upwards, so they are equally terrified with the dismal prospect of a precipice below. Thus, in the choice of a devil it has been the usual method of mankind to single out some being, either in act or in vision, which was in most antipathy to the god they had framed. Thus also the sect of Æolists possessed themselves with a dread and horror and hatred of two malignant natures, betwixt whom and the deities they adored perpetual enmity was established. The first of these was the chameleon[1], sworn foe to inspiration, who in scorn devoured large influences of their god, without refunding the smallest blast by eructation. The other was a huge terrible monster, called Moulinavent, who, with four strong arms, waged eternal battle with all their divinities, dexterously turning to avoid their blows, and repay them with interest.

1 I do not well understand what the author aims at here, any more than by the terrible monster, mention'd in the following lines, called Moulinavent, which is the French word for a windmill.

Thus furnished and set out with gods, as well as devils, was the renowned sect of Æolists, which makes at this day so illustrious a figure in the world, and whereof that polite nation of Laplanders are, beyond all doubt, a most authentic branch; of whom I therefore cannot, without injustice, here omit to make honourable mention; since they appear to be so closely allied in point of interest, as well as inclinations, with their brother Æolists among us, as not only to buy their winds by wholesale from the same merchants, but also to retail them after the same rate and method, and to customers much alike.

Now, whether this system here delivered was wholly compiled by Jack, or, as some writers believe, rather copied, from the original at Delphos, with certain additions and emendations, suited to the times and circumstances, I shall not absolutely determine. This I may affirm, that Jack gave it at least a new turn, and formed it into the same dress and model as it lies deduced by me.

I have long sought after this opportunity of doing justice to a society of men for whom I have a peculiar honour, and whose opinions, as well as practices, have been extremely misrepresented and traduced by the malice or ignorance of their adversaries. For I think it one of the greatest and best of human actions to remove prejudices, and place things in their truest and fairest light, which I therefore boldly undertake, without any regards of my own, beside the conscience, the honour, and the thanks.

SECTION IX

A Digression Concerning the Original, the Use, and Improvement of Madness in a Commonwealth

Nor shall it in any ways detract from the just reputation of this famous sect, that its rise and institution are owing to such an author as I have described Jack to be; a person whose intellectuals were overturned, and his brain shaken out of its natural position; which we commonly suppose to be a distemper, and call by the name of madness or phrensy. For if we take a survey of the greatest actions that have been performed in the world under the influence of single men, which are, the establishment of new empires by conquest, the advance and progress of new schemes in philosophy, and the contriving, as well as the propagating, of new religions; we shall find the authors of them all to have been persons whose natural reason had admitted great revolutions, from their diet, their education, the prevalency of some certain temper, together with the particular influence of air and climate. Besides, there is something individual in human minds, that easily kindles at the accidental approach and collision of certain circumstances, which, though of paltry and mean appearance, do often flame out into the greatest emergencies of life. For great turns are not always given by strong hands, but by lucky adaption, and at proper seasons; and it is of no import where the fire was kindled, if the vapour has once got up into the brain. For the upper region of man is furnished like the middle region of the air; the materials are formed from causes of the widest difference, yet produce at last the same substance and effect. Mists arise from the earth, steams from dunghills, exhalations from the sea, and smoke from fire; yet all clouds are the same in composition as well as consequences, and the fumes issuing from a jakes will furnish as comely and useful a vapour as incense from an altar. Thus far, I suppose, will easily be granted me; and then it will follow that, as the face of nature never produces rain but when it is overcast and disturbed, so human understanding, seated in the brain, must be troubled and overspread by vapours ascending from the lower faculties to water the invention and render it fruitful. Now, although these vapours (as it has been already said) are of as various original as those of the skies, yet the crops they produce differ both in kind and degree, merely according to the soil. I will produce two instances to prove and explain what I am now advancing.

A certain great prince[1] raised a mighty army, filled his coffers with infinite treasures, provided an invincible fleet, and all this without giving the least part of his design to his greatest ministers or his nearest favourites. Immediately the whole world was armed; the neighbouring crowns in trembling expectations towards what point the storm would burst; the small politicians everywhere forming profound conjectures. Some believed he had laid a scheme for universal monarchy; others, after much insight, determined the matter to be a project for pulling down the pope, and setting up the reformed religion, which had once been his own. Some, again, of a deeper sagacity, sent him into Asia to subdue the Turk and recover Palestine. In the midst of all these projects and preparations, a certain state-surgeon[2], gathering the nature of the disease by these symptoms, attempted the cure, at one blow performed the operation, broke the bag, and out flew the vapour; nor did anything want to render it a complete remedy, only that the prince unfortunately happened to die in the performance. Now, is the reader exceedingly curious to learn whence this vapour took its rise, which had so long set the nations at a gaze? what secret wheel, what hidden spring, could put into motion so wonderful an engine? It was afterwards discovered that the movement of this whole machine had been directed by an absent female, whose eyes had raised a pro-

1 This was Harry the Great of France.
2 Ravillac, who stabb'd Henry the Great in his coach.

tuberancy, and, before emission, she was removed into an enemy's country. What should an unhappy prince do in such ticklish circumstances as these? He tried in vain the poet's never-failing receipt of *corpora quæque*; for,

"Idque petit corpus mens unde est saucia amore:
Unde feritur, eo tendit, gestitque coire."—Lucr.

Having to no purpose used all peaceable endeavours, the collected part of the semen, raised and inflamed, became adust, converted to choler, turned head upon the spinal duct, and ascended to the brain: the very same principle that influences a bully to break the windows of a whore who has jilted him naturally stirs up a great prince to raise mighty armies, and dream of nothing but sieges, battles, and victories.

"——Teterrima belli
Causa——"

The other instance[1] is what I have read somewhere in a very ancient author, of a mighty king, who, for the space of about thirty years, amused himself to take and lose towns; beat armies, and be beaten; drive princes out of their dominions; fright children from their bread and butter; burn, lay waste, plunder, dragoon, massacre subject and stranger, friend and foe, male and female. It is recorded that the philosophers of each country were in grave dispute upon causes, natural, moral and political, to find out where they should assign an original solution of this phenomenon. At last, the vapour or spirit which animated the hero's brain, being in perpetual circulation, seized upon that region of the human body so renowned for furnishing the *zibeta occidentalis*[2], and, gathering there into a tumour, left the rest of the world for that time in peace. Of such mighty consequence it is where those exhalations fix, and of so little from whence they

---

1 This is meant of the present French king.
2 Paracelsus, who was so famous for chymistry, try'd an experiment upon human excrement, to make a perfume of it, which when he had brought to perfection, he called Zibeta Occidentalis, or western civet, the back parts of man (according to his division mention'd by the author, page 160) being the west.

proceed. The same spirits which, in their superior progress, would conquer a kingdom, descending upon the anus, conclude in a fistula.

Let us now examine the great introducers of new schemes in philosophy, and search till we can find from what faculty of the soul the disposition arises in mortal man of taking it into his head to advance new systems, with such an eager zeal, in things agreed on all hands impossible to be known: from what seeds this disposition springs, and to what quality of human nature these grand innovators have been indebted for their number of disciples. Because it is plain that several of the chief among them, both ancient and modern, were usually mistaken by their adversaries, and indeed by all except their own followers, to have been persons crazed, or out of their wits; having generally proceeded, in the common course of their words and actions, by a method very different from the vulgar dictates of unrefined reason; agreeing for the most part in their several models with their present undoubted sucessors in the academy of modern Bedlam, whose merits and principles I shall further examine in due place. Of this kind were Epicurus, Diogenes, Apollonius, Lucretius, Paracelsus, Des Cartes, and others; who, if they were now in the world, tied fast, and separate from their followers, would, in this our undistinguishing age, incur manifest danger of phlebotomy, and whips, and chains, and dark chambers, and straw. For what man, in the natural state or course of thinking, did ever conceive it in his power to reduce the notions of all mankind exactly to the same length, and breadth, and height of his own? yet this is the first humble and civil design of all innovators in the empire of reason. Epicurus modestly hoped that, one time or other, a certain fortuitous concourse of all men's opinions, after perpetual justlings, the sharp with the smooth, the light and the heavy, the round and the square, would, by certain clinamina, unite in the notions of atoms and void, as these did in the originals of all things. Cartesius reckoned to see, before he died, the sentiments of all philosophers, like so many lesser

121

stars in his romantic system, wrapped and drawn within his own vortex. Now, I would gladly be informed how it is possible to account for such imaginations as these in particular men, without recourse to my phenomenon of vapours ascending from the lower faculties to overshadow the brain, and there distilling into conceptions, for which the narrowness of our mother-tongue has not yet assigned any other name beside that of madness or phrensy. Let us therefore now conjecture how it comes to pass that none of these great prescribers do ever fail providing themselves and their notions with a number of implicit disciples. And I think the reason is easy to be assigned; for there is a peculiar string in the harmony of human understanding, which, in several individuals, is exactly of the same tuning. This, if you can dexterously screw up to its right key, and then strike gently upon it, whenever you have the good fortune to light among those of the same pitch, they will, by a secret necessary sympathy, strike exactly at the same time. And in this one circumstance lies all the skill or luck of the matter; for, if you chance to jar the string among those who are either above or below your own height, instead of subscribing to your doctrine, they will tie you fast, call you mad, and feed you with bread and water. It is therefore a point of the nicest conduct to distinguish and adapt this noble talent with respect to the differences of persons and of times. Cicero understood this very well, who, when writing to a friend in England, with a caution, among other matters, to beware of being cheated by our hackney-coachmen (who, it seems, in those days were as errant rascals as they are now), has these remarkable words:

Est quod gaudeas te in ista loca venisse, ubi aliquid sapere viderere[*]. For, to speak a bold truth, it is a fatal miscarriage so ill to order affairs as to pass for a fool in one company, when in another you might be treated as a philosopher. Which I desire some certain gentlemen of my acquaintance to lay up in their hearts, as a very seasonable *innuendo*.

[*] Pausan. L. 8.

This, indeed, was the fatal mistake of that worthy gentleman, my most ingenious friend, Mr. Wotton; a person, in appearance, ordained for greater designs, as well as performances: whether you will consider his notions or his looks, surely no man ever advanced into public with fitter qualifications of body and mind for the propagation of a new religion. Oh, had those happy talents, missapplied to vain philosophy, been turned into their proper channels of dreams and visions, where distortion of mind and countenance are of such sovereign use, the base detracting world would not then have dared to report that something is amiss, that his brain has undergone an unlucky shake, which even his brother modernists themselves, like ungrates, do whisper so loud, that it reaches up to the very garret I am now writing in!

Lastly, whosoever pleases to look into the fountains of enthusiasm, from whence, in all ages, have eternally proceeded such fattening streams, will find the spring-head to have been as troubled and muddy as the current: of such great emolument is a tincture of this vapour, which the world calls madness, that without its help the world would not only be deprived of these two great blessings, conquests and systems, but even all mankind would unhappily be reduced to the same belief in things invisible. Now, the former *postulatum* being held that it is of no import from what originals this vapour proceeds, but either in what angles it strikes and spreads over the understanding, or upon what species of brain it ascends; it will be a very delicate point to cut the feather, and divide the several reasons to a nice and curious reader, how this numerical difference in the brain can produce effects of so vast a difference from the same vapour as to be the sole point of individuation between Alexander the Great, Jack of Leyden, and Monsieur Des Cartes. The present argument is the most abstracted that ever I engaged in; it strains my faculties to their highest stretch: and I desire the reader to attend with the utmost propensity; for I now proceed to unravel this knotty point.

There is in mankind[1] a certain * * * * * * * * * * * *
* *
Hic multa desiderantur * * * * * * * * * * * * * * * * * *
* *
* * * * * * * * * * * * * * * And this I take to be a clear
solution of the matter.

Having therefore so narrowly passed through this intricate difficulty, the reader will, I am sure, agree with me in the conclusion, that if the moderns mean by madness only a disturbance or transposition of the brain, by force of certain vapours issuing up from the lower faculties, then has this madness been the parent of all those mighty revolutions that have happened in empire, philosophy, and in religion. For the brain in its natural position and state of serenity disposes its owner to pass his life in the common forms, without any thoughts of subduing multitudes to his own power, his reasons, or his vision; and the more he shapes his understanding by the pattern of human learning, the less he is inclined to form parties after his particular notions, because that instructs him in his private infirmities, as well as in the stubborn ignorance of the people. But when a man's fancy gets astride on his reason; when imagination is at cuffs with the senses; and common understanding, as well as common sense, is kicked out of doors; the first proselyte he makes is himself; and when that is once compassed, the difficulty is not so great in bringing over others; a strong delusion always operating from without as vigorously as from within. For cant and vision are to the ear and the eye the same that tickling is to the touch. Those entertainments and pleasures we most value in life are such as dupe and play the wag with the senses. For if we take an examination of what is generally understood by happiness, as it has respect either to the understanding or the senses, we

---

1 Here is another defect in the manuscript, but I think the author did wisely, and that the matter which thus strained his faculties, was not worth a solution; and it were well if all metaphysical cobweb problems were no otherwise answered.

shall find all its properties and adjuncts will herd under this short definition, that it is a perpetual possession of being well deceived. And first, with relation to the mind or understanding, it is manifest what mighty advantages fiction has over truth; and the reason is just at our elbow, because imagination can build nobler scenes, and produce more wonderful revolutions, than fortune or nature will be at expense to furnish. Nor is mankind so much to blame in his choice thus determining him, if we consider that the debate merely lies between things past and things conceived: and so the question is only this; whether things that have place in the imagination may not as properly be said to exist as those that are seated in the memory; which may be justly held in the affirmative, and very much to the advantage of the former, since this is acknowledged to be the womb of things, and the other allowed to be no more than the grave. Again, if we take this definition of happiness, and examine it with reference to the senses, it will be acknowledged wonderfully adapt. How fading and insipid do all objects accost us that are not conveyed in the vehicle of delusion! how shrunk is everything as it appears in the glass of nature! so that if it were not for the assistance of artificial mediums, false lights, refracted angles, varnish and tinsel, there would be a mighty level in the felicity of enjoyments of mortal men. If this were seriously considered by the world, as I have a certain reason to suspect it hardly will, men would no longer reckon among their high points of wisdom the art of exposing weak sides and publishing infirmities; an employment, in my opinion, neither better nor worse than that of unmasking, which, I think, has never been allowed fair usage either in the world or the playhouse.

In the proportion that credulity is a more peaceful possession of the mind than curiosity, so far preferable is that wisdom which converses about the surface to that pretended philosophy which enters into the depths of things, and then comes gravely back with informations and discoveries that in the inside they are good for nothing. The two senses to which all objects first address themselves are the sight and the touch; these never examine farther than the colour, the shape, the size, and whatever other qualities dwell or are drawn by art upon the outward of bodies; and then comes reason officiously with tools for cutting, and opening, and mangling, and piercing, offering to demonstrate that they are not of the same consistence quite through. Now I take all this to be the last degree of perverting nature; one of whose eternal laws it is, to put her best furniture forward. And therefore, in order to save the charges of all such expensive anatomy for the time to come, I do here think fit to inform the reader that in such conclusions as these reason is certainly in the right; and that, in most corporeal beings which have fallen under my cognizance, the outside has been infinitely preferable to the in: whereof I have been farther convinced from some late experiments. Last week I saw a woman flayed, and you will hardly believe how much it altered her person for the worse. Yesterday I ordered the carcase of a beau to be stripped in my presence; when we were all amazed to find so many unsuspected faults under one suit of clothes. Then I laid open his brain, his heart, and his spleen: but I plainly perceived at every operation, that the farther we proceeded we found the defects increase upon us in number and bulk: from all which, I justly formed this conclusion to myself, that whatever philosopher or projector can find out an art to solder and patch up the flaws and imperfections of nature will deserve much better of mankind, and teach us a more useful science, than that so much in present esteem, of widening and exposing them, like him who held anatomy to be the ultimate end of physic. And he whose fortunes and dispositions have placed him in a convenient station to enjoy the fruits of this noble art; he that can, with Epicurus, content his ideas with the films and images that fly off upon his senses from the superficies of things; such a man, truly wise, creams off nature, leaving the sour and the dregs for philosophy and reason to lap up. This is the sublime and refined point of felicity, called the possession of being well deceived; the serene, peaceful state of being a fool among knaves.

But to return to madness. It is certain that, according to the system I have above deduced, every species thereof proceeds from a redundancy of vapours; therefore, as some kinds of phrensy give double strength to the sinews, so there are of other species, which add vigour, and life, and spirit to the brain: now, it usually happens that these active spirits, getting possession of the brain, resemble those that haunt other waste and empty dwellings, which, for want of business, either vanish and carry away a piece of the house, or else stay at home and fling it all out of the windows. By which are mystically displayed the two principal branches of madness, and which some philosophers, not considering so well as I, have mistaken to be different in their causes, over hastily assigning the first to deficiency, and the other to redundance.

I think it therefore manifest, from what I have here advanced, that the main point of skill and address is, to furnish employment for this redundancy of vapour, and prudently to adjust the season of it; by which means it may certainly become of cardinal and catholic emolument in a commonwealth. Thus one man, choosing a proper juncture, leaps into a gulf, thence proceeds a hero, and is called the saviour of his country: another achieves the same enterprise, but, unluckily timing it, has left the brand of madness fixed as a reproach upon his memory: upon so nice a distinction, are we taught to repeat the name of Curtius with reverence and love; that of Empedocles with hatred and contempt. Thus also it is usually conceived that the elder Brutus only personated the fool and madman for the good of the public; but this was nothing else than a redundancy of the same vapour long misapplied, called by Latins *ingenium par negotiis**; or, to translate it as   * Tacit   ⬤$ nearly as I can, a sort of phrensy, never in its right element till you take it up in the business of the state.

Upon all which, and many other reasons of equal weight, though not equally curious, I do here gladly embrace an opportunity I have long sought for of recommending it as a very noble undertaking to Sir Edward Seymour, Sir Christopher Musgrave, Sir John Bowles, John Howe, esq., and other patriots concerned, that they would move for leave to bring in a bill for appointing commissioners to inspect into Bedlam[2] and the parts adjacent; who shall be empowered to send for persons, papers, and records; to examine into the merits and qualifications of every student and professor; to observe with utmost exactness their several dispositions and behaviour; by which means, duly distinguishing and adapting their talents, they might produce admirable instruments for the several offices in a state, civil and military: proceeding in such methods as I shall here humbly propose. And I hope the gentle reader will give some allowance to my great solicitudes in this important affair, upon account of the high esteem I have borne that honourable society, whereof I had some time the happiness to be an unworthy member.

Is any student tearing his straw in piecemeal, swearing and blaspheming, biting his grate, foaming at the mouth, and emptying his piss-pot in the spectators' faces? let the right worshipful the commissioners of inspection give him a regiment of dragoons, and send him into Flanders among the rest. Is another eternally talking, spluttering, gaping, bawling in a sound without period or article? what wonderful talents are here mislaid! let him be furnished immediately with a green bag and papers, and threepence* in his pocket, and away with him to Westminster Hall. You will find a third gravely taking the dimensions of his kennel; a person of foresight and insight, though kept quite in the dark; for why, like Moses, *ecce cornuta*[1] *erat ejus facies*. He walks duly in one place, entreats your penny with due gravity and ceremony; talks much of hard times, and taxes, and the whore of Babylon; bars up the wooden window of his cell

* A lawyer's coach-hire.

---

1 Cornutus, is either horned or shining, and by this term, Moses is described in the vulgar Latin of the Bible.

constantly at eight o'clock; dreams of fire, and shoplifters, and court-customers, and privileged places. Now, what a figure would all these acquirements amount to if the owner were sent into the city among his brethren! Behold a fourth, in much and deep conversation with himself, biting his thumbs at proper junctures; his countenance checkered with business and design; sometimes walking very fast, with his eyes nailed to a paper that he holds in his hands: a great saver of time, somewhat thick of hearing, very short of sight, but more of memory: a man ever in haste, a great hatcher and breeder of business, and excellent at the famous art of whispering nothing; a huge idolator of monosyllables and procrastination; so ready to give his word to everybody, that he never keeps it: one that has forgot the common meaning of words, but an admirable retainer of the sound: extremely subject to the looseness, for his occasions are perpetually calling him away. If you approach his grate in his familiar intervals; Sir, says he, give me a penny, and I'll sing you a song: but give me the penny first. (Hence comes the common saying, and commoner practice, of parting with money for a song.) What a complete system of court skill is here described in every branch of it, and all utterly lost with wrong application! Accost the hole of another kennel (first stopping you nose), you will behold a surly, gloomy, nasty, slovenly mortal, raking in his own dung, and dabbling in his urine. The best part of his diet is the reversion of his own ordure, which, expiring into steams, whirls perpetually about, and at last reinfunds. His complexion is of a dirty yellow, with a thin scattered beard, exactly agreeable to that of his diet upon its first declination; like other insects, who, having their birth and education in an excrement, from thence borrow their colour and their smell. The student of this apartment is very sparing of his words, but somewhat over-liberal of his breath: he holds his hand out ready to receive your penny, and immediately upon receipt withdraws to his former occupations. Now, is it not amazing to think the society of Warwick Lane should have no more concern for the recovery of so useful a member, who, if one may judge from these appearances, would become the greatest ornament to that illustrious body? Another student struts up fiercely to your teeth, puffing with his lips, half squeezing out his eyes, and very graciously holds you out his hand to kiss. The keeper desires you not to be afraid of this professor, for he will do you no hurt: to him alone is allowed the liberty of the ante-chamber, and the orator of the place gives you to understand that this solemn person is a tailor run mad with pride. This considerable student is adorned with many other qualities, upon which at present I shall not farther enlarge. - - - - - - - - - - Hark in your ear[1] - I am strangely mistaken if all his address, his motions, and his airs, would not then be very natural, and in their proper element.

I shall not descend so minutely as to insist upon the vast number of beaux, fiddlers, poets, and politicians that the world might recover by such a reformation; but what is more material, beside the clear gain redounding to the common-wealth, by so large an acquisition of persons to employ, whose talents and acquirements, if I may be so bold as to affirm it, are now buried, or at least misapplied; it would be a mighty advantage accruing to the public from this inquiry, that all these would very much excel, and arrive at great perfection in their several kinds; which, I think, is manifest from what I have already shown, and shall enforce by this one plain instance; that even I myself, the author of these momentous truths, am a person whose imaginations are not hard-mouthed and exceedingly disposed to run away with his reason, which I have observed, from long experience, to be a very light rider, and easily shaken off; upon which account my friends will never trust me alone, without a solemn promise to vent my speculations in this or the like manner, for the universal

---

1 I cannot conjecture what the author means here, or how this chasm could be fill'd, tho' it is capable of more than one interpretation.

131

benefit of humankind; which perhaps the gentle, courteous, and candid reader, brimful of that modern charity and tenderness usually annexed to his office, will be very hardly persuaded to believe.

SECTION X

A Tale of a Tub

It is an unanswerable argument of a very refined age, the wonderful civilities that have passed of late years between the nation of authors and that of readers. There can hardly pop out a play[1], a pamphlet, or a poem, without a preface full of acknowledgment to the world for the general reception and applause they have given it, which the Lord knows where, or when, or how, or from whom it received. In due deference to so laudable a custom, I do here return my humble thanks to his majesty and both houses of parliament, to the lords of the king's most honourable privy-council, to the reverend the judges, to the clergy, and gentry, and yeomanry of this land; but in a more especial manner, to my worthy brethren and friends at Will's coffee-house, and Gresham College, and Warwick Lane, and Moorfields, and Scotland Yard, and Westminster Hall, and Guildhall; in short, to all the inhabitants and retainers whatsoever, either in court, or church, or camp, or city, or country, for their generous and universal acceptance of this divine treatise. I accept their approbation and good opinion with extreme gratitude, and, to the utmost of my poor capacity, shall take hold of all opportunities to return the obligation.

I am also happy that fate has flung me into so blessed an age for the mutual felicity of booksellers and authors, whom I may safely affirm to be at this day the two only satisfied parties in England. Ask an author how his last piece has succeeded; why, truly, he thanks his stars the world has been very favourable, and he has not the least reason to complain: and yet, by G—, he wrote it in a week, at bits and starts, when he could steal an hour from his urgent affairs; as it is a hundred to one, you may see farther in the preface, to which he refers you; and for the rest to the bookseller. There you go as a customer, and make

---

1 This is literally true, as we may observe in the prefaces to most plays, poems, &c.

133

the same question: he blesses his God the thing takes wonderfully, he is just printing the second edition, and has but three left in his shop. You beat down the price: "Sir, we shall not differ;" and, in hopes of your custom another time, lets you have it as reasonable as you please; and "pray send as many of your acquaintance as you will, I shall, upon your account, furnish them all at the same rate."

Now, it is not well enough considered to what accidents and occasions the world is indebted for the greatest part of those noble writings which hourly start up to entertain it. If it were not for a rainy day, a drunken vigil, a fit of the spleen, a course of physic, a sleepy Sunday, an ill run at dice, a long tailor's bill, a beggar's purse, a factious head, a hot sun, costive diet, want of books, and a just contempt of learning: but for these events, I say, and some others too long to recite (especially a prudent neglect of taking brimstone inwardly), I doubt the number of authors and of writings would dwindle away to a degree most woeful to behold. To confirm this opinion, hear the words of the famous Troglodyte philosopher: It is certain (said he) some grains of folly are of course annexed, as part of the composition of human nature, only the choice is left us, whether we please to wear them inlaid or embossed: and we need not to go very far to seek how that is usually determined, when we remember it is with human faculties as with liquors, the lightest will be ever at the top.

There is in this famous island of Britain a certain paltry scribbler, very voluminous, whose character the reader cannot wholly be a stranger to. He deals in a pernicious kind of writings, called *second parts*; and usually passes under the name of the author of the first. I easily foresee, that as soon as I lay down my pen this nimble operator will have stolen it, and treat me as inhumanly as he has already done Dr. Blackmore, Lestrange, and many others, who shall here be nameless; I therefore fly for justice and relief into the hands of that great rectifier of saddles, and lover of mankind, Dr. Bentley, begging he will take this enormous grievance into his most modern consideration: and if it should so happen that the furniture of an ass, in the shape of second part, must, for my sins, be clapped by a mistake upon my back, that he will immediately please, in the presence of the world, to lighten me of the burden, and take it home to his own house, till the true beast thinks fit to call for it.

In the meantime I do here give this public notice, that my resolutions are to circumscribe within this discourse the whole stock of matter I have been so many years providing. Since my vein is once opened, I am content to exhaust it all at a running, for the peculiar advantage of my dear country, and for the universal benefit of mankind. Therefore, hospitably considering the number of my guests, they shall have my whole entertainment at a meal; and I scorn to set up the leavings in the cupboard. What the guests cannot eat may be given to the poor; and the dogs[1] under the table may gnaw the bones. This I understand for a more generous proceeding than to turn the company's stomach, by inviting them again tomorrow to a scurvy meal of scraps.

If the reader fairly considers the strength of what I have advanced in the foregoing section, I am convinced it will produce a wonderful revolution in his notions and opinions; and he will be abundantly better prepared to receive and to relish the concluding part of this miraculous treatise. Readers may be divided into three classes—the superficial, the ignorant, and the learned: and I have with much felicity fitted my pen to the genius and advantage of each. The superficial reader will be strangely provoked to laughter; which clears the breast and the lungs, is sovereign against the spleen, and the most innocent of all diuretics. The ignorant reader, between whom and the former the distinction is extremely nice, will find himself disposed to stare; which is an admirable remedy for ill eyes, serves to raise and enliven the spirits, and wonderfully helps perspiration. But the reader truly learned, chiefly for whose

---

1 By dogs, the author means common injudicious critics, as he explains it himself before in his digression upon critics (page 96).

benefit I wake when others sleep, and sleep when others wake, will here find sufficient matter to employ his speculations for the rest of his life. It were much to be wished, and I do here humbly propose for an experiment, that every prince in Christendom will take seven of the deepest scholars in his dominions, and shut them up close for seven years in seven chambers, with a command to write seven ample commentaries on this comprehensive discourse. I shall venture to affirm that, whatever difference may be found in their several conjectures, they will be all, without the least distortion, manifestly deducible from the text. Meantime, it is my earnest request that so useful an undertaking may be entered upon, if their majesties please, with all convenient speed; because I have a strong inclination, before I leave the world, to taste a blessing which we mysterious writers can seldom reach till we have gotten into our graves: whether it is, that fame, being a fruit grafted on the body, can hardly grow, and much less ripen, till the stock is in the earth; or whether she be a bird of prey, and is lured, among the rest, to pursue after the scent of a carcase; or whether she conceives her trumpet sounds best and farthest when she stands on a tomb, by the advantage of a rising ground and the echo of a hollow vault.

It is true, indeed, the republic of dark authors, after they once found out this excellent expedient of dying, have been peculiarly happy in the variety as well as extent of their reputation. For night being the universal mother of things, wise philosophers hold all writings to be fruitful in the proportion that they are dark; and therefore, the true illuminated* (that is to say, the darkest of all) have met with such numberless commen-tators, whose scholastic midwifery has delivered them of meanings that the authors themselves perhaps never conceived, and yet may very justly be allowed the lawful parents of them; the words of such writers being like seed[1],

* A name of the Rosycrucians.

1 Nothing is more frequent than for commentators to force interpretation, which the author never meant.

136

which, however scattered at random, when they light upon a fruitful ground, will multiply far beyond either the hopes or imagination of the sower.

And therefore, in order to promote so useful a work, I will here take leave to glance a few innuendoes that may be of great assistance to those sublime spirits who shall be appointed to labour in a universal comment upon this wonderful discourse. And first, I have couched a very profound mystery[1] in the number of O's multiplied by seven and divided by nine. Also, if a devout brother of the rosy cross will pray fervently for sixty-three mornings, with a lively faith, and then transpose certain letters and syllables, according to prescription, in the second and fifth section, they will certainly reveal into a full receipt of the *opus magnum*. Lastly, whoever will be at the pains to calculate the whole number of each letter in this treatise, and sum up the difference exactly between the several numbers, assigning the true natural cause for every such difference, the discoveries in the product will plentifully reward his labour. But then he must beware of Bythus and Sigé[2], and be sure not to forget the qualities of Achamoth; *à cujus lacrymis humecta prodit substantia, à risu lucida, à tristitia, et à timore mobilis*; wherein Eugenius Philalethes*[3] hath committed an unpardonable mistake.

* Vid. Anima magica abscondita.

1 This is what the Cabbalists among the Jews have done with the Bible, and pretend to find wonderful mysteries by it.

2 I was told by an eminent divine, whom I consulted on this point, that these two barbarous words, with that of Acamoth and its qualities, as here set down, are quoted from Irenæus. This he discover'd by searching that ancient writer for another quotation of our author, which he has placed in the title page, and refers to the book and chapter; the curious were very inquisitive, whether those barbarous words, Basima Eacabasa, &c. are really in Irenæus, and upon enquiry 'twas found they were a sort of cant or jargon of certain heretics, and therefore very properly prefix'd to such a book as this of our author.

3 To the abovementioned treatise, called *Anthroposophia Theomagica*, there is another annexed, called *Anima Magica Abscondita*, written by the same author Vaughan, under the name of Eugenius Philalethes, but in neither of those treatises is there any mention of Acamoth or its qualities, so that this is nothing but amusement, and a ridicule of dark, unintelligible writers; only the words, *à cujus lacrymis* &c., are as we have said, transcribed from Irenæus, tho' I know not from what part. I believe one of the author's designs was to set curious men a hunting thro' indexes, and enquiring for books out of the common road.

SECTION XI

A Tale of a Tub

After so wide a compass as I have wandered, I do now gladly overtake and close in with my subject, and shall henceforth hold on with it an even pace to the end of my journey, except some beautiful prospect appears within sight of my way; whereof though at present I have neither warning nor expectation, yet upon such an accident, come when it will, I shall beg my reader's favour and company, allowing me to conduct him through it along with myself. For in writing it is as in travelling; if a man is in haste to be at home (which I acknowledge to be none of my case, having never so little business as when I am there), and his horse be tired with long riding and ill ways, or naturally a jade, I advise him clearly to make the straightest and the commonest road, be it ever so dirty; but then surely we must own such a man to be a scurvy companion at best; he spatters himself and his fellow-travellers at every step; all their thoughts, and wishes, and conversation turn entirely upon the subject of their journey's end; and at every splash, and plunge, and stumble, they heartily wish one another at the devil.

On the other side, when a traveller and his horse are in heart and plight, when his purse is full and the day before him, he takes the road only where it is clean and convenient; entertains his company there as agreeably as he can; but, upon the first occasion, carries them along with him to every delightful scene in view, whether of art, of nature, or of both; and if they chance to refuse, out of stupidity or weariness, let them jog on by themselves and be d——n'd; he'll overtake them at the next town; at which arriving, he rides furiously through; the men, women, and children, run out to gaze; a hundred noisy curs[1] run barking after him, of which, if he honours the boldest with

1 By these are meant what the author calls, the true critics, page 96.

a lash of his whip, it is rather out of sport than revenge; but should some sourer mongrel dare too near an approach, he receives a salute on the chaps by an accidental stroke from the courser's heels, nor is any ground lost by the blow, which sends him yelping and limping home.

I now proceed to sum up the singular adventures of my renowned Jack: the state of whose dispositions and fortunes the careful reader does, no doubt, most exactly remember, as I last parted with them in the conclusion of a former section. Therefore, his next care must be, from two of the foregoing, to extract a scheme of notions that may best fit his understanding for a true relish of what is to ensue.

JACK had not only calculated the first revolution of his brain so prudently as to give rise to that epidemic sect of Æolists, but succeeding also into a new and strange variety of conceptions, the fruitfulness of his imagination led him into certain notions, which, although in appearance very unaccountable, were not without their mysteries and their meanings, nor wanted followers to countenance and improve them. I shall therefore be extremely careful and exact in recounting such material passages of this nature as I have been able to collect, either from undoubted tradition or indefatigable reading; and shall describe them as graphically as it is possible, and as far as notions of that height and latitude can be brought within the compass of a pen. Nor do I at all question but they will furnish plenty of noble matter for such whose converting imaginations dispose them to reduce all things into types; who can make shadows, no thanks to the sun; and then mould them into substances, no thanks to philosophy; whose peculiar talent lies in fixing tropes and allegories to the letter, and refining what is literal into figure and mystery.

JACK had provided a fair copy of his father's will, engrossed in form upon a large skin of parchment; and resolving to act the part of a most dutiful son, he became the fondest creature of it imaginable. For although, as I have often told the reader, it consisted wholly in certain plain, easy directions, about the management and wearing of their coats, with legacies, and penalties in case of obedience or neglect, yet he began to entertain a fancy that the matter was deeper and darker, and therefore must needs have a great deal more of mystery at the bottom. "Gentlemen," said he, "I will prove this very skin of parchment to be meat, drink, and cloth, to be the philosopher's stone and the universal medicine[1]." In consequence of which raptures, he resolved to make use of it in the necessary as well as the most paltry occasions of life. He had a way of working it into any shape he pleased; so that it served him for a nightcap when he went to bed, and for an umbrella in rainy weather. He would lap a piece of it about a sore toe, or, when he had fits, burn two inches under his nose; or, if anything lay heavy on his stomach, scrape off and swallow as much of the powder as would lie on a silver penny; they were all infallible remedies. With analogy to these refinements, his common talk and conversation[2] ran wholly in the phrase of his will, and he circumscribed the utmost of his eloquence within that compass, not daring to let slip a syllable without authority from that. Once, at a strange house, he was suddenly taken short upon an urgent juncture, whereon it may not be allowed too particularly to dilate; and being not able to call to mind, with that suddenness the occasion required, an authentic phrase for demanding the way to the back-side, he chose rather, as the most prudent course, to incur the penalty in such cases usually annexed. Neither was it possible for the united rhetoric of mankind to prevail with him to make himself clean again; because, having consulted the will upon this emergency, he met with a passage near the bottom[3] (whether foisted in by the transcriber is not known) which seemed to forbid it.

---

1 The author here lashes those pretenders to purity, who place so much merit in using Scripture phrases on all occasions.

2 The Protestant dissenters use Scripture phrases in their serious discourses, and composures more than the Church of England men, accordingly Jack is introduced making his common talk and conversation to run wholly in the phrase of his will. W. Wotton.

3 I cannot guess the author's meaning here, which I would be very glad to know, because it seems to be of importance.

He made it a part of his religion never to say grace[1] to his meat; nor could all the world persuade him, as the common phrase is, to eat his victuals like a Christian[2].

He bore a strange kind of appetite to snap-dragon[3], and to the livid snuffs of a burning candle, which he would catch and swallow with an agility wonderful to conceive; and, by this procedure, maintained a perpetual flame in his belly, which, issuing in a glowing steam from both his eyes, as well as his nostrils and his mouth, made his head appear, in a dark night, like the skull of an ass, wherein a roguish boy had conveyed a farthing candle, to the terror of his majesty's liege subjects. Therefore, he made use of no other expedient to light himself home, but was wont to say that a wise man was his own lantern.

He would shut his eyes as he walked along the streets, and if he happened to bounce his head against a post, or fall into a kennel, as he seldom missed either to do one or both, he would tell the gibing apprentices who looked on that he submitted with entire resignation as to a trip or a blow of fate, with whom he found, by long experience, how vain it was either to wrestle or to cuff; and whoever durst undertake to do either would be sure to come off with a swinging fall or a bloody nose. "It was ordained," said he, "some few days before the creation, that my nose and this very post should have a rencounter; and therefore nature thought fit to send us both into the world in the same age, and to make us countrymen and fellow-citizens. Now, had my eyes been open, it is very likely the business might have been a great deal worse; for how many a confounded slip is daily got by a man with all his foresight about him? Besides, the eyes of the understanding see best when those of the senses

---

1 The slovenly way of receiving the sacrament among the fanatics.
2 This is a common phrase to express eating cleanly, and is meant for an invective against that undecent manner among some people in receiving the sacrament, so in the lines before, which is to be understood of the dissenters refusing to kneel at the sacrament.
3 I cannot well find the author's meaning here, unless it be the hot, untimely, blind zeal of enthusiasts.

are out of the way; and therefore blind men are observed to tread their steps with much more caution, and conduct, and judgment, than those who rely with too much confidence upon the virtue of the visual nerve, which every little accident shakes out of order, and a drop or a film can wholly disconcert; like a lantern among a pack of roaring bullies when they scour the streets, exposing its owner and itself to outward kicks and buffets, which both might have escaped if the vanity of appearing would have suffered them to walk in the dark. But farther, if we examine the conduct of these boasted lights, it will prove yet a great deal worse than their fortune. It is true, I have broke my nose against this post, because fortune either forgot, or did not think it convenient, to twitch me by the elbow, and give me notice to avoid it. But let not this encourage either the present age or posterity to trust their noses into the keeping of their eyes, which may prove the fairest way of losing them for good and all. For, O ye eyes, ye blind guides; miserable guardians are ye of our frail noses; ye, I say, who fasten upon the first precipice in view, and then tow our wretched willing bodies after you to the very brink of destruction: and alas! that brink is rotten, our feet slip, and we tumble down prone into a gulf, without one hospitable shrub in the way to break the fall; a fall to which not any nose of mortal make is equal, except that of the giant Laurcalco*, who was lord of the silver bridge. Most properly, therefore, O eyes, and with great justice, may you be compared to those foolish lights which conduct men through dirt and darkness, till they fall into a deep pit or a noisome bog."

* Vide Don Quixot.

This I have produced as a scantling of Jack's great eloquence, and the force of his reasoning upon such abstruse matters.

He was, besides, a person of great design and improvement in affairs of devotion, having introduced a new deity, who has since met with a vast number of worshippers; by some called Babel, by others Chaos, who had an ancient temple of Gothic structure upon Salisbury plain, famous for its shrine and celebration by pilgrims.

When he had some roguish trick[1] to play, he would down with his knees, up with his eyes, and fall to prayers, though in the midst of the kennel. Then it was that those who understood his pranks would be sure to get far enough out of his way; and whenever curiosity attracted strangers to laugh or to listen, he would, of a sudden, with one hand, out with his gear and piss full in their eyes, and with the other all bespatter them with mud.

In winter[2] he went always loose and unbuttoned, and clad as thin as possible to let in the ambient heat; and in summer lapped himself close and thick to keep it out.

In all revolutions[3] of government he would make his court for the office of hangman general; and in the exercise of that dignity, wherein he was very dexterous, would make use of no other vizard than a long prayer[4].

He had a tongue so musculous and subtile, that he could twist it up into his nose, and deliver a strange kind of speech from thence. He was also the first in these kingdoms who began to improve the Spanish accomplishment of braying; and having large ears, perpetually exposed and erected, he carried his art to such a perfection, that it was a point of great difficulty to distinguish, either by the view or the sound, between the original and the copy.

He was troubled with a disease reverse to that called the stinging of the tarantula; and would run dog-mad[5] at the noise of music, especially a pair of bagpipes. But he would cure himself again by taking two or three turns in Westminster Hall, or Billingsgate, or in a boarding-school, or the Royal Exchange, or a state coffee-house.

He was a person that feared no colours[6], but mortally hated

1 The villanies and cruelties committed by enthusiasts and fanatics among us, were all performed under the disguise of religion and long prayers.
2 They affect differences in habit and behaviour.
3 They are severe persecutors, and all in a form of cant and devotion.
4 Cromwell and his confederates went, as they called it, to seek God, when they resolved to murther the king.
5 This is to expose our dissenters' aversion to instrumental music in churches. W. Wotton.
6 They quarrel at the most innocent decency and ornament, and defaced the statues and paintings on all the churches in England.

all, and, upon that account, bore a cruel aversion against painters, insomuch that, in his paroxysms, as he walked the streets, he would have his pockets loaden with stones to pelt at the signs.

Having, from this manner of living, frequent occasion to wash himself, he would often leap over head and ears into water, though it were in the midst of the winter, but was always observed to come out again much dirtier, if possible, than he went in.

He was the first that ever found out the secret of contriving a soporiferous medicine[1] to be conveyed in at the ears; it was a compound of sulphur and balm of Gilead, with a little pilgrim's salve.

He wore a large plaster of artificial caustics on his stomach, with the fervour of which he could set himself a-groaning, like the famous board upon application of a red-hot iron.

He would stand in the turning of a street[2], and, calling to those who passed by, would cry to one, "Worthy sir, do me the honour of a good slap in the chaps." To another, "Honest friend, pray favour me with a handsome kick on the arse: Madam, shall I entreat a small box on the ear from your ladyship's fair hands? Noble captain, lend a reasonable thwack, for the love of God, with that cane of yours over these poor shoulders." And when he had, by such earnest solicitations, made a shift to procure a basting sufficient to swell up his fancy and his sides, he would return home extremely comforted, and full of terrible accounts of what he had undergone for the public good. "Observe this stroke" (said he, showing his bare shoulders); "a plaguy janizary gave it me this very morning, at seven o'clock, as, with much ado, I was driving off the great Turk. Neighbours, mind, this broken head deserves a plaster;

---

1 Fanatic preaching, composed either of hell and damnation, or a fulsome description of the joys of heaven, both in such a dirty, nauseous style, as to be well resembled to pilgrim's salve.
2 The fanatics have always had a way of affecting to run into persecution, and count vast merit upon every little hardship they suffer.

had poor Jack been tender of his noddle, you would have seen the pope and the French king, long before this time of day, among your wives and your warehouses. Dear christians, the great Mogul was come as far as Whitechapel, and you may thank these poor sides that he hath not (God bless us!) already swallowed up man, woman, and child."

It was highly worth observing the singular effects of that aversion[1] or antipathy which Jack and his brother Peter seemed, even to an affectation, to bear against each other. Peter had lately done some rogueries that forced him to abscond, and he seldom ventured to stir out before night, for fear of bailiffs. Their lodgings were at the two most distant parts of the town from each other; and whenever their occasions or humours called them abroad, they would make choice of the oddest unlikely times, and most uncouth rounds they could invent, that they might be sure to avoid one another; yet, after all this, it was their perpetual fortune to meet. The reason of which is easy enough to apprehend; for, the phrenzy and the spleen of both having the same foundation, we may look upon them as two pair of compasses, equally extended, and the fixed foot of each remaining in the same centre, which, though moving contrary ways at first, will be sure to encounter somewhere or other in the circumference. Besides, it was among the great misfortunes of Jack to bear a huge personal resemblance with his brother Peter. Their humour and dispositions were not only the same, but there was a close analogy in their shape, their size, and their mien. Insomuch, as nothing was more frequent than for a bailiff to seize Jack by the shoulders, and cry, "Mr. Peter, you are the king's prisoner." Or, at other times, for one of Peter's nearest friends to accost Jack with open arms, "Dear Peter, I am glad to

---

1 The Papists and fanatics, tho' they appear the most averse to each other, yet bear a near resemblance in many things, as has been observed by learned men.

Ibid. The agreement of our dissenters and the Papists in that which Bishop Stillingfleet called, the fanaticism of the Church of Rome, is ludicrously described for several pages together by Jack's likeness to Peter, and their being often mistaken for each other, and their frequent meeting, when they least intended it. W. Wotton.

see thee; pray send me one of your best medicines for the worms." This, we may suppose, was a mortifying return of those pains and proceedings Jack had laboured in so long; and finding how directly opposite all his endeavours had answered to the sole end and intention which he had proposed to himself, how could it avoid having terrible effects upon a head and heart so furnished as his? However, the poor remainders of his coat bore all the punishment; the orient sun never entered upon his diurnal progress without missing a piece of it. He hired a tailor to stitch up the collar so close that it was ready to choke him, and squeezed out his eyes at such a rate as one could see nothing but the white. What little was left of the main substance of the coat he rubbed every day for two hours against a rough-cast wall, in order to grind away the remnants of lace and embroidery; but at the same time went on with so much violence that he proceeded a heathen philosopher. Yet, after all he could do of this kind, the success continued still to disappoint his expectation. For, as it is the nature of rags to bear a kind of mock resemblance to finery, there being a sort of fluttering appearance in both which is not to be distinguished at a distance, in the dark, or by short-sighted eyes, so, in those junctures, it fared with Jack and his tatters, that they offered to the first view a ridiculous flaunting, which, assisting the resemblance in person and air, thwarted all his projects of separation, and left so near a similitude between them as frequently deceived the very disciples and followers of both.   *
* *
* *
Desunt nonnulla   *
* *
* *

The old Sclavonian proverb said well, that it is with men as with asses; whoever would keep them fast must find a very good hold at their ears. Yet I think we may affirm that it has been verified by repeated experience that—

Effugiet tamen hæc sceleratus vincula Proteus.

It is good, therefore, to read the maxims of our ancestors, with great allowances to times and persons; for, if we look into primitive records, we shall find that no revolutions have been so great or so frequent as those of human ears. In former days there was a curious invention to catch and keep them, which I think we may justly reckon among the *artes perditœ*; and how can it be otherwise, when in the latter centuries the very species is not only diminished to a very lamentable degree, but the poor remainder is also degenerated so far as to mock our skilfullest tenure? For, if the only slitting of one ear in a stag has been found sufficient to propagate the defect through a whole forest, why should we wonder at the greatest consequences from so many loppings and mutilations to which the ears of our fathers, and our own, have been of late so much exposed? It is true, indeed, that while this island of ours was under the dominion of grace, many endeavours were made to improve the growth of ears once more among us. The proportion of largeness was not only looked upon as an ornament of the outward man, but as a type of grace in the inward. Besides, it is held by naturalists that, if there be a protuberancy of parts in the superior region of the body, as in the ears and nose, there must be a parity also in the inferior: and, therefore, in that truly pious age, the males in every assembly, according as they were gifted, appeared very forward in exposing their ears to view, and the regions about them; because * Lib. de aëre locis & Hippocrates* tells us that, when the vein aquis. behind the ear happens to be cut, a man becomes an eunuch; and the females were nothing backwarder in beholding and edifying by them; whereof those who had already used the means looked about them with great concern, in hopes of conceiving a suitable offspring by such a prospect: others, who stood candidates for benevolence, found there a plentiful choice, and were sure to fix upon such as discovered the largest ears, that the breed might not dwindle between them. Lastly, the devouter sisters, who looked upon all extraordinary dilatations of that member as protrusions of zeal, or spiritual excrescences, were sure to honour every head they sat upon as if they had been marks of grace; but especially that of the preacher, whose ears were usually of the prime magnitude; which, upon that account, he was very frequent and exact in exposing with all advantages to the people; in his rhetorical paroxysms turning sometimes to hold forth the one, and sometimes to hold forth the other: from which custom the whole operation of preaching is to this very day, among their professors, styled by the phrase of holding forth.

Such was the progress of the saints for advancing the size of that member; and it is thought the success would have been every way answerable, if, in process of time, a cruel king[1] had not arisen, who raised a bloody persecution against all ears above a certain standard: upon which, some were glad to hide their flourishing sprouts in a black border, others crept wholly under a periwig; some were slit, others cropped, and a great number sliced off to the stumps. But of this more hereafter in my general history of ears, which I design very speedily to bestow upon the public.

From this brief survey of the falling state of ears in the last age, and the small care had to advance their ancient growth in the present, it is manifest how little reason we can have to rely upon a hold so short, so weak, and so slippery, and that whoever desires to catch mankind fast must have recourse to some other methods. Now, he that will examine human nature with circumspection enough may discover several handles, whereof the six senses* afford one a-piece,

*Including Scaliger's.

beside a great number that are screwed to the passions, and some few riveted to the intellect. Among these last, curiosity is one, and of all others, affords the firmest grasp: curiosity, that spur in the side, that bridle in the mouth, that

1 This was King Charles the Second, who at his restoration, turned out all the dissenting teachers that would not conform.

ring in the nose, of a lazy and impatient and a grunting reader. By this handle it is, that an author should seize upon his readers; which as soon as he has once compassed, all resistance and struggling are in vain; and they become his prisoners as close as he pleases, till weariness or dulness force him to let go his gripe.

And therefore, I, the author of this miraculous treatise, having hitherto, beyond expectation, maintained, by the aforesaid handle, a firm hold upon my gentle readers, it is with great reluctance that I am at length compelled to remit my grasp; leaving them, in the perusal of what remains, to that natural oscitancy inherent in the tribe. I can only assure thee, courteous reader, for both our comforts, that my concern is altogether equal to thine for my unhappiness in losing, or mislaying among my papers, the remaining part of these memoirs; which consisted of accidents, turns, and adventures, both new, agreeable, and surprising; and therefore calculated, in all due points, to the delicate taste of this our noble age. But, alas! with my utmost endeavours, I have been able only to retain a few of the heads. Under which, there was a full account how Peter got a protection out of the king's bench; and of a reconcilement[1] between Jack and him, upon a design they had, in a certain rainy night, to trepan brother Martin into a spunging-house, and there strip him to the skin. How Martin, with much ado, showed them both a fair pair of heels. How a new warrant came out against Peter; upon which, how Jack left him in the lurch, stole his protection, and made use of it himself. How Jack's tatters came into fashion in court and city; how he got upon a great

---

1 In the reign of King James the Second, the Presbyterians by the King's invitation, joined with the Papists, against the Church of England, and addrest him for repeal of the penal laws and Test. The King by his dispensing power, gave liberty of conscience, which both Papists and Presbyterians made use of, but upon the Revolution, the Papists being down of course, the Presbyterians freely continued their assemblies, by virtue of King James's indulgence, before they had a toleration by law; this I believe the author means by Jack's stealing Peter's protection, and making use of it himself.

horse[1], and eat custard[2]. But the particulars of all these, with several others which have now slid out of my memory, are lost beyond all hopes of recovery. For which misfortune, leaving my readers to condole with each other, as far as they shall find it to agree with their several constitutions, but conjuring them by all the friendship that has passed between us, from the title-page to this, not to proceed so far as to injure their healths for an accident past remedy—I now go on to the ceremonial part of an accomplished writer, and therefore, by a courtly modern, least of all others to be omitted.

1 Sir Humphrey Edwyn, a Presbyterian, was some years ago Lord Mayor of London, and had the insolence to go in his formalities to a conventicle, with the ensigns of his office.
2 Custard is a famous dish at a Lord Mayor's feast.

Going too long is a cause of abortion as effectual, though not so frequent, as going too short, and holds true especially in the labours of the brain. Well fare the heart of that noble Jesuit* who first adventured to * Pere d'Orleans. confess in print that books must be suited to their several seasons, like dress, and diet, and diversions; and better fare our noble nation for refining upon this among other French modes. I am living fast to see the time when a book that misses its tide shall be neglected, as the moon by day, or like mackerel a week after the season. No man has more nicely observed our climate than the bookseller who bought the copy of this work; he knows to a tittle what subjects will best go off in a dry year, and which it is proper to expose foremost when the weather-glass is fallen to much rain. When he had seen this treatise, and consulted his almanac upon it, he gave me to understand that he had manifestly considered the two principal things, which were, the bulk and the subject, and found it would never take but after a long vacation, and then only in case it should happen to be a hard year for turnips. Upon which I desired to know, considering my urgent necessities, what he thought might be acceptable this month. He looked westward and said, I doubt we shall have a fit of bad weather; however, if you could prepare some pretty little banter (but not in verse), or a small treatise upon the ——, it would run like wildfire. But if it hold up, I have already hired an author to write something against Dr. Bentley, which I am sure will turn to account.

At length we agreed upon this expedient; that when a customer comes from one of these, and desires in confidence to know the author, he will tell him very privately as a friend, naming whichever of the wits shall happen to be that week in vogue; and if Durfey's last play shall be in course, I would as lieve he may be the person as Congreve. This I mention, because I am wonderfully well acquainted with the present relish of our courteous readers; and have often observed with singular pleasure, that a fly driven from a honey-pot will immediately, with very good appetite, alight and finish his meal on an excrement.

I have one word to say upon the subject of profound writers, who are grown very numerous of late; and I know very well the judicious world is resolved to list me in that number. I conceive therefore, as to the business of being profound, that it is with writers as with wells—a person with good eyes may see to the bottom of the deepest, provided any water be there: and often when there is nothing in the world at the bottom besides dryness and dirt, though it be but a yard and a-half under-ground, it shall pass, however, for wondrous deep, upon no wiser a reason than because it is wondrous dark.

I am now trying an experiment very frequent among modern authors, which is to write upon nothing; when the subject is utterly exhausted, to let the pen still move on: by some called the ghost of wit, delighting to walk after the death of its body. And to say the truth, there seems to be no part of knowledge in fewer hands than that of discerning when to have done. By the time that an author has written out a book he and his readers are become old acquaintance, and grow very loth to part; so that I have sometimes known it to be in writing as in visiting, where the ceremony of taking leave has employed more time than the whole conversation before. The conclusion of a treatise resembles the conclusion of human life, which has sometimes been compared to the end of a feast, where few are satisfied to depart, *ut plenus vitæ conviva*; for men will sit down after the fullest meal, though it be only to doze or to sleep out the rest of the day. But in this latter I differ extremely from other writers; and shall be too proud if, by all my labours, I can have anyways contributed to the repose of mankind in times so turbulent[1] and unquiet as these. Neither do I think such an employment so very alien from the office of a wit as some would suppose. For, among a very polite nation

1 This was writ before the peace of Riswick.

in Greece*, there were the same temples built and consecrated to Sleep and the Muses; * Trezenii Pausan. l. 2.
between which two deities they believed the strictest friendship was established.

I have one concluding favour to request of my reader, that he will not expect to be equally diverted and informed by every line or every page of this discourse; but give some allowance to the author's spleen and short fits or intervals of dulness, as well as his own; and lay it seriously to his conscience, whether, if he were walking the streets in dirty weather or a rainy day, he would allow it fair dealing in folks at their ease from a window to criticise his gait and ridicule his dress at such a juncture.

In my disposure of employments of the brain I have thought fit to make invention the master, and to give method and reason the office of its lackeys. The cause of this distribution was, from observing it my peculiar case to be often under a temptation of being witty, upon occasions where I could be neither wise, nor sound, nor anything to the matter in hand. And I am too much a servant of the modern way to neglect any such opportunities, whatever pains or improprieties I may be at to introduce them. For I have observed that, from a laborious collection of seven hundred and thirty-eight flowers and shining hints of the best modern authors, digested with great reading into my book of common-places, I have not been able, after five years, to draw, book, or force into common conversation, any more than a dozen. Of which dozen, the one moiety failed of success by being dropped among unsuitable company; and the other cost me so many strains and traps and ambages to introduce, that I at length resolved to give it over. Now, this disappointment (to discover a secret), I must own, gave me the first hint of setting up for an author; and I have since found among some particular friends, that it is become a very general complaint, and has produced the same effects upon many others. For I have remarked many a towardly word to be wholly neglected or despised in discourse, which has passed very smoothly with some consideration and esteem after its preferment and sanction in print. But now, since by the liberty and encouragement of the press, I am grown absolute master of the occasions and opportunities to expose the talents I have acquired, I already discover that the issues of my *observanda* begin to grow too large for the receipts. Therefore I shall here pause a while, till I find, by feeling the world's pulse and my own, that it will be of absolute necessity for us both to resume my pen.

THE BATTLE OF THE BOOKS

A FULL AND TRUE ACCOUNT
OF THE BATTLE
FOUGHT LAST FRIDAY
BETWEEN THE ANCIENT
AND THE MODERN BOOKS
IN SAINT JAMES'S LIBRARY

THE BOOKSELLER TO THE READER

The following discourse, as it is unquestionably of the same author, so it seems to have been written about the same time, with the former; I mean the year 1697, when the famous dispute was on foot about ancient and modern learning. The controversy took its rise from an essay of Sir William Temple's upon that subject; which was answered by W. Wotton, B.D., with an appendix by Dr. Bentley, endeavouring to destroy the credit of Æsop and Phalaris for authors, whom Sir William Temple had, in the essay before mentioned, highly commended. In that appendix the doctor falls hard upon a new edition of Phalaris, put out by the Honourable Charles Boyle, now Earl of Orrery, to which Mr. Boyle replied at large with great learning and wit; and the doctor voluminously rejoined. In this dispute the town highly resented to see a person of Sir William Temple's character and merits roughly used by the two reverend gentlemen aforesaid, and without any manner of provocation. At length, there appearing no end of the quarrel, our author tells us that the BOOKS in St. James's Library, looking upon themselves as parties principally concerned, took up the controversy, and came to a decisive battle; but the manuscript, by the injury of fortune or weather, being in several places imperfect, we cannot learn to which side the victory fell.

I must warn the reader to beware of applying to persons what is here meant only of books, in the most literal sense. So, when Virgil is mentioned, we are not to understand the person of a famous poet called by that name; but only certain sheets of paper bound up in leather, containing in print the works of the said poet: and so of the rest.

THE PREFACE OF THE AUTHOR

Satire is a sort of glass wherein beholders do generally discover everybody's face but their own; which is the chief reason for that kind reception it meets with in the world, and that so very few are offended with it. But, if it should happen otherwise, the danger is not great; and I have learned from long experience never to apprehend mischief from those understandings I have been able to provoke: for anger and fury, though they add strength to the sinews of the body, yet are found to relax those of the mind, and to render all its efforts feeble and impotent.

There is a brain that will endure but one scumming; let the owner gather it with discretion, and manage his little stock with husbandry; but, of all things, let him beware of bringing it under the lash of his betters, because that will make it all bubble up into impertinence, and he will find no new supply. Wit without knowledge being a sort of cream, which gathers in a night to the top, and by a skilful hand may be soon whipped into froth; but once scummed away, what appears underneath will be fit for nothing but to be thrown to the hogs.

THE BATTLE OF THE BOOKS

Whoever examines, with due circumspection, into the annual records of time*, will find it re-marked that war is the child of pride, and pride the daughter of riches:—

the former of which assertions may be soon granted, but one cannot so easily subscribe to the latter; for pride is nearly related to beggary and want, either by father or mother, and sometimes by both: and, to speak naturally, it very seldom happens among men to fall out when all have enough; invasions usually travelling from north to south, that is to say, from poverty to plenty. The most ancient and natural grounds of quarrels are lust and avarice; which, though we may allow to be brethren, or collateral branches of pride, are certainly the issues of want. For, to speak in the phrase of writers upon politics, we may observe in the republic of dogs, which in its original seems to be an institution of the many, that the whole state is ever in the profoundest peace after a full meal; and that civil broils arise among them when it happens for one great bone to be seized on by some leading dog, who either divides it among the few, and then it falls to an oligarchy, or keeps it to himself, and then it runs up to a tyranny. The same reasoning also holds place among them in those dissensions we behold upon a turgescency in any of their females. For the right of possession lying in common (it being impossible to establish a property in so delicate a case), jealousies and suspicions do so abound, that the whole commonwealth of that street is reduced to a manifest state of war, of every citizen against every citizen, till some one of more courage, conduct, or fortune than the rest seizes and enjoys the prize: upon which naturally arises plenty of heart-burning, and envy, and snarling against the happy dog. Again, if we look upon any of these republics engaged in a foreign war, either of invasion or defence, we shall find the same reasoning will serve as to the grounds and occasions of each; and that poverty or want, in

some degree or other (whether real or in opinion, which makes no alteration in the case), has a great share, as well as pride, on the part of the aggressor.

Now, whoever will please to take this scheme, and either reduce or adapt it to an intellectual state or commonwealth of learning, will soon discover the first ground of disagreement between the two great parties at this time in arms, and may form just conclusions upon the merits of either cause. But the issue or events of this war are not so easy to conjecture at; for the present quarrel is so inflamed by the warm heads of either faction, and the pretensions somewhere or other so exorbitant, as not to admit the least overtures of accommodation. This quarrel first began, as I have heard it affirmed by an old dweller in the neighbourhood, about a small spot of ground, lying and being upon one of the two tops of the hill Parnassus; the highest and largest of which had, it seems, been time out of mind in quiet possession of certain tenants, called the Ancients; and the other was held by the Moderns. But these, disliking their present station, sent certain ambassadors to the ancients, complaining of a great nuisance; how the height of that part of Parnassus quite spoiled the prospect of theirs, especially toward the *east*; and therefore, to avoid a war, offered them the choice of this alternative, either that the ancients would please to remove themselves and their effects down to the lower summit, which the moderns would graciously surrender to them, and advance into their place; or else the said ancients will give leave to the moderns to come with shovels and mattocks, and level the said hill as low as they shall think it convenient. To which the ancients made answer, how little they expected such a message as this from a colony whom they had admitted, out of their own free grace, to so near a neighbourhood. That, as to their own seat, they were aborigines of it, and therefore to talk with them of a removal or surrender was a language they did not understand. That, if the height of the hill on their side shortened the prospect of the moderns, it was a disadvantage they could not help; but desired them to consider whether that injury (if it be any) were not largely recompensed by the shade and shelter it afforded them. That, as to the levelling or digging down, it was either folly or ignorance to propose it if they did or did not know how that side of the hill was an entire rock, which would break their tools and hearts, without any damage to itself. That they would therefore advise the moderns rather to raise their own side of the hill than dream of pulling down that of the ancients; to the former of which they would not only give licence, but also largely contribute. All this was rejected by the moderns with much indignation, who still insisted upon one of the two expedients; and so this difference broke out into a long and obstinate war, maintained on the one part by resolution, and by the courage of certain leaders and allies; but, on the other, by the greatness of their number, upon all defeats affording continual recruits. In this quarrel whole rivulets of ink have been exhausted, and the virulence of both parties enormously augmented. Now, it must be here understood that ink is the great missive weapon in all battles of the learned, which, conveyed through a sort of engine called a quill, infinite numbers of these are darted at the enemy by the valiant on each side, with equal skill and violence, as if it were an engagement of *porcupines*. This malignant liquor was compounded, by the engineer who invented it, of two ingredients, which are, gall and copperas; by its bitterness and venom to suit, in some degree, as well as to foment, the genius of the combatants. And as the Grecians, after an engagement, when they could not agree about the victory, were wont to set up trophies on both sides, the beaten party being content to be at the same expense, to keep itself in countenance (a laudable and ancient custom, happily revived of late in the art of war), so the learned, after a sharp and bloody dispute, do, on both sides, hang out their trophies too, whichever comes by the worst. These trophies have largely inscribed on them the merits of the cause; a full impartial account of such a *battle*, and how the victory fell clearly to the party that set them up.

They are known to the world under several names; as disputes, arguments, rejoinders, brief considerations, answers, replies, remarks, reflections, objections, confutations. For a very few days they are fixed up in all public places, either by themselves or their representatives*, for passengers to gaze at; whence the chiefest and largest are removed to certain magazines they call libraries, there to remain in a quarter purposely assigned them, and thenceforth begin to be called books of controversy.

* Their title pages.

In these books is wonderfully instilled and preserved the spirit of each warrior while he is alive; and after his death his soul transmigrates thither to inform them. This at least is the more common opinion; but I believe it is with libraries as with other cemeteries; where some philosophers affirm that a certain spirit, which they call *brutum hominis*, hovers over the monument, till the body is corrupted and turns to dust or to worms, but then vanishes or dissolves; so, we may say, a restless spirit haunts over every book, till dust or worms have seized upon it; which to some may happen in a few days, but to others later: and therefore books of controversy, being, of all others, haunted by the most disorderly spirits, have always been confined in a separate lodge from the rest; and for fear of a mutual violence against each other, it was thought prudent by our ancestors to bind them to the peace with strong iron chains. Of which invention the original occasion was this: When the works of Scotus first came out, they were carried to a certain library, and had lodgings appointed them; but this author was no sooner settled than he went to visit his master, Aristotle; and there both concerted together to seize Plato by main force, and turn him out from his ancient station among the divines, where he had peaceably dwelt near eight hundred years. The attempt succeeded, and the two usurpers have reigned ever since in his stead; but, to maintain quiet for the future, it was decreed that all *polemics* of the larger size should be held fast with a chain.

By this expedient the public peace of libraries might

certainly have been preserved if a new species of controversial books had not arisen of late years, instinct with a more malignant spirit, from the war above mentioned between the learned about the higher summit of *Parnassus*.

When these books were first admitted into the public libraries, I remember to have said, upon occasion, to several persons concerned, how I was sure they would create broils wherever they came, unless a world of care were taken: and therefore I advised that the champions of each side should be coupled together, or otherwise mixed, that, like the blending of contrary poisons, their malignity might be employed among themselves. And it seems I was neither an ill prophet nor an ill counsellor; for it was nothing else but the neglect of this caution which gave occasion to the terrible fight that happened on Friday last between the ancient and modern books in the king's library. Now, because the talk of this battle is so fresh in everybody's mouth, and the expectation of the town so great to be informed in the particulars, I, being possessed of all qualifications requisite in an historian, and retained by neither party, have resolved to comply with the urgent importunity of my friends, by writing down a full impartial account thereof.

The guardian of the regal library, a person of great valour, but chiefly renowned for his humanity[1], had been a fierce champion for the moderns; and, in an engagement upon Parnassus, had vowed, with his own hands to knock down two of the ancient chiefs, who guarded a small pass on the superior rock; but, endeavouring to climb up, was cruelly obstructed by his own unhappy weight and tendency towards his centre; a quality to which those of the modern party are extremely subject; for, being light-headed, they have, in speculation, a wonderful agility, and conceive nothing too high for them to mount; but, in reducing to practice, discover a mighty pressure

---

1 The Honourable Mr. Boyle, in the preface to his edition of Phalaris, says, he was refus'd a manuscript by the library keeper, *pro solita humanitate suâ*.

about their posteriors and their heels. Having thus failed in his design, the disappointed champion bore a cruel rancour to the ancients; which he resolved to gratify by showing all marks of his favour to the books of their adversaries, and lodging them in the fairest apartments; when, at the same time, whatever book had the boldness to own itself for an advocate of the ancients was buried alive in some obscure corner, and threatened, upon the least displeasure, to be turned out of doors. Besides, it so happened that about this time there was a strange confusion of place among all the books in the library; for which several reasons were assigned. Some imputed it to a great heap of learned dust, which a perverse wind blew off from a shelf of moderns into the keeper's eyes. Others affirmed he had a humour to pick the worms out of the schoolmen, and swallow them fresh and fasting: whereof some fell upon his spleen, and some climbed up into his head, to the great perturbation of both. And lastly, others maintained that, by walking much in the dark about the library, he had quite lost the situation of it out of his head; and therefore, in replacing his books, he was apt to mistake, and clap Des Cartes next to Aristotle; poor Plato had got between Hobbes and the Seven Wise Masters, and Virgil was hemmed in with Dryden on one side and Withers on the other.

Meanwhile those books that were advocates for the moderns chose out one from among them to make a progress through the whole library, examine the number and strength of their party, and concert their affairs. This messenger performed all things very industriously, and brought back with him a list of their forces, in all, fifty thousand, consisting chiefly of light-horse, heavy-armed foot, and mercenaries; whereof the foot were in general but sorrily armed and worse clad; their horses large, but extremely out of case and heart; however, some few, by trading among the ancients, had furnished themselves tolerably enough.

While things were in this ferment, discord grew extremely high; but words passed on both sides, and ill blood was plentifully bred. Here a solitary ancient, squeezed up among a whole shelf of moderns, offered fairly to dispute the case, and to prove by manifest reason that the priority was due to them from long possession, and in regard of their prudence, antiquity, and, above all, their great merits toward the moderns. But these denied the premises, and seemed very much to wonder how the ancients could pretend to insist upon their antiquity, when it was so plain (if they went to that) that the moderns were much the more ancient* of the two. As for any obligations they owed to the ancients, they renounced them all. It is true, said they, we are informed some few of our party have been so mean to borrow their subsistence from you; but the rest, infinitely the greater number (and especially we French and English), were so far from stooping to so base an example, that there never passed, till this very hour, six words between us. For our horses were of our own breeding, our arms of our own forging, and our clothes of our own cutting out and sewing. Plato was by chance up on the next shelf, and observing those that spoke to be in the ragged plight mentioned a while ago; their jades lean and foundered, their weapons of rotten wood, their armour rusty, and nothing but rags underneath; he laughed loud, and in his pleasant way swore, by ——, he believed them.

* According to the modern paradox.

Now, the moderns had not proceeded in their late negotiation with secrecy enough to escape the notice of the enemy. For those advocates who had begun the quarrel, by setting first on foot the dispute of precedency, talked so loud of coming to a battle, that Sir William Temple happened to overhear them, and gave immediate intelligence to the ancients: who thereupon drew up their scattered troops together, resolving to act upon the defensive; upon which, several of the moderns fled over to their party, and among the rest Temple himself. This Temple, having been educated and long conversed among the ancients, was, of all the moderns, their greatest favourite, and became their greatest champion.

Things were at this crisis when a material accident fell out.

For upon the highest corner of a large window there dwelt a certain spider, swollen up to the first magnitude by the destruction of infinite numbers of flies, whose spoils lay scattered before the gates of his palace, like human bones before the cave of some giant. The avenues to his castle were guarded with turnpikes and palisadoes, all after the modern way of fortification. After you had passed several courts you came to the centre, wherein you might behold the constable himself in his own lodgings, which had windows fronting to each avenue, and ports to sally out upon all occasions of prey or defence. In this mansion he had for some time dwelt in peace and plenty, without danger to his person by swallows from above, or to his palace by brooms from below; when it was the pleasure of fortune to conduct thither a wandering bee, to whose curiosity a broken pane in the glass had discovered itself, and in he went; where, expatiating a while, he at last happened to alight upon one of the outward walls of the spider's citadel; which, yielding to the unequal weight, sunk down to the very foundation. Thrice he endeavoured to force his passage, and thrice the centre shook. The spider within, feeling the terrible convulsion, supposed at first that nature was approaching to her final dissolution; or else, that Beelzebub, with all his legions, was come to revenge the death of many thousands of his subjects whom his enemy had slain and devoured. However, he at length valiantly resolved to issue forth and meet his fate. Meanwhile the bee had acquitted himself of his toils, and, posted securely at some distance, was employed in cleansing his wings, and disengaging them from the ragged remants of the cobweb. By this time the spider was adventured out, when, beholding the chasms, the ruins, and dilapidations of his fortress, he was very near at his wits' end; he stormed and swore like a madman, and swelled till he was ready to burst. At length, casting his eye upon the bee, and wisely gathering causes from events (for they knew each other by sight): A plague split you, said he, for a giddy son of a whore; is it you, with a vengeance, that have made this litter here? could not you look before you, and be d——d? do you think I have nothing else to do (in the devil's name) but to mend and repair after your arse?—Good words, friend, said the bee (having now pruned himself, and being disposed to droll): I'll give you my hand and word to come near your kennel no more; I was never in such a confounded pickle since I was born.—Sirrah, replied the spider, if it were not for breaking an old custom in our family, never to stir abroad against an enemy, I should come and teach you better manners.—I pray have patience, said the bee, or you'll spend your substance, and, for aught I see, you may stand in need of it all, toward the repair of your house.—Rogue, rogue, replied the spider, yet methinks you should have more respect to a person whom all the world allows to be so much your betters.—By my troth, said the bee, the comparison will amount to a very good jest; and you will do me a favour to let me know the reasons that all the world is pleased to use in so hopeful a dispute. At this the spider, having swelled himself into the size and posture of a disputant, began his argument in the true spirit of controversy, with resolution to be heartily scurrilous and angry to urge on his own reasons, without the least regard to the answers or objections of his opposite; and fully predetermined in his mind against all conviction.

Not to disparage myself, said he, by the comparison with such a rascal, what art thou but a vagabond without house or home, without stock or inheritance? born to no possession of your own, but a pair of wings and a drone-pipe. Your livelihood is a universal plunder upon nature; a freebooter over fields and gardens; and, for the sake of stealing will rob a nettle as easily as a violet. Whereas I am a domestic animal, furnished with a native stock within myself. This large castle (to show my improvements in the mathematics) is all built with my own hands, and the materials extracted altogether out of my own person.

I am glad, answered the bee, to hear you grant at least that I am come honestly by my wings and my voice; for then, it seems, I am obliged to Heaven alone for my flights and my music; and Providence would never have bestowed on me two such gifts, without designing them for the noblest ends. I visit indeed all the flowers and blossoms of the field and garden; but whatever I collect thence enriches myself, without the least injury to their beauty, their smell, or their taste. Now, for you and your skill in architecture and other mathematics, I have little to say: in that building of yours there might, for aught I know, have been labour and method enough; but, by woeful experience for us both, it is too plain the materials are naught; and I hope you will henceforth take warning, and consider duration and matter, as well as method and art. You boast indeed of being obliged to no other creature, but of drawing and spinning out all from yourself; that is to say, if we may judge of the liquor in the vessel by what issues out, you possess a good plentiful store of dirt and poison in your breast; and, though I would by no means lessen or disparage your genuine stock of either, yet I doubt you are somewhat obliged, for an increase of both, to a little foreign assistance. Your inherent portion of dirt does not fail of acquisitions, by sweepings exhaled from below; and one insect furnishes you with a share of poison to destroy another. So that, in short, the question comes all to this; whether is the nobler being of the two, that which, by a lazy contemplation of four inches round, by an overweening pride, feeding and engendering on itself, turns all into excrement and venom, producing nothing at all but flybane and a cobweb; or that which, by a universal range, with long search, much study, true judgment, and distinction of things, brings home honey and wax.

This dispute was managed with such eagerness, clamour, and warmth, that the two parties of books, in arms below, stood silent a while, waiting in suspense what would be the issue; which was not long undetermined; for the bee, grown impatient at so much loss of time, fled straight away to a bed of roses, without looking for a reply, and left the spider, like an orator, collected in himself, and just prepared to burst out.

It happened upon this emergency that Æsop broke silence first. He had been of late most barbarously treated by a strange effect of the regent's humanity, who had torn off his title-page, sorely defaced one half of his leaves, and chained him fast among a shelf of moderns. Where, soon discovering how high the quarrel was likely to proceed, he tried all his arts, and turned himself to a thousand forms. At length, in the borrowed shape of an ass, the regent mistook him for a modern; by which means he had time and opportunity to escape to the ancients, just when the spider and the bee were entering into their contest; to which he gave his attention with a world of pleasure, and when it was ended, swore in the loudest key that in all his life he had never known two cases so parallel and adapt to each other as that in the window and this upon the shelves. The disputants, said he, have admirably managed the dispute between them, have taken in the full strength of all that is to be said on both sides, and exhausted the substance of every argument *pro* and *con*. It is but to adjust the reasonings of both to the present quarrel, then to compare and apply the labours and fruits of each, as the bee has learnedly deduced them, and we shall find the conclusion fall plain and close upon the moderns and us. For pray, gentlemen, was ever anything so modern as the spider in his air, his turns, and his paradoxes? he argues in the behalf of you, his brethren, and himself with many boastings of his native stock and great genius; that he spins and spits wholly from himself, and scorns to own any obligation or assistance from without. Then he displays to you his great skill in architecture and improvement in the mathematics. To all this the bee, as an advocate retained by us the ancients, thinks fit to answer, that, if one may judge of the great genius or inventions of the moderns by what they have produced, you will hardly have countenance to bear you out in boasting of either. Erect your schemes with as much method and skill as you please; yet, if the materials be nothing but dirt, spun out of your own entrails (the guts of modern brains), the edifice will conclude at last in a cobweb; the duration of which, like that of other spiders' webs, may be imputed to their being forgotten, or neglected, or hid in a corner. For anything else of genuine that the moderns may pretend to, I cannot recollect; unless it be a large vein of wrangling and satire, much of a nature and substance with the spider's poison; which, however, they pretend to spit wholly out of themselves, is improved by the same arts, by feeding upon the insects and vermin of the age. As for us the ancients, we are content, with the bee, to pretend to nothing of our own beyond our wings and our voice: that is to say, our flights and our language. For the rest, whatever we have got has been by infinite labour and search, and ranging through every corner of nature; the difference is, that, instead of dirt and poison, we have rather chosen to fill our hives with honey and wax; thus furnishing mankind with the two noblest of things, which are sweetness and light.

It is wonderful to conceive the tumult arisen among the books upon the close of this long descant of Æsop: both parties took the hint, and heightened their animosities so on a sudden, that they resolved it should come to a battle. Immediately the two main bodies withdrew, under their several ensigns, to the farther parts of the library, and there entered into cabals and consults upon the present emergency. The moderns were in very warm debates upon the choice of their leaders; and nothing less than the fear impending from their enemies could have kept them from mutinies upon this occasion. The difference was greatest among the horse, where every private trooper pretended to the chief command, from Tasso and Milton to Dryden and Withers. The light-horse were commanded by Cowley and Despreaux. There came the bowmen under their valiant leaders, Des Cartes, Gassendi, and Hobbes; whose strength was such that they could shoot their arrows beyond the atmosphere, never to fall down again, but turn like that of Evander, into meteors; or, like the cannon-ball, into stars. Paracelsus brought a squadron of stinkpot-flingers from the snowy mountains of Rhætia. There came a vast body of dragoons, of different nations, under the leading of Harvey their great aga: part armed with scythes, the weapons of death; part with lances and long knives, all steeped in poison; part shot bullets of a most malignant nature, and used white powder, which infallibly killed without report. There came several bodies of heavy-armed foot, all mercenaries, under the ensigns of Guicciardini, Davila, Polydore, Virgil, Buchanan, Mariana, Camden, and others. The engineers were command-ed by Regiomontanus and Wilkins. The rest was a confused multitude, led by Scotus, Aquinas, and Bellarmine; of mighty bulk and stature, but without either arms, courage, or discipline. In the last place came infinite swarms of calones*, a disorderly rout led by L'Estrange; rogues and ragamuffins, that follow the camp for nothing but the plunder, all without coats to cover them.

* These are pamphlets, which are not bound or cover'd.

The army of the ancients was much fewer in number; Homer led the horse, and Pindar the light-horse; Euclid was chief engineer; Plato and Aristotle commanded the bowmen; Herodotus and Livy the foot; Hippocrates the dragoons; the allies, led by Vossius and Temple, brought up the rear.

All things violently tending to a decisive battle, Fame, who much frequented, and had a large apartment formerly assigned her in the regal library, fled up straight to Jupiter, to whom she delivered a faithful account of all that passed between the two parties below; for among the gods she always tells truth. Jove, in great concern, convokes a council in the milky way. The senate assembled, he declares the occasion of convening them; a bloody battle just impendent between two mighty armies of ancient and modern creatures, called books, wherein the celestial interest was but too deeply concerned. Momus, the patron of the moderns, made an excellent speech in their favour, which was answered by Pallas, the protectress of the ancients. The assembly was divided in their affections; when Jupiter commanded the book of fate to be laid before him. Immediately were brought by Mercury three large volumes in folio, containing memoirs of all things past present, and to come. The clasps were of silver double gilt, the covers of celestial turkey leather, and the paper such as here on earth might pass almost for vellum. Jupiter, having silently read the decree, would communicate the import to none, but presently shut up the book.

Without the doors of this assembly there attended a vast number of light, nimble gods, menial servants to Jupiter: these are his ministering instruments in all affairs below. They travel in a caravan, more or less together, and are fastened to each other, like a link of galley-slaves, by a light chain, which passes from them to Jupiter's great toe: and yet, in receiving or delivering a message, they may never approach above the lowest step of his throne, where he and they whisper to each other through a large hollow trunk. These deities are called by mortal men accidents or events; but the gods call them second causes. Jupiter having delivered his message to a certain number of these divinities, they flew immediately down to the pinnacle of the regal library, and consulting a few minutes, entered unseen, and disposed the parties according to their orders.

Meanwhile Momus, fearing the worst, and calling to mind an ancient prophecy which bore no very good face to his children the moderns, bent his flight to the region of a malignant deity called Criticism. She dwelt on the top of a snowy mountain in Nova Zembla; there Momus found her extended in her den, upon the spoils of numberless volumes, half devoured. At her right hand sat Ignorance, her father and husband, blind with age; at her left, Pride, her mother, dressing her up in the scraps of paper herself had torn. There was opinion, her sister, light of foot, hoodwinked, and headstrong, yet giddy and perpetually turning. About her played her children, Noise and Impudence, Dulness and Vanity, Positiveness, Pedantry, and Ill-manners. The goddess herself had claws like a cat; her head, and ears, and voice, resembled those of an ass; her teeth fallen out before, her eyes turned inward, as if she looked only upon herself; her diet was the overflowing of her own gall; her spleen was so large as to stand prominent, like a dug of the first rate; nor wanted excrescencies in form of teats, at which a crew of ugly monsters were greedily sucking; and, what is wonderful to concerve, the bulk of spleen increased faster than the sucking could diminish it. Goddess, said Monus, can you sit idly here while our devout worshippers, the moderns, are this minute entering into a cruel battle, and perhaps now lying under the swords of their enemies? who then hereafter will ever sacrifice or build altars to our divinities? Haste, therefore, to the British isle, and, if possible, prevent their destruction; while I make factions among the gods, and gain them over to our party.

Momus, having thus delivered himself, staid not for an answer, but left the goddess to her own resentment. Up she rose in a rage, and, as it is the form upon such occasions, began a soliloquy: It is I (said she) who give wisdom to infants and idiots; by me children grow wiser than their parents, by me beaux become politicians, and school-boys judges of philosophy: by me sophisters debate and conclude upon the depths of knowledge; and coffee-house wits, instinct by me, can correct an author's style, and display his minutest errors without understanding a syllable of his matter or his language; by me striplings spend their judgment, as they do their estate, before it comes into their hands. It is I who have deposed wit and knowledge from their empire over poetry, and advanced myself in their stead. And shall a few upstart ancients dare to oppose me?—But come, my aged parent, and you my children dear, and thou, my beauteous sister; let us ascend my chariot, and haste to assist our devout moderns, who are now sacrificing to us a hecatomb, as I perceive by that grateful smell which from thence reaches my nostrils.

The goddess and her train, having mounted the chariot, which was drawn by tame geese, flew over infinite regions, shedding her influence in due places, till at length she arrived at her beloved island of Britain; but in hovering over its metropolis, what blessings did she not let fall upon her seminaries of Gresham and Covent Garden! And now she reached the fatal plain of St. James's library, at what time the two armies were upon the point to engage: where, entering with all her caravan unseen, and landing upon a case of shelves, now desert, but once inhabited by a colony of virtuosoes, she staid a while to observe the posture of both armies.

But here the tender cares of a mother began to fill her thoughts and move in her breast: for at the head of a troop of modern bowmen she cast her eyes upon her son Wotton, to whom the fates had assigned a very short thread. Wotton, a young hero, whom an unknown father of mortal race begot by stolen embraces with this goddess. He was the darling of his mother above all her children, and she resolved to go and comfort him. But first, according to the good old custom of deities, she cast about to change her shape, for fear the divinity of her countenance might dazzle his mortal sight and overcharge the rest of his senses. She therefore gathered up her person into an octavo compass: her body grew white and arid, and split in pieces with dryness; the thick turned into pasteboard, and the thin into paper; upon which her parents and children artfully strewed a black juice, or decoction of gall and soot, in form of letters: her head, and voice, and spleen, kept their primitive form; and that which before was a cover of skin did still continue so. In this guise she marched on towards the moderns, undistinguishable in shape and dress from the divine Bentley, Wotton's dearest friend. Brave Wotton, said the goddess, why do our troops stand idle here, to spend their present vigour and opportunity of the day? away, let us haste to the generals, and advise to give the onset immediately. Having spoken thus, she took the ugliest of her monsters, full glutted from her spleen, and flung it invisibly into his mouth, which, flying straight up into his head, squeezed out his eye-balls, gave him a distorted look, and half over-turned his brain. Then she privately ordered two of her beloved children, Dulness and Ill-manners, closely to attend his person in all encounters. Having thus accoutred him, she vanished in a mist, and the hero perceived it was the goddess his mother.

The destined hour of fate being now arrived, the fight began; whereof, before I dare adventure to make a particular description, I must, after the example of other authors, petition for a hundred tongues, and mouths, and hands, and pens, which would all be too little to perform so immense a work. Say, goddess, that presidest over history, who it was that first advanced in the field of battle! Paracelsus, at the head of his dragoons, observing Galen in the adverse wing, darted his javelin with a mighty force, which the brave ancient received upon his shield, the point breaking in the second fold.

* * * * * * * * * * * * * * * * * * * *

Hic pauca desunt. * * * * * * * * * * * * * * * * * * *

* * * * * * * * * * * * * * * * * * * *

They bore the wounded aga on their shields to his chariot *

* * * * * * * * * * * * * * * * * * * *

Desunt nonnulla. * * * * * * * * * * * * * * * * * * *

* * * * * * * * * * * * * * * * * * * *

Then Aristotle, observing Bacon advance with a furious mien, drew his bow to the head, and let fly his arrow, which missed the valiant modern and went whizzing over his head; but Des Cartes it hit; the steel point quickly found a defect in his headpiece; it pierced the leather and the pasteboard, and went in at his right eye. The torture of the pain whirled the valiant bowman round till death, like a star of superior influence, drew him into his own vortex.

* *

* * * * * * * * * * * * * * * * *

* * * * * * * * * * * * * * * * * Ingens hiatus hic in MS.

* * * * * * * * * * * * * * * *

when Homer appeared at the head of the cavalry, mounted on a furious horse, with difficulty managed by the rider himself, but which no other mortal durst approach; he rode among the enemy's ranks, and bore down all before him. Say, goddess, whom he slew first and whom he slew last! First,

Gondibert advanced against him, clad in heavy armour and mounted on a staid, sober gelding, not so famed for his speed as his docility in kneeling whenever his rider would mount or alight. He had made a vow to Pallas that he would never leave the field till he had spoiled Homer* of his armour: madman, who had never once seen ^{* Vid. Homer.} the wearer, nor understood his strength! Him Homer overthrew, horse and man, to the ground, there to be trampled and choked in the dirt. Then with a long spear he slew Denham, a stout modern, who from his father's side[1] derived his lineage from Apollo, but his mother was of mortal race. He fell, and bit the earth. The celestial part Apollo took, and made it a star; but the terrestrial lay wallowing upon the ground. Then Homer slew Sam Wesley with a kick of his horse's heel; he took Perrault by mighty force out of his saddle, then hurled him at Fontenelle, with the same blow dashing out both their brains.

On the left wing of the horse Virgil appeared, in shining armour, completely fitted to his body: he was mounted on a dapple grey steed, the slowness of whose pace was an effect of the highest mettle and vigour. He cast his eye on the adverse wing, with a desire to find an object worthy of his valour, when behold upon a sorrel gelding of a monstrous size appeared a foe, issuing from among the thickest of the enemy's squadrons; but his speed was less than his noise; for his horse, old and lean, spent the dregs of his strength in a high trot, which, though it made slow advances, yet caused a loud clashing of his armour terrible to hear. The two cavaliers had now approached within the throw of a lance, when the stranger desired a parley, and, lifting up the vizor of his helmet, a face hardly appeared from within which, after a pause, was known for that of the renowned Dryden. The brave ancient suddenly started, as one possessed with surprise and

---

1 Sir John Denham's poems are very unequal, extremely good, and very indifferent, so that his detractors said, he was not the real author of *Cooper's Hill*.

disappointment together; for the helmet was nine times too large for the head, which appeared situate far in the hinder part, even like the lady in a lobster, or like a mouse under a canopy of state, or like a shrivelled beau from within the penthouse of a modern periwig; and the voice was suited to the visage, sounding weak and remote. Dryden, in a long harangue, soothed up the good ancient; called him father, and, by a large deduction of genealogies, made it plainly appear that they were nearly related. Then he humbly proposed an exchange of armour, as a lasting mark of hospitality between them. Virgil* consented (for the goddess Diffidence came unseen, and cast a mist before his eyes), though his was of gold and cost a hundred beeves, the other's but of rusty iron. However, this glittering armour became the modern yet worse than his own. Then they agreed to exchange horses; but, when it came to the trial, Dryden was afraid and utterly unable to mount. * * * * *

* Vid Homer.

Alter hiatus in MS.

* * * * * * * * * * * * * * * * * * *
* * * * * * * * * * * * * * * * * * *
* * * * * * * * * * * * * * * * * * *

Lucan appeared upon a fiery horse of admirable shape, but headstrong, bearing the rider where he list over the field; he made a mighty slaughter among the enemy's horse; which destruction to stop, Blackmore, a famous modern (but one of the mercenaries), strenuously opposed himself, and darted his javelin with a strong hand, which, falling short of its mark, struck deep in the earth. Then Lucan threw a lance; but Æsculapius came unseen and turned off the point. Brave modern, said Lucan, I perceive some god protects you, for never did my arm so deceive me before: but what mortal can contend with a god? Therefore, let us fight no longer, but present gifts to each other. Lucan then bestowed the modern a pair of spurs, and Blackmore gave Lucan a bridle.

Pauca desunt.

* * * * * * * * * * * * * * * * * * *
* * * * * * * * * * * * * * * * * * *
* * * * * * * * * * * * * * * * * * *

Creech: but the goddess Dulness took a cloud, formed into the shape of Horace, armed and mounted, and placed in a flying posture before him. Glad was the cavalier to begin a combat with a flying foe, and pursued the image, threatening aloud; till at last it led him to the peaceful bower of his father, Ogleby, by whom he was disarmed and assigned to his repose.

Then Pindar slew —, and —, and Oldham, and —, and Afra the Amazon, light of foot; never advancing in a direct line, but wheeling with incredible agility and force, he made a terrible slaughter among the enemy's light horse. Him, when Cowley observed, his generous heart burnt within him, and he advanced against the fierce ancient, imitating his address, his pace, and career, as well as the vigour of his horse and his own skill would allow. When the two cavaliers had approached within the length of three javelins, first Cowley threw a lance, which missed Pindar, and, passing into the enemy's ranks, fell ineffectual to the ground. Then Pindar darted a javelin so large and weighty, that scarce a dozen cavaliers, as cavaliers are in our degenerate days, could raise it from the ground; yet he threw it with ease, and it went, by an unerring hand, singing through the air; nor could the modern have avoided present death if he had not luckily opposed the shield that had been given him by Venus. And now both heroes drew their swords; but the modern was so aghast and disordered that he knew not where he was; his shield dropped from his hands; thrice he fled, and thrice he could not escape; at last he turned, and lifting up his hand in the posture of a suppliant, Godlike Pindar, said he, spare my life, and possess my horse, with these arms, beside the ransom which my friends will give when they hear I am alive and your prisoner. Dog! said Pindar, let your ransom stay with your friends; but your carcase shall be left for the fowls of the air and the beasts of the field. With that he raised his sword, and, with a mighty stroke, cleft the wretched modern in twain, the sword pursuing the blow; and one half lay panting on the ground, to be trod in pieces by the horses' feet; the other half was borne by the frighted steed through the

field. This Venus[1] took, washed it seven times in ambrosia, then struck it thrice with a sprig of amaranth; upon which the leather grew round and soft, and the leaves turned into feathers, and, being gilded before, continued gilded still; so it became a dove, and she harnessed it to her chariot.* * * * *
* *

Hiatus valde deflendus in MS.* * * * * * * * * * * * * *
* *

Day being far spent, and the numerous forces of the moderns half inclining to a retreat, there issued forth from a squadron of their heavy-armed foot a captain* whose name was Bentley, the most deformed of all the moderns; tall, but without shape or comeliness; large, but without strength or proportion. His armour was patched up of a thousand incoherent pieces; and the sound of it, as he marched, was loud and dry, like that made by the fall of a sheet of lead, which an Etesian wind blows suddenly down from the roof of some steeple. His helmet was of old rusty iron, but the vizor was brass, which, tainted by his breath, corrupted into copperas, nor wanted gall from the same fountain; so that, whenever provoked by anger or labour, an atramentous quality, of most malignant nature, was seen to distil from his lips. In his right hand[2] he grasped a flail, and (that he might never be unprovided of an offensive weapon) a vessel full of ordure in his left. Thus completely armed, he advanced with a slow and heavy pace where the modern chiefs were holding a consult upon the sum of things; who, as he came onwards, laughed to behold his crooked leg and humped shoulder, which his boot and armour*, vainly endeavouring to hide, were forced to comply with and expose. The generals made use of him for his talent of railing; which, kept within government,

*The episode of Bentley and Wotton.

* Vid. Homer de Thersite.

---

1 I do not approve the author's judgment in this, for I think Cowley's pindarics are much preferable to his mistress.
2 The person here spoken of, is famous for letting fly at every body without distinctions, and using mean and foul scurrilities.

proved frequently of great service to their cause, but, at other times, did more mischief than good; for, at the least touch of offence, and often without any at all, he would, like a wounded elephant, convert it against his leaders. Such, at this juncture, was the disposition of Bentley; grieved to see the enemy prevail, and dissatisfied with everybody's conduct but his own. He humbly gave the modern generals to understand that he conceived, with great submission, they were all a pack of rogues, and fools, and sons of whores, and d—d cowards, and confounded loggerheads, and illiterate whelps, and non-sensical scoundrels; that, if himself had been constituted general, those presumptuous dogs, the ancients, would long before this have been beaten out of the field. You, said he, sit here idle; but when I, or any other valiant modern, kill an enemy, you are sure to seize the spoil. But I will not march one foot against the foe till you all swear to me that whomever I take or kill, his arms I shall quietly possess. Bentley having spoken thus, Scaliger, bestowing him a sour look, Miscreant prater! said he, eloquent only in thine own eyes, thou railest without wit, or truth, or discretion. The malignity of thy temper perverteth nature; thy learning makes thee more barbarous; thy study of humanity more inhuman; thy converse among poets more grovelling, miry, and dull. All arts of civilising others render thee rude and untractable; courts have taught thee ill manners, and polite conversation has finished thee a pedant. Besides, a greater coward burdeneth not the army. But never despond; I pass my word, whatever spoil thou takest shall certainly be thy own; though I hope that vile carcase will first become a prey to kites and worms.

Bentley durst not reply; but, half choked with spleen and rage, withdrew, in full resolution of performing some great achievement. With him, for his aid and companion, he took his beloved Wotton; resolving by policy or surprise to attempt some neglected quarter of the ancient's army. They began their march over carcases of their slaughtered friends; then to the right of their own forces; then wheeled northward, till

181

they came to Aldrovandus's tomb, which they passed on the side of the declining sun. And now they arrived, with fear, toward the enemy's outguards; looking about, if haply they might spy the quarters of the wounded, or some straggling sleepers, unarmed and remote from the rest. As when two mongrel curs, whom native greediness and domestic want provoke and join in partnership, though fearful, nightly to invade the folds of some rich grazier, they, with tails depressed and lolling tongues, creep soft and slow; meanwhile the conscious moon, now in her zenith, on their guilty heads darts perpendicular rays; nor dare they bark, though much provoked at her refulgent visage, whether seen in puddle by reflection or in sphere direct; but one surveys the region round, while the other scouts the plain, if haply to discover, at distance from the flock, some carcase half devoured, the refuse of gorged wolves or ominous ravens. So marched this lovely, loving pair of friends, nor with less fear and circumspection, when at a distance they might perceive two shining suits of armour hanging upon an oak, and the owners not far off in a profound sleep. The two friends drew lots, and the pursuing of this adventure fell to Bentley; on he went, and in his van Confusion and Amaze, while Horror and Affright brought up the rear. As he came near, behold two heroes of the ancient's army, Phalaris and Æsop, lay fast asleep; Bentley would fain have despatched them both, and, stealing close, aimed his flail at Phalaris's breast. But then the goddess Affright, interposing, caught the modern in her icy arms, and dragged him from the danger she foresaw; both the dormant heroes happened to turn at the same instant, though soundly sleeping, and busy in a dream[1]. For Phalaris was just that minute dreaming how a most vile poetaster had lampooned him, and how he had got him roaring in his bull. And Æsop dreamed that, as he and the ancient chiefs were lying on the ground, a wild ass broke loose, ran about,

1 This is according to Homer, who tells the dreams of those who were kill'd in their sleep.

trampling and kicking and dunging in their faces. Bentley, leaving the two heroes asleep, seized on both their armours, and withdrew in quest of his darling Wotton.

He, in the meantime, had wandered long in search of some enterprise, till at length he arrived at a small rivulet that issued from a fountain hard by, called, in the language of mortal men, Helicon. Here he stopped, and, parched with thirst, resolved to allay it in this limpid stream. Thrice with profane hands he essayed to raise the water to his lips, and thrice it slipped all through his fingers. Then he stooped prone on his breast, but, ere his mouth had kissed the liquid crystal, Apollo came, and in the channel held his shield betwixt the modern and the fountain, so that he drew up nothing but mud. For, although no fountain on earth can compare with the clearness of Helicon, yet there lies at bottom a thick sediment of slime and mud; for so Apollo begged of Jupiter, as a punishment to those who durst attempt to taste it with unhallowed lips, and for a lesson to all not to draw too deep or far from the spring.

At the fountain-head Wotton discerned two heroes; the one he could not distinguish, but the other was soon known for Temple, general of the allies to the ancients. His back was turned, and he was employed in drinking large draughts in his helmet from the fountain, where he had withdrawn himself to rest from the toils of the war. Wotton, observing him, with quaking knees and trembling hands, spoke thus to himself: O that I could kill* this destroyer of our army, what renown should I purchase   * Vid. Homer.
among the chiefs! but to issue out against him, man against man, shield against shield, and lance against lance, what modern of us dare? for he fights like a god, and Pallas or Apollo are ever at his elbow. But, O mother! if what Fame reports be true, that I am the son of so great a goddess, grant me to hit Temple with this lance, that the stroke may send him to hell, and that I may return in safety and triumph, laden with his spoils. The first part of this prayer the gods granted at the intercession of his mother and of Momus; but the rest,

by a perverse wind sent from Fate, was scattered in the air. Then Wotton grasped his lance, and, brandishing it thrice over his head, darted it with all his might; the goddess, his mother, at the same time adding strength to his arm. Away the lance went hizzing, and reached even to the belt of the averted ancient, upon which lightly grazing, it fell to the ground. Temple neither felt the weapon touch him nor heard it fall: and Wotton might have escaped to his army, with the honour of having remitted his lance against so great a leader unrevenged; but Apollo, enraged that a javelin flung by the assistance of so foul a goddess should pollute his fountain, put on the shape of ——, and softly came to young Boyle, who then accompanied Temple: he pointed first to the lance, then to the distant modern that flung it, and commanded the young hero to take immediate revenge. Boyle, clad in a suit of armour which had been given him by all the gods, immediately advanced against the trembling foe, who now fled before him. As a young lion in the Libyan plains, or Araby desert, sent by his aged sire to hunt for prey, or health, or exercise, he scours along, wishing to meet some tiger from the mountains, or a furious boar; if chance a wild ass, with brayings importune, affronts his ear, the generous beast, though loathing to distain his claws with blood so vile, yet, much provoked at the offensive noise, which Echo, foolish nymph, like her ill-judging sex, repeats much louder, and with more delight than Philomela's song, he vindicates the honour of the forest, and hunts the noisy long-eared animal. So Wotton fled, so Boyle pursued. But Wotton, heavy armed and slow of foot, began to slack his course, when his lover Bentley appeared, returning laden with the spoils of the two sleeping ancients. Boyle observed him well, and soon discovering the helmet and shield of Phalaris his friend, both which he had lately with his own hands new polished and gilt, rage sparkled in his eyes, and, leaving his pursuit after Wotton, he furiously rushed on against this new approacher. Fain would he be revenged on both; but both now fled different ways:

and, as a woman*[1] in a little house that gets   * Vid. Homer.
a painful livelihood by spinning, if chance
her geese be scattered o'er the common, she courses round
the plain from side to side, compelling here and there the
stragglers to the flock; they cackle loud, and flutter o'er the
champaign; so Boyle pursued, so fled this pair of friends:
finding at length their flight was vain, they bravely joined,
and drew themselves in phalanx. First Bentley threw a spear
with all his force, hoping to pierce the enemy's breast; but
Pallas came unseen, and in the air took off the point, and
clapped on one of lead, which, after a dead bang against the
enemy's shield, fell blunted to the ground. Then Boyle,
observing well his time, took up a lance of wondrous length
and sharpness; and, as this pair of friends compacted, stood
close side to side, he wheeled him to the right, and, with
unusual force, darted the weapon. Bentley saw his fate
approach, and flanking down his arms close to his ribs,
hoping to save his body, in went the point, passing through
arm and side, nor stopped or spent its force till it had also
pierced the valiant Wotton, who, going to sustain his dying
friend, shared his fate. As when a skilful cook has trussed a
brace of woodcocks, he with iron skewer pierces the tender
sides of both, their legs and wings close pinioned to the ribs;
so was this pair of friends transfixed, till down they fell,
joined in their lives, joined in their deaths; so closely joined
that Charon would mistake them both for one, and waft them
over Styx for half his fare. Farewell, beloved, loving pair; few
equals have you left behind: and happy and immortal shall
you be, if all my wit and eloquence can make you.

And now *
* *
* *
* * * * * * * Desunt cœtera.

1 This is also, after the manner of Homer; the woman's getting a painful livelihood by
spinning, has nothing to do with the similitude, nor would be excusable without such an
authority.

AN ARGUMENT

TO PROVE THAT THE ABOLISHING OF
CHRISTIANITY IN ENGLAND
MAY, AS THINGS NOW STAND,
BE ATTENDED WITH SOME INCONVENIENCES,
AND PERHAPS NOT PRODUCE THOSE MANY
GOOD EFFECTS PROPOSED THEREBY.

I am very sensible what a weakness and presumption it is to reason against the general humour and disposition of the world. I remember it was, with great justice, and due regard to the freedom both of the public and the press, forbidden, upon several penalties, to write, or discourse, or lay wagers against the Union, even before it was confirmed by parliament; because that was looked upon as a design to oppose the current of the people, which, beside the folly of it, is a manifest breach of the fundamental law, that makes this majority of opinion the voice of God. In like manner, and for the very same reasons, it may perhaps be neither safe nor prudent to argue against the abolishing of Christianity, at a juncture when all parties appear so unanimously determined upon the point, as we cannot but allow from their actions, their discourses, and their writings. However, I know not how, whether from the affectation of singularity, or the perverseness of human nature, but so it unhappily falls out, that I cannot be entirely of this opinion. Nay, though I were sure an order were issued for my immediate prosecution by the attorney-general, I should still confess that, in the present posture of our affairs at home or abroad, I do not yet see the absolute necessity of extirpating the Christian religion from among us.

This, perhaps, may appear too great a paradox even for our wise and paradoxical age to endure; therefore I shall handle it with all tenderness, and with the utmost deference to that great and profound majority which is of another sentiment.

And yet the curious may please to observe how much the genius of a nation is liable to alter in half an age. I have heard it affirmed for certain, by some very old people, that the contrary opinion was, even in their memories, as much in vogue as the other is now; and that a project for the abolishing of Christianity would then have appeared as singular, and been thought as absurd, as it would be, at this time, to write or discourse in its defence.

Therefore I freely own that all appearances are against me. The system of the gospel, after the fate of other systems, is generally antiquated and exploded: and the mass or body of the common people, among whom it seems to have had its latest credit, are now grown as much ashamed of it as their betters; opinions like fashions always descending from those of quality to the middle sort, and thence to the vulgar, where at length they are dropped and vanish.

But here I would not be mistaken, and must therefore be so bold as to borrow a distinction from the writers on the other side, when they make a difference between nominal and real Trinitarians. I hope no reader imagines me so weak to stand up in the defence of real Christianity, such as used in primitive times (if we may believe the authors of those ages) to have an influence upon men's belief and actions: to offer at the restoring of that would indeed be a wild project; it would be to dig up foundations; to destroy at one blow all the wit and half the learning of the kingdom; to break the entire frame and constitution of things; to ruin trade, extinguish arts and sciences, with the professors of them; in short, to turn our courts, exchanges, and shops into deserts; and would be full as absurd as the proposal of Horace, where he advises the Romans all in a body to leave their city, and seek a new seat in some remote part of the world, by way of cure for the corruption of their manners.

Therefore I think this caution was in itself altogether unnecessary (which I have inserted only to prevent all possibility of cavilling), since every candid reader will easily understand my discourse to be intended only in defence of nominal Christianity; the other having been for some time wholly laid aside by general consent, as utterly inconsistent with our present schemes of wealth and power.

But why we should therefore cast off the name and title of Christians, although the general opinion and resolution be so violent for it, I confess I cannot (with submission) apprehend, nor is the consequence necessary. However, since the undertakers propose such wonderful advantages to the nation by this project, and advance many plausible objections against the system of Christianity, I shall briefly consider the strength of both, fairly allow them their greatest weight, and offer such answers as I think most reasonable. After which I will beg leave to show what inconveniences may possibly happen by such an innovation, in the present posture of our affairs.

First, one great advantage proposed by the abolishing of Christianity is, that it would very much enlarge and establish liberty of conscience, that great bulwark of our nation, and of the Protestant religion; which is still too much limited by priestcraft, notwihtstanding all the good intentions of the legislature, as we have lately found by a severe instance. For it is confidently reported that two young gentlemen of real hopes, bright wit, and profound judgment, who, upon a thorough examination of causes and effects, and by the mere force of natural abilities, without the least tincture of learning, having made a discovery that there was no God, and generously communicating their thoughts for the good of the public, were some time ago, by an unparalleled severity, and upon I know not what obsolete law, broke for blasphemy. And as it has been wisely observed, if persecution once begins, no man alive knows how far it may reach or where it will end.

In answer to all which, with deference to wiser judgments, I think this rather shows the necessity of a nominal religion among us. Great wits love to be free with the highest objects; and if they cannot be allowed a God to revile or renounce, they will speak evil of dignities, abuse the government, and reflect upon the ministry; which I am sure few will deny to be of much more pernicious consequence, according to the saying of Tiberius, *deorum offensa diis curæ*. As to the particular fact related, I think it is not fair to argue from one instance, perhaps another cannot be produced: yet (to the comfort of all those who may be apprehensive of persecution) blasphemy, we know, is freely spoken a million of times in every coffee-house and tavern, or wherever else good company meet. It must be allowed, indeed, that, to break an English free-born officer only for blasphemy was, to speak the gentlest of such an action, a very high strain of absolute power. Little can be said in excuse for the general: perhaps he was afraid it might give offence to the allies, among whom, for aught we know, it may be the custom of the country to believe a God. But if he argued, as some have done, upon a mistaken principle, that an officer who is guilty of speaking blasphemy may some time or other proceed so far as to raise a mutiny, the consequence is by no means to be admitted; for surely the commander of an English army is likely to be but ill obeyed whose soldiers fear and reverence him as little as they do a Deity.

It is further objected against the gospel system, that it obliges men to the belief of things too difficult for freethinkers, and such who have shaken off the prejudices that usually cling to a confined education. To which I answer, that men should be cautious how they raise objections which reflect upon the wisdom of the nation. Is not everybody freely allowed to believe whatever he pleases, and to publish his belief to the world whenever he thinks fit, especially if it serves to strengthen the party which is in the right? Would any indifferent foreigner, who should read the trumpery lately written by Asgill, Tindall, Toland, Coward, and forty more, imagine the gospel to be our rule of faith, and confirmed by parliaments? Does any man either believe, or say he believes, or desire to have it thought that he says he believes, one syllable of the matter? And is any man worse received upon that score, or does he find his want of nominal faith a disadvantage to him in the pursuit of any civil or military employment? What if there be an old dormant statute or two against him, are they not now obsolete to a degree, that Epsom and Dudley themselves, if they were now alive, would find it impossible to put them in execution?

It is likewise urged that there are, by computation, in this kingdom, above ten thousand parsons, whose revenues, added to those of my lords the bishops, would suffice to maintain at least two hundred young gentlemen of wit and pleasure, and free-thinking, enemies to priestcraft, narrow principles, pedantry, and prejudices, who might be an ornament to the court and town: and then again, so great a number of able divines might be a recruit to our fleet and armies. This, indeed, appears to be a consideration of some weight; but then, on the other side, several things deserve to be considered likewise: as first, whether it may not be thought necessary that in certain tracts of country, like what we call parishes, there shall be one man at least of abilities to read and write. Then it seems a wrong computation, that the revenues of the church throughout this island would be large enough to maintain two hundred young gentlemen, or even half that number, after the present refined way of living; that is, to allow each of them such a rent as, in the modern form of speech, would make them easy. But still there is in this project a greater mischief behind; and we ought to beware of the woman's folly, who killed the hen that every morning laid her a golden egg. For, pray what would become of the race of men in the next age, if we had nothing to trust to beside the scrofulous, consumptive productions furnished by our men of wit and pleasure, when, having squandered away their vigour, health, and estates, they are forced, by some disagreeable marriage, to piece up their broken fortunes, and entail rottenness and politeness on their posterity? Now, here are ten thousand persons reduced, by the wise regulations of Henry VIII., to the necessity of a low diet and moderate exercise, who are the only great restorers of our breed, without which the nation would in an age or two become one great hospital.

Another advantage proposed by the abolishing of Christianity, is the clear gain of one day in seven, which is now entirely lost, and consequently the kingdom one-seventh less considerable in trade, business, and pleasure; besides the loss to the public of so many stately structures, now in the hands of the clergy, which might be converted into play-houses, market-houses, exchanges, common dormitories, and other public edifices.

I hope I shall be forgiven a hard word, if I call this a perfect cavil. I readily own there has been an old custom, time out of mind, for people to assemble in the churches every Sunday, and that shops are still frequently shut, in order, as it is conceived, to preserve the memory of that ancient practice; but how this can prove a hindrance to business or pleasure is hard to imagine. What if the men of pleasure are forced, one day in the week, to game at home instead of the chocolate-houses? are not the taverns and coffee-houses open? can there be a more convenient season for taking a dose of physic? are fewer claps got upon Sundays than other days? is not that the chief day for traders to sum up the accounts of the week, and for lawyers to prepare their briefs? But I would fain know how it can be pretended that the churches are misapplied? where are more appointments and rendezvouses of gallantry? where more care to appear in the foremost box, with greater advantage of dress? where more meetings for business? where more bargains driven of all sorts? and where so many conveniences or incitements to sleep?

There is one advantage greater than any of the foregoing proposed by the abolishing of Christianity; that it will utterly extinguish parties among us, by removing those factious distinctions of high and low church, of Whig and Tory, Presbyterian and Church of England, which are now so many grievous clogs upon public proceedings, and are apt to dispose men to prefer the gratifying of themselves, or depressing of their adversaries, before the most important interests of the state.

I confess, if it were certain that so great an advantage would redound to the nation by this expedient, I would submit and be silent; but will any man say that, if the words whoring, drinking, cheating, lying, stealing were, by act of parliament, ejected out of the English tongue and dictionaries, we should all awake next morning chaste and temperate, honest and just, and lovers of truth? Is this a fair consequence? Or, if the physicians would forbid us to pronounce the words pox, gout, rheumatism, and stone, would that expedient serve, like so many talismans, to destroy the diseases themselves? Are party and faction rooted in men's hearts no deeper than phrases borrowed from religion, or founded upon no firmer principles? and is our language so poor that we cannot find other terms to express them? Are envy, pride, avarice, and ambition such ill nomenclators, that they cannot furnish appellations for their owners? Will not heydukes, and mamalukes, mandarins, and patshaws, or any other words formed at pleasure, serve to distinguish those who are in the ministry, from others, who would be in it if they could? What, for instance, is easier than to vary the form of speech, and instead of the word church make it a question in politics whether the monument be in danger? Because religion was nearest at hand to furnish a few convenient phrases, is our invention so barren, we can find no other? Suppose, for argument sake, that the Tories favoured Margarita, the Whigs Mrs. Tofts, and the trimmers Valentini; would not Margaritians, Toftians, and Valentinians be very tolerable marks of distinction? The Prasini and Veniti, two most virulent factions in Italy, began (if I remember right) by a distinction of colours in ribbons; and we might contend with as good a grace about the dignity of the blue and the green, which would serve as properly to divide the court, the parliament, and the kingdom between them as any terms of art whatsoever borrowed from religion. And therefore I think there is little force in this objection against Christianity, or prospect of so great an advantage, as is proposed in the abolishing of it.

It is again objected, as a very absurd, ridiculous custom, that a set of men should be suffered, much less employed and hired, to bawl one day in seven against the lawfulness of those methods most in use, toward the pursuit of greatness, riches, and pleasure, which are the constant practice of all men alive on the other six. But this objection is, I think, a little unworthy of so refined an age as ours. Let us argue this matter calmly: I appeal to the breast of any polite free-thinker, whether, in the pursuit of gratifying a predominant passion, he has not always felt a wonderful incitement, by reflecting it was a thing forbidden; and therefore we see, in order to cultivate this taste, the wisdom of the nation has taken special care that the ladies should be furnished with prohibited silks, and the men with prohibited wine. And indeed it were to be wished that some other prohibitions were promoted, in order to improve the pleasures of the town; which for want of such expedients begin already, as I am told, to flag and grow languid, giving way daily to cruel inroads from the spleen.

It is likewise proposed as a great advantage to the public, that if we once discard the system of the gospel, all religion will of course be banished for ever; and consequently along with it those grievous prejudices of education, which under the names of virtue, conscience, honour, justice, and the like, are so apt to disturb the peace of human minds, and the notions whereof are so hard to be eradicated, by right reason or free-thinking, sometimes during the whole course of our lives.

Here first I observe, how difficult it is to get rid of a phrase which the world is once grown fond of, though the occasion that first produced it be entirely taken away. For several years past, if a man had but an ill-favoured nose, the deep-thinkers of the age would some way or other contrive to impute the cause to the prejudice of his education. From this fountain were said to be derived all our foolish notions of justice, piety, love of our country; all our opinions of God or a future state, heaven, hell, and the like; and there might formerly, perhaps, have been some pretence for this charge. But so effectual care has been taken to remove those prejudices by an entire change in the methods of education, that (with honour I mention it to our polite innovators) the young gentlemen who are now on the scene seem to have not the least tincture of those infusions, or string of those weeds; and by consequence, the reason for abolishing nominal Christianity upon that pretext is wholly ceased.

For the rest, it may perhaps admit a controversy whether the banishing of all notions of religion whatsoever would be convenient for the vulgar. Not that I am in the least of opinion with those who hold religion to have been the invention of politicians to keep the lower part of the world in awe, by the fear of invisible powers; unless mankind were then very different to what it is now: for I look upon the mass or body of our people here in England to be as free-thinkers, that is to say, as staunch unbelievers, as any of the highest rank. But I conceive some scattered notions about a superior power to be of singular use for the common people, as furnishing excellent materials to keep children quiet when they grow peevish, and providing topics of amusement in a tedious winter-night.

Lastly, it is proposed as a singular advantage, that the abolishing of Christianity will very much contribute to the uniting of Protestants, by enlarging the terms of communion, so as to take in all sorts of dissenters, who are now shut out of the pale upon account of a few ceremonies, which all sides confess to be things indifferent; that this alone will effectually answer the great ends of a scheme for comprehension, by opening a large noble gate, at which all bodies may enter; whereas the chaffering with dissenters, and dodging about this or the other ceremony, is but like opening a few wickets, and leaving them at jar, by which no more than one can get in at a time, and that not without stooping, and sideling, and squeezing his body.

To all this I answer, that there is one darling inclination of mankind which usually affects to be a retainer to religion, though she be neither its parent, its godmother, or its friend; I mean the spirit of opposition, that lived long before Christianity, and can easily subsist without it. Let us, for instance, examine wherein the opposition of sectaries among us consists; we shall find Christianity to have no share in it at all. Does the gospel anywhere prescribe a starched, squeezed countenance, a stiff formal gait, a singularity of manners and habit, or any affected modes of speech, different from the reasonable part of mankind? Yet, if Christianity did not lend its name to stand in the gap, and to employ or divert these humours, they must of necessity be spent in contraventions to the laws of the land, and disturbance of the public peace.

There is a portion of enthusiasm assigned to every nation, which, if it has not proper objects to work on, will burst out and set all in a flame. If the quiet of a state can be bought by only flinging men a few ceremonies to devour, it is a purchase no wise man would refuse. Let the mastiffs amuse themselves about a sheep's skin stuffed with hay, provided it will keep them from worrying the flock. The institution of convents abroad seems in one point a strain of great wisdom; there being few irregularities in human passions that may not have recourse to vent themselves in some of those orders, which are so many retreats for the speculative, the melancholy, the proud, the silent, the politic, and the morose, to spend themselves, and evaporate the noxious particles; for each of whom we in this island are forced to provide a several sect of religion, to keep them quiet; and whenever Christianity shall be abolished, the legislature must find some other expedient to employ and entertain them. For what imports it how large a gate you open, if there will be always left a number, who place a pride and a merit in refusing to enter?

Having thus considered the most important objections against Christianity, and the chief advantages proposed by the abolishing thereof, I shall now, with equal deference and submission to wiser judgments, as before, proceed to mention a few inconveniences that may happen, if the gospel should be repealed, which perhaps the projectors may not have sufficiently considered.

And first, I am very sensible how much the gentlemen of wit and pleasure are apt to murmur, and be choked at the sight of so many daggled-tail parsons, who happen to fall in their way and offend their eyes; but, at the same time, these wise reformers do not consider what an advantage and felicity it is for great wits to be always provided with objects of scorn and contempt, in order to exercise and improve their talents, and divert their spleen from falling on each other or on themselves; especially when all this may be done without the least imaginable danger to their persons.

And to urge another argument of a parallel nature: if Christianity were once abolished, how could the free-thinkers, the strong reasoners, and the men of profound learning, be able to find another subject, so calculated in all points, whereon to display their abilities? what wonderful productions of wit should we be deprived of from those whose genius, by continual practice, has been wholly turned upon raillery and invectives against religion, and would therefore never be able to shine or distinguish themselves upon any other subject? we are daily complaining of the great decline of wit among us, and would we take away the greatest, perhaps the only, topic we have left? Who would ever have suspected Asgill for a wit, or Toland for a philosopher, if the inexhaustible stock of Christianity had not been at hand to provide them with materials? What other subject, through all art or nature, could have produced Tindall for a profound author, or furnished him with readers? It is the wise choice of the subject that alone adorns and distinguishes the writer. For had a hundred such pens as these been employed on the side of religion, they would have immediately sunk into silence and oblivion.

Nor do I think it wholly groundless, or my fears altogether imaginary, that the abolishing Christianity may perhaps bring the church into danger, or at least put the senate to the trouble of another securing vote. I desire I may not be mistaken; I am far from presuming to affirm or think that the church is in danger at present, or as things now stand; but we know not how soon it may be so, when the Christian religion is repealed. As plausible as this project seems, there may be a dangerous design lurking under it. Nothing can be more notorious than that the atheists, deists, socinians, anti-trinitarians, and other sub-divisions of free-thinkers, are persons of little zeal for the present ecclesiastical establishment; their declared opinion is for repealing the sacramental test; they are very indifferent with regard to ceremonies, nor do they hold the jus divinum of episcopacy; therefore this may be intended as one politic step toward altering the constitution of the church established, and setting up presbytery in the stead, which I leave to be further considered by those at the helm.

In the last place, I think nothing can be more plain than that, by this expedient, we shall run into the evil we chiefly pretend to avoid, and that the abolishment of the Christian religion will be the readiest course we can take to introduce popery. And I am the more inclined to this opinion, because we know it has been the constant practice of the Jesuits to send over emissaries with instructions to personate themselves members of the several prevailing sects among us. So it is recorded that they have at sundry times appeared in the disguise of presbyterians, anabaptists, independents, and quakers, according as any of these were most in credit; so, since the fashion has been taken up of exploding religion, the popish missionaries have not been wanting to mix with the free-thinkers; among whom Toland, the great oracle of the anti-christians, is an Irish priest, the son of an Irish priest, and the most learned and ingenious author of a book called "The Rights of the Christian Church," was in a proper juncture reconciled to the Romish faith, whose true son, as appears by a hundred passages in his treatise, he still continues. Perhaps I could add some others to the number, but the fact is beyond dispute, and the reasoning they proceed by is right; for, supposing Christianity to be extinguished, the people will never be at ease till they find out some other method of worship, which will as infallibly produce superstition, as superstition will end in popery.

And therefore if, notwithstanding all I have said, it still be thought necessary to have a bill brought in for repealing Christianity, I would humbly offer an amendment, that instead of the word Christianity, may be put religion in general, which, I conceive, will much better answer all the good ends proposed by the projectors of it. For, as long as we leave in being a God and his providence, with all the necessary consequences which curious and inquisitive men will be apt to draw from such premises, we do not strike at the root of the evil, though we should ever so effectually annihilate the present scheme of the gospel: for of what use is freedom of thought, if it will not produce freedom of action? which is the sole end, how remote soever in appearance, of all objections against Christianity; and therefore the free-thinkers consider it as a sort of edifice, wherein all the parts have such a mutual dependence on each other, that if you happen to pull out one single nail, the whole fabric must fall to the ground. This was happily expressed by him, who had heard of a text brought for proof of the Trinity, which in an ancient manuscript was differently read; he thereupon immediately took the hint, and by a sudden deduction of a long sorites most logically concluded—"Why, if it be as you say, I may safely whore and drink on, and defy the parson." From which, and many the like instances easy to be produced, I think nothing can be more manifest than that the quarrel is not against any particular points of hard digestion in the Christian system, but against religion in general; which, by laying restraints on human nature, is supposed the great enemy to the freedom of thought and action.

Upon the whole, if it shall still be thought for the benefit of church and state that Christianity be abolished, I conceive, however, it may be more convenient to defer the execution to a time of peace, and not venture, in this conjuncture, to disoblige our allies, who, as it falls out, are all Christians, and many of them, by the prejudices of their education, so bigoted as to place a sort of pride in the appellation. If, upon being rejected by them, we are to trust to an alliance with the Turk, we shall find ourselves much deceived; for, as he is too remote, and generally engaged in war with the Persian Emperor, so his people would be more scandalised at our infidelity than our Christian neighbours. For the Turks are not only strict observers of religious worship, but, what is worse, believe a God; which is more than is required of us, even while we preserve the name of Christians.

To conclude: whatever some may think of the great advantages to trade by this favourite scheme, I do very much apprehend that, in six months time after the act is passed for the extirpation of the gospel, the Bank and East India stock may fall at least one per cent. And since that is fifty times more than ever the wisdom of our age thought fit to venture for the preservation of Christianity, there is no reason we should be at so great a loss, merely for the sake of destroying it.

A MODEST PROPOSAL

FOR PREVENTING THE CHILDREN OF POOR PEOPLE
IN IRELAND FROM BEING A BURDEN
TO THEIR PARENTS OR COUNTRY,
AND FOR MAKING THEM BENEFICIAL
TO THE PUBLIC. 1729.

It is a melancholy object to those who walk through this great town or travel in the country, when they see the streets, the roads, and cabin doors, crowded with beggars of the female sex, followed by three, four, or six children, all in rags and importuning every passenger for an alms. These mothers, instead of being able to work for their honest livelihood, are forced to employ all their time in strolling to beg sustenance for their helpless infants: who as they grow up either turn thieves for want of work, or leave their dear native country to fight for the pretender in Spain, or sell themselves to the Barbadoes.

I think it is agreed by all parties that this prodigious number of children in the arms, or on the backs, or at the heels of their mothers, and frequently of their fathers, is in the present deplorable state of the kingdom a very great additional grievance; and, therefore, whoever could find out a fair, cheap, and easy method of making these children sound, useful members of the commonwealth, would deserve so well of the public as to have his statue set up for a preserver of the nation.

But my intention is very far from being confined to provide only for the children of professed beggars; it is of a much greater extent, and shall take in the whole number of infants at a certain age who are born of parents in effect as little able to support them as those who demand our charity in the streets.

As to my own part, having turned my thoughts for many years upon this important subject, and maturely weighed the several schemes of our projectors, I have always found them grossly mistaken in their computation. It is true, a child just dropped from its dam may be supported by her milk for a solar year, with little other nourishment; at most not above the value of two shillings, which the mother may certainly get, or the value in scraps, by her lawful occupation of begging; and it is exactly at one year old that I propose to provide for them in such a manner as instead of being a charge upon their parents or the parish, or wanting food and raiment for the rest of their lives, they shall on the contrary contribute to the feeding, and partly to the clothing, of many thousands.

There is likewise another great advantage in my scheme, that it will prevent those voluntary abortions, and that horrid practice of women murdering their bastard children, alas! too frequent among us; sacrificing the poor innocent babes, I doubt, more to avoid the expense than the shame, which would move tears and pity in the most savage and inhuman breast.

The number of souls in this kingdom being usually reckoned one million and a half, of these I calculate there may be about two hundred thousand couple whose wives are breeders; from which number I subtract thirty thousand couple who are able to maintain their own children (although I apprehend there cannot be so many, under the present distresses of the kingdom); but this being granted, there will remain an hundred and seventy thousand breeders. I again subtract fifty thousand for those women who miscarry, or whose children die by accident or disease within the year. There only remains an hundred and twenty thousand children of poor parents annually born. The question therefore is, how this number shall be reared and provided for? which, as I have already said, under the present situation of affairs, is utterly impossible by all the methods hitherto proposed. For we can neither employ them in handicraft or agriculture; we neither build houses (I mean in the country) nor cultivate land; they can very seldom pick up a livelihood by stealing, till they arrive at six years old, except where they are of towardly parts; although I confess they learn the rudiments much earlier; during which time, they can however be properly looked upon only as probationers; as I have been informed by a principal gentleman in the county of Cavan, who protested to me that he never knew above one or two instances under the age of six, even in a part of the kingdom so renowned for the quickest proficiency in that art.

I am assured by our merchants, that a boy or a girl before twelve years old is no saleable commodity; and even when they come to this age they will not yield above three pounds or three pounds and half a crown at most on the exchange; which cannot turn to account either to the parents or kingdom, the charge of nutriment and rags having been at least four times that value.

I shall now therefore humbly propose my own thoughts, which I hope will not be liable to the least objection.

I have been assured by a very knowing American of my acquaintance in London, that a young healthy child well nursed is at a year old a most delicious, nourishing, and wholesome food, whether stewed, roasted, baked, or boiled; and I make no doubt that it will equally serve in a fricassee or a ragout.

I do therefore humbly offer it to public consideration that of the hundred and twenty thousand children already computed, twenty thousand may be reserved for breed, whereof only one-fourth part to be males; which is more than we allow to sheep, black cattle or swine; and my reason is, that these children are seldom the fruits of marriage, a circumstance not much regarded by our savages, therefore one male will be sufficient to serve four females. That the remaining hundred thousand may, at a year old, be offered in sale to the persons of quality and fortune through the kingdom; always advising the mother to let them suck plentifully in the last month, so as to render them plump and fat for a good table. A child will make two dishes at an entertainment for friends; and when the family dines alone, the fore or hind quarter will make a reasonable dish, and seasoned with a little pepper or salt will be very good boiled on the fourth day, especially in winter.

I have reckoned upon a medium that a child just born will weigh twelve pounds, and in a solar year, if tolerably nursed, will increase to twenty-eight pounds.

I grant this food will be somewhat dear, and therefore very proper for landlords, who, as they have already devoured most of the parents, seem to have the best title to the children.

Infant's flesh will be in season throughout the year, but more plentifully in March, and a little before and after: for we are told by a grave author[1], an eminent French physician, that fish being a prolific diet, there are more children born in Roman Catholic countries about nine months after Lent than at any other season; therefore, reckoning a year after Lent, the markets will be more glutted than usual, because the number of popish infants is at least three to one in this kingdom: and therefore it will have one other collateral advantage, by lessening the number of papists among us.

I have already computed the charge of nursing a beggar's child (in which list I reckon all cottagers, labourers, and four-fifths of the farmers) to be about two shillings per annum, rags included; and I believe no gentleman would repine to give ten shillings for the carcass of a good fat child, which, as I have said, will make four dishes of excellent nutritive meat, when he has only some particular friend or his own family to dine with him. Thus the squire will learn to be a good landlord, and grow popular among the tenants; the mother will have eight shillings net profit, and be fit for work till she produces another child.

Those who are more thrifty (as I must confess the times require) may flay the carcass; the skin of which artificially dressed will make admirable gloves for ladies, and summer boots for fine gentlemen.

As to our city of Dublin, shambles may be appointed for this purpose in the most convenient parts of it, and butchers we may be assured will not be wanting; although I rather recommend buying the children alive than dressing them hot from the knife as we do roasting pigs.

A very worthy person, a true lover of his country, and whose virtues I highly esteem, was lately pleased in discoursing on this matter to offer a refinement upon my scheme. He said that many gentlemen of this kingdom, having of late destroyed

1 Rabelais.

their deer, he conceived that the want of venison might be well supplied by the bodies of young lads and maidens, not exceeding fourteen years of age nor under twelve; so great a number of both sexes in every country being now ready to starve for want of work and service; and these to be disposed of by their parents, if alive, or otherwise by their nearest relations. But with due deference to so excellent a friend and so deserving a patriot, I cannot be altogether in his sentiments; for as to the males, my American acquaintance assured me, from frequent experience, that their flesh was generally tough and lean, like that of our school-boys by continual exercise, and their taste disagreeable; and to fatten them would not answer the charge. Then as to the females, it would, I think, with humble submission be a loss to the public, because they soon would become breeders themselves: and besides, it is not improbable that some scrupulous people might be apt to censure such a practice (although indeed very unjustly), as a little bordering upon cruelty; which, I confess, has always been with me the strongest objection against any project, how well soever intended.

But in order to justify my friend, he confessed that this expedient was put into his head by the famous Psalmanazar, a native of the island Formosa, who came from thence to London above twenty years ago: and in conversation told my friend, that in his country when any young person happened to be put to death, the executioner sold the carcass to persons of quality as a prime dainty; and that in his time the body of a plump girl of fifteen, who was crucified for an attempt to poison the emperor, was sold to his imperial majesty's prime minister of state, and other great mandarins of the court, in joints from the gibbet, at four hundred crowns. Neither indeed can I deny, that if the same use were made of several plump young girls in this town, who without one single groat to their fortunes cannot stir abroad without a chair, and appear at playhouse and assemblies in foreign fineries which they never will pay for, the kingdom would not be the worse.

Some persons of a desponding spirit are in great concern about that vast number of poor people, who are aged, diseased, or maimed, and I have been desired to employ my thoughts what course may be taken to ease the nation of so grievous an encumbrance. But I am not in the least pain upon that matter, because it is very well known that they are every day dying and rotting by cold and famine, and filth and vermin, as fast as can be reasonably expected. And as to the young labourers, they are now in as hopeful a condition; they cannot get work, and consequently pine away for want of nourishment, to a degree that if at any time they are accidentally hired to common labour, they have not strength to perform it; and thus the country and themselves are happily delivered from the evils to come.

I have too long digressed, and therefore shall return to my subject. I think the advantages by the proposal which I have made are obvious and many, as well as of the highest importance.

For first, as I have already observed, it would greatly lessen the number of papists, with whom we are yearly overrun, being the principal breeders of the nation as well as our most dangerous enemies; and who stay at home on purpose to deliver the kingdom to the pretender, hoping to take their advantage by the absence of so many good protestants, who have chosen rather to leave their country than stay at home and pay tithes against their conscience to an episcopal curate.

Secondly, The poor tenants will have something valuable of their own, which by law may be made liable to distress and help to pay their landlord's rent, their corn and cattle being already seized, and money a thing unknown.

Thirdly, Whereas the maintenance of an hundred thousand children, from two years old and upward, cannot be computed at less than ten shillings a-piece per annum, the nation's stock will be thereby increased fifty thousand pounds per annum, beside the profit of a new dish introduced to the tables of all gentlemen of fortune in the kingdom who have any refinement in taste. And the money will circulate among ourselves, the goods being entirely of our own growth and manufacture.

Fourthly, The constant breeders, beside the gain of eight shillings sterling per annum by the sale of their children, will be rid of the charge of maintaining them after the first year.

Fifthly, This food would likewise bring great custom to taverns; where the vintners will certainly be so prudent as to procure the best receipts for dressing it to perfection, and consequently have their houses frequented by all the fine gentlemen, who justly value themselves upon their knowledge in good eating: and a skilful cook, who understands how to oblige his guests, will contrive to make it as expensive as they please.

Sixthly, This would be a great inducement to marriage, which all wise nations have either encouraged by rewards or enforced by laws and penalties. It would increase the care and tenderness of mothers toward their children, when they were sure of a settlement for life to the poor babes, provided in some sort by the public, to their annual profit or expense. We should see an honest emulation among the married women, which of them could bring the fattest child to the market. Men would become as fond of their wives during the time of their pregnancy as they are now of their mares in foal, their cows in calf, their sows when they are ready to farrow; nor offer to beat or kick them (as is too frequent a practice) for fear of a miscarriage.

Many other advantages might be enumerated. For instance, the addition of some thousand carcasses in our exportation of barreled beef, the propagation of swine's flesh, and improvement in the art of making good bacon, so much wanted among us by the great destruction of pigs, too frequent at our table; which are no way comparable in taste or magnificence to a well-grown, fat, yearling child, which roasted whole will make a considerable figure at a lord mayor's feast or any other public entertainment. But this and many others I omit, being studious of brevity.

Supposing that one thousand families in this city would be constant customers for infants' flesh, beside others who might have it at merry-meetings, particularly at weddings and christenings, I compute that Dublin would take off annually about twenty thousand carcasses; and the rest of the kingdom (where probably they will be sold somewhat cheaper) the remaining eighty thousand.

I can think of no one objection that will possibly be raised against this proposal, unless it should be urged that the number of people will be thereby much lessened in the kingdom. This I freely own, and it was indeed one principal design in offering it to the world. I desire the reader will observe, that I calculate my remedy for this one individual kingdom of Ireland and for no other that ever was, is, or I think ever can be upon earth. Therefore let no man talk to me of other expedients: of taxing our absentees at five shillings a pound: of using neither clothes nor household furniture except what is of our own growth and manufacture: of utterly rejecting the materials and instruments that promote foreign luxury: of curing the expensiveness of pride, vanity, idleness, and gaming in our women: of introducing a vein of parsimony, prudence, and temperance: of learning to love our country, in the want of which we differ even from Laplanders and the inhabitants of Topinamboo: of quitting our animosities and factions, nor acting any longer like the Jews, who were murdering one another at the very moment their city was taken: of being a little cautious not to sell our country and conscience for nothing: of teaching landlords to have at least one degree of mercy toward their tenants: lastly, of putting a spirit of honesty, industry, and skill into our shopkeepers; who, if a resolution could now be taken to buy only our negative goods, would immediately unite to cheat and exact upon us in the price, the measure, and the goodness, nor could ever yet be brought to make one fair proposal of just dealing, though often and earnestly invited to it.

Therefore I repeat, let no man talk to me of these and the like expedients, till he has at least some glimpse of hope that there will be ever some hearty and sincere attempt to put them in practice.

But as to myself, having been wearied out for many years with offering vain, idle, visionary thoughts, and at length utterly despairing of success I fortunately fell upon this proposal; which, as it is wholly new, so it has something solid and real, of no expense and little trouble, full in our own power, and whereby we can incur no danger in disobliging England. For this kind of commodity will not bear exportation, the flesh being of too tender a consistence to admit a long continuance in salt, although perhaps I could name a country which would be glad to eat up our whole nation without it.

After all, I am not so violently bent upon my own opinion as to reject any offer proposed by wise men, which shall be found equally innocent, cheap, easy, and effectual. But before something of that kind shall be advanced in contradiction to my scheme, and offering a better, I desire the author or authors will be pleased maturely to consider two points. First, as things now stand, how they will be able to find food and raiment for an hundred thousand useless mouths and backs. And secondly, there being a round million of creatures in human figure throughout this kingdom, whose whole subsistence put into a common stock would leave them in debt two millions of pounds sterling, adding those who are beggars by profession to the bulk of farmers, cottagers, and labourers, with the wives and children who are beggars in effect; I desire those politicians who dislike my overture, and may perhaps be so bold as to attempt an answer, that they will first ask the parents of these mortals, whether they would not at this day think it a great happiness to have been sold for food at a year old in the manner I prescribe, and thereby have avoided such a perpetual scene of misfortunes as they have since gone through by the oppression of landlords, the impossibility of paying rent without money or trade, the want of common sustenance, with neither house nor clothes to cover them from the inclemencies of the weather, and the most inevitable prospect of entailing the like or greater miseries upon their breed for ever.

I profess, in the sincerity of my heart, that I have not the least personal interest in endeavouring to promote this necessary work, having no other motive than the public good of my country, by advancing our trade, providing for infants, relieving the poor, and giving some pleasure to the rich. I have no children by which I can propose to get a single penny; the youngest being nine years old, and my wife past child-bearing.

A TRUE AND FAITHFUL NARRATIVE

OF WHAT PASSED IN LONDON
DURING THE GENERAL CONSTERNATION
OF ALL RANKS AND DEGREES OF MANKIND,
ON TUESDAY, WEDNESDAY, THURSDAY,
AND FRIDAY LAST.

On Tuesday, the 13th of October, Mr Whiston held a lecture near the Royal Exchange to an audience of fourteen worthy citizens, his subscribers and constant hearers. Besides these there were five chance auditors for that night only, who had paid their shillings apiece. I think myself obliged to be very particular in this relation lest my veracity should be suspected, which makes me appeal to the men who were present, of which number I myself was one. Their names are—

Henry Watson, haberdasher.
George Hancock, druggist.
John Lewis, dry-salter.
William Jones, corn-chandler.
Henry Theobald, watchmaker.
James Peters, draper.
Thomas Floyer, silversmith.
John Wells, brewer.
Samuel Greg, soap-boiler.
William Cooley, fishmonger.
James Harper, hosier.
Robert Tucker, stationer.
George Ford, ironmonger.
Daniel Lynch, apothecary.
William Bennet,
David Somers,
Charles Lock, } apprentices.
Leonard Daval,
Henry Croft,

Mr. Whiston began by acquainting us that (contrary to his advertisement) he thought himself in duty and conscience obliged to change the subject-matter of his intended discourse. Here he paused, and seemed for a short space, as it were, lost in devotion and mental prayer, after which, with great earnestness and vehemence, he spake as follows:—

"Friends and fellow-citizens, all speculative science is at an end; the period of all things is at hand: on Friday next this world shall be no more. Put not your confidence in me, brethren, for tomorrow morning, five minutes after five, the truth will be evident; in that instant the comet shall appear of which I have heretofore warned you. As ye have heard, believe. Go hence and prepare your wives, your families, and friends for the universal change."

At this solemn and dreadful prediction the whole society appeared in the utmost astonishment: but it would be unjust not to remember that Mr. Whiston himself was in so calm a temper as to return a shilling a-piece to the youths, who had been disappointed of their lecture, which I thought, from a man of his integrity, a convincing proof of his own faith in the prediction.

As we thought it a duty in charity to warn all men, in two or three hours the news had spread through the city. At first, indeed, our report met with but little credit, it being by our greatest dealers in stocks thought only a court artifice to sink them, that some choice favourites might purchase at a lower rate; for the South Sea that very evening fell five per cent., the Indian eleven, and all the other funds in proportion. But at the court end of the town our attestations were entirely disbelieved or turned into ridicule, yet nevertheless the news spread everywhere and was the subject-matter of all conversation.

That very night (as I was credibly informed) Mr. Whiston was sent for to a great lady who is very curious in the learned sciences, and addicted to all the speculative doubts of the most able philosophers, but he was not now to be found; and since at other times he has been known not to decline that honour, I make no doubt he concealed himself to attend the great business of his soul: but whether it was the lady's faith or inquisitiveness that occasioned her to send is a point I shall not presume to determine. As for his being sent for to the secretary's office by a messenger, it is now known to be a matter notoriously false, and indeed at first it had little credit with me that so zealous and honest a man should be ordered into custody as a seditious preacher, who is known to be so well-affected to the present happy establishment.

It was now I reflected, with exceeding trouble and sorrow, that I had disused family prayers for above five years, and (though it has been a custom of late entirely neglected by men of any business or station) I determined within myself no longer to omit so reasonable and religious a duty. I acquainted my wife with my intentions, but two or three neighbours having been engaged to sup with us that night, and many hours being unwarily spent at cards, I was prevailed upon by her to put it off till the next day; she reasoning that it would be time enough to take off the servants from their business (which this practice must infallibly occasion for an hour or two every day) after the comet had made its appearance.

Zachary Bowen, a Quaker, and my next neighbour, had no sooner heard of the prophecy but he made me a visit. I informed him of everything I had heard, but found him quite obstinate in his unbelief; for, said he, be comforted, friend, thy tidings are impossibilities, for were these things to happen they must have been foreseen by some of our brethren. This indeed (as in all other spiritual cases with this set of people) was his only reason against believing me; and as he was fully persuaded that the prediction was erroneous, he in a very neighbourly manner admonished me against selling my stock at the present low price, which, he said, beyond dispute must have a rise before Monday, when this unreasonable consternation should be over.

But on Wednesday morning (I believe to the exact calculation of Mr. Whiston) the comet appeared; for at three minutes after five by my own watch I saw it. He, indeed, foretold that it would be seen at five minutes after five; but as the best watches may be a minute or two too slow, I am apt to think his calculation just to a minute.

In less than a quarter of an hour all Cheapside was crowded with a vast concourse of people, and notwithstanding it was so early, it is thought that through all that part of the town there was not man, woman, or child, except the sick or infirm, left in their beds. From my own balcony I am confident I saw several thousands in the street, and counted at least seventeen who were upon their knees, and seemed in actual devotion. Eleven of them, indeed, appeared to be old women of about fourscore; the six others were men in advanced life, but (as I could guess) two of them might be under seventy.

It is highly probable that an event of this nature may be passed over by the greater historians of our times, as conducing very little or nothing to the unravelling and laying open the deep schemes of politicians and mysteries of state; for which reason I thought it might not be unacceptable to record the facts which in the space of three days came to my knowledge, either as an eye-witness or from unquestionable authorities; nor can I think this narrative will be entirely without its use, as it may enable us to form a more just idea of our countrymen in general, particularly in regard to their faith, religion, morals, and politics.

Before Wednesday noon the belief was universal that the day of judgment was at hand, insomuch that a waterman of my acquaintance told me he counted no less than one hundred and twenty-three clergymen who had been ferried over to Lambeth before twelve o'clock; these, it is said, went thither to petition that a short prayer might be penned and ordered, there being none in the service upon that occasion. But as in things of this nature it is necessary that the council be consulted, their request was not immediately complied with, and this I affirm to be the true and only reason that the churches were not that morning so well attended, and is in noways to be imputed to the fears and consternation of the clergy, with which the free-thinkers have since very unjustly reproached them.

My wife and I went to church (where we had not been for many years on a week-day), and with a very large congregation were disappointed of the service. But (what will be scarce credible) by the carelessness of a 'prentice, in our absence we had a piece of fine cambric carried off by a shoplifter, so little impression was yet made on the minds of those wicked women!

I cannot omit the care of a particular director of the bank; I hope the worthy and wealthy knight will forgive me that I endeavour to do him justice; for it was unquestionably owing to Sir Gilbert Heathcote's sagacity that all the fire offices were required to have a particular eye upon the bank of England. Let it be recorded to his praise, that in the general hurry this struck him as his nearest and tenderest concern; but the next day in the evening, after having taken due care of all his books, bills, and bonds, I was informed his mind was wholly turned upon spiritual matters, yet ever and anon he could not help expressing his resentment against the Tories and Jacobites, to whom he imputed that sudden run upon the bank which happened on this occasion.

A great man (whom at this time it may not be prudent to name) employed all the Wednesday morning to make up such an account as might appear fair in case he should be called upon to produce it on the Friday; but was forced to desist, after having for several hours together attempted it, not being able to bring himself to a resolution to trust the many hundred articles of his secret transactions upon paper.

Another seemed to be very melancholy, which his flatterers imputed to his dread of losing his power in a day or two; but I rather take it that his chief concern was the terror of being tried in a court that could not be influenced, and where a majority of voices could avail him nothing. It was observed, too, that he had but few visitors that day. This added so much to his mortification, that he read through the first chapter of the book of Job, and wept over it bitterly; in short, he seemed a true penitent in everything but in charity to his neighbour. No business was that day done in his counting-house. It is said, too, that he was advised to restitution, but I never heard that he complied with it, any further than in giving half-a-crown a-piece to several crazed and starving creditors who attended in the outward room.

Three of the maids-of-honour sent to countermand their birthday clothes; two of them burnt all their collections of novels and romances, and sent to a bookseller's in Pallmall to buy each of them a bible and *Taylor's Holy Living and Dying*. But I must do all of them the justice to acknowledge that they showed a very decent behaviour in the drawing-room, and restrained themselves from those innocent freedoms and little levities so commonly incident to young ladies of their profession. So many birthday suits were countermanded the next day, that most of the tailors and mantua-makers discharged all their journeymen and women. A grave elderly lady of great erudition and modesty, who visits these young ladies, seemed to be extremely shocked by the apprehensions that she was to appear naked before the whole world; and no less so, that all mankind was to appear naked before her; which might so much divert her thoughts as to incapacitate her to give ready and apt answers to the interrogatories that might be made her. The maids-of-honour, who had both modesty and curiosity, could not imagine the sight so disagreeable as was represented; nay, one of them went so far as to say she perfectly longed to see it; for it could not be so indecent when everybody was to be alike; and they had a day or two to prepare themselves to be seen in that condition. Upon this reflection, each of them ordered a bathing-tub to be got ready that evening, and a looking-glass to be set by it. So much are these young ladies, both by nature and custom, addicted to cleanly appearance.

A west-country gentleman told me he got a church-lease filled up that morning for the same sum which had been refused for three years successively. I must impute this merely to accident; for I cannot imagine that any divine could take the advantage of his tenant in so unhandsome a manner, or that the shortness of the life was in the least his consideration; though I have heard the same worthy prelate aspersed and maligned since upon this very account.

The term being so near, the alarm among the lawyers was inexpressible, though some of them, I was told, were so vain as to promise themselves some advantage in making their defence by being versed in the practice of our earthly courts. It is said, too, that some of the chief pleaders were heard to express great satisfaction that there had been but few state trials of late years. Several attorneys demanded the return of fees that had been given the lawyers; but it was answered, the fee was undoubtedly charged to their client, and that they could not connive at such injustice as to suffer it to be sunk in the attorneys' pockets. Our sage and learned judges had great consolation, insomuch as they had not pleaded at the bar for several years; the barristers rejoiced in that they were not attorneys, and the attorneys felt no less satisfaction that they were not pettifoggers, scriveners, and other meaner officers of the law.

As to the army, far be it from me to conceal the truth. Every soldier's behaviour was as undismayed and undaunted as if nothing was to happen; I impute not this to their want of faith, but to their martial disposition; though I cannot help thinking they commonly accompany their commands with more oaths than are requisite, of which there was no remarkable diminution this morning on the parade in St. James's Park. But possibly it was by choice and on consideration that they continued this way of expression, not to intimidate the common soldiers, or give occasion to suspect that even the fear of damnation could make any impression upon their superior officers. A duel was fought the same morning between two colonels, not occasioned (as was reported) because the one was put over the other's head; that being a point which might at such a juncture have been accommodated by the mediation of friends; but as this was upon the account of a lady, it was judged it could not be put off at this time above all others, but demanded immediate satisfaction. I am apt to believe that a young officer, who desired his surgeon to defer putting him into a salivation till Saturday, might make this request out of some opinion he had of the truth of the prophecy: for the apprehensions of any danger in the operation could not be his motive, the surgeon himself having assured me that he had before undergone three severe operations of the like nature with great resignation and fortitude.

There was an order issued that the chaplains of the several regiments should attend their duty; but as they were dispersed about in several parts of England, it was believed that most of them could not be found, or so much as heard of, till the great day was over.

Most of the considerable physicians, by their outward demeanour, seemed to be unbelievers; but at the same time they everywhere insinuated that there might be a pestilential malignancy in the air, occasioned by the comet, which might be armed against by proper and timely medicines. This caution had but little effect; for as the time approached, the Christian resignation of the people increased, and most of them (which was never before known) had their souls more at heart than their bodies.

If the reverend clergy showed more concern than others, I charitably impute it to their great charge of souls; and what confirmed me in this opinion was, that the degrees of apprehension and terror could be distinguished to be greater or less according to their ranks and degrees in the church.

The like might be observed in all sorts of ministers, though not of the Church of England; the higher their rank, the more was their fear.

I speak not of the court, for fear of offence; and I forbear inserting the names of particular persons, to avoid the imputation of slander; so that the reader will allow the narrative must be deficient, and is therefore desired to accept hereof rather as a sketch than a regular circumstantial history.

I was not informed of any persons who showed the least joy; except three malefactors who were to be executed on the Monday following, and one old man, a constant churchgoer, who, being at the point of death, expressed some satisfaction at the news.

On Thursday morning there was little or nothing transacted in 'Change-alley; there were a multitude of sellers, but so few buyers that one cannot affirm the stocks bore any certain price except among the Jews, who this day reaped great profit by their infidelity. There were many who called themselves Christians, who offered to buy for time; but as these were people of great distinction, I choose not to mention them, because in effect it would seem to accuse them both of avarice and infidelity.

The run upon the bank is too well known to need a particular relation; for it never can be forgotten that no one person whatever (except the directors themselves and some of their particular friends and associates) could convert a bill all that day into specie; all hands being employed to serve them.

In the several churches of the city and suburbs there were seven thousand two hundred and forty-five who publicly and solemnly declared before the congregation that they took to wife their several kept mistresses, which was allowed as valid marriage, the priest not having time to pronounce the ceremony in form.

At St. Bride's church in Fleet Street Mr. Woolston (who writ against the miracles of our Saviour), in the utmost terrors of conscience, made a public recantation. Dr. Mandeville (who had been groundlessly reported formerly to have done the same) did it now in good earnest at St. James's Gate; as did also at the Temple church several gentlemen who frequent coffee-houses near the bar. So great was the faith and fear of two of them that they dropped dead on the spot; but I will not record their names, lest I should be thought invidiously to lay an odium on their families and posterity.

Most of the players who had very little faith before were now desirous of having as much as they could, and therefore embraced the Roman Catholic religion: the same thing was observed of some bawds and ladies of pleasure.

An Irish gentleman out of pure friendship came to make me a visit, and advised me to hire a boat for the ensuing day, and told me that unless I gave earnest for one immediately he feared it might be too late; for his countrymen had secured almost every boat upon the river, as judging that, in the general conflagration, to be upon the water would be the safest place.

There were two lords and three commoners who, out of scruple of conscience, very hastily threw up their pensions, as imagining a pension was only an annual retaining bribe. All the other great pensioners I was told had their scruples quieted by a clergyman or two of distinction, whom they happily consulted.

It was remarkable that several of our very richest tradesmen of the city in common charity gave away shillings and sixpences to the beggars who plied about the church doors; and at a particular church in the city a wealthy churchwarden with his own hands distributed fifty twelvepenny loaves to the poor, by way of restitution for the many great and costly feasts which he had eaten of at their expense.

Three great ladies, a valet-de-chambre, two lords, a custom-house officer, five half-pay captains, and a baronet (all noted gamesters) came publicly into a church at Westminster, and deposited a very considerable sum of money in the minister's hands; the parties whom they had defrauded being either out of town or not to be found. But so great is the hardness of heart of this fraternity, that among either the noble or vulgar gamesters (though the profession is so general) I did not hear of any other restitution of this sort. At the same time I must observe that (in comparison of these), through all parts of the town, the justice and penitence of the highwaymen, housebreakers, and common pickpockets were very remarkable.

The directors of our public companies were in such dreadful apprehensions that one would have thought a parliamentary inquiry was at hand; yet so great was their presence of mind, that all the Thursday morning was taken up in private transfers, which by malicious people was thought to be done with design to conceal their effects.

I forbear mentioning the private confessions of particular

ladies to their husbands; for as their children were born in wedlock, and of consequence are legitimate, it would be an invidious task to record them as bastards; and particularly after their several husbands have so charitably forgiven them.

The evening and night through the whole town were spent in devotions both public and private; the churches for this one day were so crowded by the nobility and gentry, that thousands of common people were seen praying in the public streets. In short, one would have thought the whole town had been really and seriously religious. But what was very remarkable, all the different persuasions kept by themselves, for, as each thought the other would be damned, not one would join in prayer with the other.

At length Friday came, and the people covered all the streets; expecting, watching, and praying. But as the day wore away their fears first began to abate, then lessened every hour; at night they were almost extinct, till the total darkness that hitherto used to terrify, now comforted every free-thinker and atheist. Great numbers went together to the taverns, bespoke suppers, and broke up whole hogsheads for joy. The subject of all wit and conversation was to ridicule the prophecy and rally each other. All the quality and gentry were perfectly ashamed, nay, some utterly disowned that they had manifested any signs of religion.

But the next day, even the common people as well as their betters appeared in their usual state of indifference. They drank, they whored, they swore, they lied, they cheated, they quarrelled, they murdered. In short, the world went on in the old channel.

I need not give any instances of what will so easily be credited; but I cannot omit relating that Mr. Woolston advertised in that very Saturday's *Evening Post*, a *New Treatise against the Miracles of our Saviour*; and that the few who had given up their pensions the day before solicited to have them continued; which, as they had not been thrown up upon any ministerial point, I am informed was readily granted.

A MEDITATION
UPON A BROOMSTICK

This single stick, which you now behold ingloriously lying in that neglected corner, I once knew in a flourishing state in a forest: it was full of sap, full of leaves, and full of boughs: but now, in vain does the busy art of man pretend to vie with nature, by tying that withered bundle of twigs to its sapless trunk: it is now, at best, but the reverse of what it was, a tree turned upside down, the branches on the earth, and the root in the air; it is now handled by every dirty wench, condemned to do her drudgery, and, by a capricious kind of fate, destined to make other things clean, and be nasty itself: at length, worn to the stumps in the service of the maids, it is either thrown out of doors, or condemned to the last use, of kindling a fire. When I beheld this I sighed, and said within myself, Surely mortal man is a Broomstick! Nature sent him into the world strong and lusty, in a thriving condition, wearing his own hair on his head, the proper branches of this reasoning vegetable, until the axe of intemperance has lopped off his green boughs, and left him a withered trunk: he then flies to art, and puts on a periwig, valuing himself upon an unnatural bundle of hairs, all covered with powder, that never grew on his head; but now, should this our broomstick pretend to enter the scene, proud of those birchen spoils it never bore, and all covered with dust, though the sweepings of the finest lady's chamber, we should be apt to ridicule and despise its vanity. Partial judges that we are of our own excellencies, and other men's defaults!

But a broomstick, perhaps, you will say, is an emblem of a tree standing on its head; and pray what is man, but a topsy-turvy creature, his animal faculties perpetually mounted on his rational, his head where his heels should be, grovelling on the earth! and yet, with all his faults, he sets up to be a universal reformer and corrector of abuses, a remover of grievances, rakes into every slut's corner of nature, bringing hidden corruption to the light, and raises a mighty dust where there was none before; sharing deeply all the while in the very same pollutions he pretends to sweep away: his last days are spent in slavery to women, and generally the least deserving; till, worn to the stumps, like his brother besom, he is either kicked out of doors, or made use of to kindle flames for others to warm themselves by.

NOTES

"I have ever hated all nations, professions and communities, and all my love is towards individuals," Swift wrote to his friend Alexander Pope on 29 September 1725; "for instance, I hate the tribe of lawyers, but I love councillor such a one, judge such a one, for so with physicians (I will not speak of my own trade), soldiers, English, Scotch, French; and the rest, but principally I hate and detest that animal called man, although I heartily love John, Peter, Thomas and so forth."

The satirist's lash in the six pieces selected for the present volume, which covers the full span of Swift's writing life, scourged collective abuses of various kinds. The evolution of different strains of Christianity provided his principal butt in *A Tale of a Tub*; the controversy over the respective virtues of ancient and modern authors prompted by Sir William Temple's *Essay on Ancient and Modern Learning* was his occasion for *The Battle of the Books*; the foolishness of would-be prophets together with the hypocrisy of eleventh-hour penitence earned his ribald derision in the *True and Faithful Narrative*; and the pitiless English exploitation of Ireland inspired a notorious cannibal proposal advanced in modest, seemingly rational tones, in what is surely the most perfect expression of Swift's savage indignation.

Dr. Samuel Johnson in his *Life of Swift* felt that *A Tale of a Tub* was "of dangerous example" and exhibited "want of knowledge or want of integrity", though he conceded, in characteristic back-handed fashion, that it "exhibits a vehemence and rapidity of mind, a copiousness of images and vivacity of diction such as he afterwards never possessed or never exerted". Boswell (24 March 1775) recorded Johnson as stating, in the same conversation that saw his notorious dismissal of *Gulliver's Travels* ("When once you have thought of big men and little men, it is very easy to do all the rest"), that *A Tale of a Tub* "is so much superior to his other writings that one can hardly believe he was the author of it." Swift himself, towards the end of his life, is reported to have murmured ruefully, on looking once more at his early *Tale*, "Good God! What a genius I had when I wrote that book!" 20th century critics have agreed, from Herbert Davis to Hugh Kenner.

Of the other satires in the present volume, the most notable is *A Modest Proposal*, which F.W. Bateson nominated "perhaps the greatest of the prose ironies". The thrust of Swift's satire, Bateson argued, goes deeper than merely the Irish policy of the Whig government: "It is an exposure of a whole social philosophy, of which the English economic discrimination against Ireland was only one instance [...] *A Modest Proposal* [...] talks the actual language of Cheapside and Threadneedle Street. It is to all appearances another essay in the 'political arithmetic' that was so popular in the City of London during the later seventeenth and early eighteenth centuries. The tone of voice, the method of argument, the statistical approach are exactly the kind of thing that the business world of the time had been accustomed to meet in the pamphlets of Sir William Petty, Charles Davenant and Daniel Defoe. Here was their old friend the Economic Man! The opening paragraphs have lulled any suspicions that Swift's authorship might have aroused, and the reader, who finds the Economic Man disposing of his surplus children to the butcher, is brought suddenly face to face with the contradiction between his own weekday and Sunday religions. It is the Augustan paradox, the familiar formula of the poetry of the squirearchy, but here it operates on a grander scale, charged with a higher intensity, than any of Swift's contemporaries were able to command."

In the present selection, the texts are given in modern spelling. The *Tale of a Tub* includes the 'Apology' first published in the fifth edition (1710) but not 'The History of Martin' and other material of doubtful authenticity added to an edition printed in Holland in 1720. The side-notes and foot-notes are almost certainly all Swift's, or at the very least were approved by him; other notes added to the editions of 1720 and 1734 were *probably* his too, but only a selection of these is included here. The notes to the present edition are not intended to be exhaustive; for example, it would be beyond the scope of this book to gloss in individual detail the many allusions to Homer that so delightfully enrich the epic rhetoric of *The Battle of the Books*. The most meticulous edition of *A Tale of a Tub* and *The Battle of the Books* (together with *The Mechanical Operation of the Spirit*, with which those pieces were first published in 1704) is that edited by A.C. Guthkelch and D. Nichol Smith (second edn., Oxford, 1958), and to that outstanding work of editorial scholarship the reader is directed for further help. The present volume includes six of the illustrations that first appeared in the fifth edition (1710) of *A Tale of a Tub*. Words found in any good dictionary are not glossed in the notes that follow.   *Ed.*

A TALE OF A TUB

p. 9   *treatises written expressly against it*: principally, William King's *Remarks on the Tale of a Tub* (1704) and William Wotton's *Observations upon the Tale of a Tub* (1705).

p. 9   *a late discourse*: The Principles of Deism Truly represented and set in a clear Light, in Two Dialogues between a Sceptick and a Deist (1708), attributed to Francis Gastrell.

p. 10   *nondum tibi defuit hostis*: "you have never yet lacked an external enemy", from Lucan's *De Bello Civili*, I, 23.

p. 11   *the weightiest men in the weightiest stations*: the Archbishop of York showed *A Tale of a Tub* to the Queen, so debarring Swift (so Johnson reports in the *Lives of the Poets*) from a bishopric.

p. 11   *another book*: Shaftesbury's *A Letter concerning Enthusiasm to My Lord ***** [Somers]* (1708).

p. 12   *one instance*: p. 52 of the present edition.

p. 12   *one of his prefaces*: Dryden's *Discourse concerning*

Satire, written as the preface to his translation of Juvenal.

p. 13   *Dr. Eachard ... his book*: *The Grounds & Occasions of the Contempt of the Clergy and Religion Enquired into* (1679), by John Eachard (?1636-1697).

p. 13   *Marvell's answer to Parker*: i.e. *The Rehearsal Transpros'd* (1672-3), his response to Samuel Parker's *A Discourse of Ecclesiastical Politie* (1670).

p. 13   *the Earl of Orrery's remarks*: *Dr. Bentley's Dissertations on the Epistle of Phalaris, and the Fables of Æsop, examin'd by the Honourable Charles Boyle, Esq.* (1698). Boyle became fourth Earl of Orrery in 1703.

p. 14   *a person*: King (cf. note to p. 9).

p. 14   *a person of a graver character*: Wotton (cf. note to p. 9). Wotton was rector of Middleton Keynes in Buckinghamshire and chaplain to the Earl of Nottingham.

p. 14   *Sir William Temple*: English diplomat and essay writer (1628-99). Swift began his own professional life as Temple's secretary.

p. 15   *idem trecenti juravimus*: "three hundred of us have vowed to attempt the same", the words of a captured Roman assassin to the Etruscan king Porsenna.

p. 15   *another antagonist*: Richard Bentley (1662-1742), a classical scholar whose commanding reputation was tarnished by his arrogance and chicanery. Swift's reference here is to the controversy satirized in *The Battle of the Books*.

p. 16   *Alsatia*: a part of Whitefriars that enjoyed sanctuary and was therefore a criminal haunt.

p. 16   *Combat des Livres*: i.e. the *Histoire Poëtique de la Guerre nouvellement declarée entre les Anciens et les Modernes* (1688) by François de Callières.

p. 18   *Minellius, or Farnaby*: the classical scholars Jean Minell (1625-83) and Thomas Farnaby (?1575-1647).

p. 18   *optat ephippia bos piger*: the words, paraphrased as Swift continues, are from Horace, *Epistles* I, 14.

p. 20   *the 153d. page*: p. 109 of the present edition.

p. 20   *Whitefriars*: cf. note to Alsatia, p. 16. The privilege of sanctuary was abolished in 1697.

p. 21   *a prostitute bookseller*: Swift means Edmund Curll (1675–1747), later satirized by Pope in *The Dunciad*, a bookseller whose practices were often less than scrupulous.

p. 22   *John Lord Sommers*: "John Lord Somers [*sic*], Chancellor of England in 1697, was one of the greatest men of his age and nation, and a great patron of learning, which induced many learned men to dedicate their works to him, and this author in particular who had great obligations to him." (Swift's note, 1720.)

p. 23   *the second place*: the principle described by Swift originates in the election of Themistocles, in the *Histories* of Herodotus, VIII, 123–4.

p. 24   *at the head of an army*: "'Tis a ridiculous custom of most authors in their dedications, to praise their patrons for many qualitys they have not, and oftimes need not to have." (Swift's note, 1720.)

p. 24   *your enemies*: Sommers was impeached by the Commons in 1701, but a trial was delayed, leaving the Lords free to proceed to trial and acquit him.

p. 24   *a late reign*: "That of K. William, who had a great value for this Lord and took much of his advice." (Swift's note, 1720.)

p. 27   *the person*: "Time." (Swift's note, 1720.)

p. 28   *maître du palais*: Guthkelch and Nichol Smith point out that the French master of the royal household is correctly designated the *maire du palais*.

p. 29   *Moloch*: cf. Jeremiah 23, 35.

p. 31   *lately printed*: Dryden's translation of Virgil appeared in 1697.

p. 31   *Nahum Tate*: the Irish poet (1652–1715) succeeded Shadwell as Poet Laureate in 1692.

p. 31 *Tom Durfey*: English dramatist (1653–1723) known chiefly for his popular comedies.

p. 31 *a friend of your governor*: the governor is "Antiquity" (Swift's note, 1720) and the friend Sir William Temple (cf. note to p. 14).

p. 33 *Hobbes's Leviathan*: "A book sufficiently known; very much esteemed by some, and held by others very dangerous for the maxims of religion and government it contains." (Swift's note, 1720.)

p. 34 *the principal schools*: "Academy and schools proper for different sorts of rakes and beaus [1720] that pretend to be wits [1734]." (Swift's notes.)

p. 35 *insigne, recens, indictum ore alio*: Horace, *Odes*, III, xxv, 7–8.

p. 37 *Leicester Fields*: what is now Leicester Square.

p. 38 *the first monarch of this island*: i.e. James I.

p. 40 *pork*: in Plutarch's *Life of Titus Quintius Flaminius*, and in various analogues described by Guthkelch and Nichol Smith, the fact that the same meat prepared in different ways remains one and the same meat is presented as an argument against shallow taste that is forever falling for novelty.

p. 40 *the Attic commonwealth*: Swift is referring to a political pamphlet, *On the Polity of the Athenians*, once attributed to Xenophon but in fact written before his own writing life began.

p. 40 *there is none that doth good, no not one*: "Psalm xiv. 3." (Swift's note, 1720.)

p. 41 *splendida bilis*: Horace, *Satires* II, iii, 141.

p. 43 *Virgil*: the lines are from the *Aeneid*, VI, 128–9, and the footnote translation is Dryden's (1697).

p. 45 *senes ut in otia tuta recedant*: "so that when they are old they may retire in peace of mind"; Horace, *Satires* I, ii, 31.

p. 46 *sylva Caledonia*: Scottish forests.

p. 47 *Epicurus*: Greek philosopher (341–271 B.C.). Lucretius in particular, with Cicero and Plutarch, provides most of what we now know of his views.

p. 47   *Corpoream quoque ... sensus*: the footnote translation of Lucretius, *De Natura Rerum*, IV, 526–7 is from the English rendering published in 1683 by Thomas Creech (1659–1700).

p. 49   *Gresham*: the Royal Society met in Gresham College until 1710. Cf. *The Battle of the Books*, p. 136.

p. 50   *briguing*: intriguing.

p. 53   *a famous writer now living*: Dryden.

p. 53   *Tommy Potts*: a popular ballad of the time, published c. 1675.

p. 54   *a conscience void of offence*: "Acts xxiv. 16." (Swift's note, 1720.)

p. 54   *a multiplicity of godfathers*: in dividing the dedication of his English rendering of Virgil between three patrons, Dryden (as Guthkelch and Nichol Smith make clear) was following a 17th century tendency that could sometimes go to ludicrous lengths, one publication carrying no fewer than forty-one dedicatory epistles.

p. 56   *a man who had three sons*: Swift's tale of a father bequeathing a coat to each of his three sons varies the much-told tale of the father bequeathing rings, which conventionally stand for the Jewish, Christian and Mohammedan religions. This story was already old when Boccaccio used it (Day 1, Third Tale, in the *Decameron*); it made a striking late reappearance in Lessing's play *Nathan the Wise*.

p. 56   *nor was born to any*: "See Math. viii. 20." (Swift's note, 1734.)

p. 57   *the good qualities*: "A list of some of the good qualitys of the town rakes." (Swift's note, 1720.)

p. 57   *bulks*: stalls outside shops.

p. 57   *Locket's*: a popular eating-house at Charing Cross.

p. 57   *sub dio*: in the open.

p. 58   *goose*: i.e. a tailor's smoothing-iron, so called from the shape of its handle, which resembled the neck of a goose.

p. 58 *hell*: the place into which a tailor throws shreds.

p. 59 *water-tabby*: watered silk.

p. 59 *honesty a pair of shoes*: "Such comparisons are frequent with some Divines, who think them authorized by several places of Scripture. See Ephes. vi. 1-17." (Swift's note, 1720.)

p. 60 *the soul was the outward, and the body the inward clothing*: cf. *All's Well That Ends Well*, II, v, 49.

p. 60 *ex traduce*: according to the doctrine of traduction, not only the body but also the soul is transmitted from parents.

p. 60 *because in them we live ... our being*: cf. Acts 17, 28.

p. 60 *a strict observance after times and fashions*: "Those of a refined taste presently judge of every one's genius, by their dress." (Swift's note, 1720.)

p. 61 *not to add to or diminish from their coats one thread*: "See Apocal. xxii. 18, 19." (Swift's note, 1734.)

p. 61 *shoulder-knots*: knots of ribbon or lace were worn on the shoulders of the fashionable in the closing decades of the 17th century.

p. 61 *ruelles*: boudoirs.

p. 64 *jure paterno*: "What ever serves the present turn or occasion must be made out to be *Jure divino*." (Swift's note, 1720.) The expression means "in accordance with the paternal law".

p. 64 *altum silentium*: profound silence. The phrase is from Virgil's *Aeneid*, X, 63.

p. 64 *aliquo modo essentiæ adhærere*: in some measure adhere to the essence.

p. 64 *si idem affirmetur de nuncupatorio, negatur*: if the same is affirmed regarding oral statement, it is denied.

p. 67 *a mystery*: "When church men find their account in any doctrine or custom introduced, tho directly against the plain literal meaning of Scripture, whoever speaks against it shall be cried down as a libertin or despiser of mysterys and religion." (Swift's note, 1720.)

p. 68   *multa absurda sequerentur*: many absurdities would follow.

p. 69   *Edinburgh streets*: even after Swift's time, Edinburgh was a byword for insanitary conditions. In the opening pages of his *Journal of a Tour to the Hebrides* (1785), Boswell wrote, "I could not prevent [Johnson's] being assailed by the evening effluvia of Edinburgh. I heard a late baronet, of some distinction in the political world in the beginning of the present reign, observe, that 'walking the streets of Edinburgh at night was pretty perilous, and a good deal odoriferous.' The peril is much abated, by the care which the magistrates have taken to enforce the city laws against throwing foul water from the windows: but, from the structure of the houses in the old town, which consist of many stories, in each of which a different family lives, and there being no covered sewers, the odour still continues."

p. 70   *Zoilus ... Tigellius*: Zoilus, a Cynic of the 4th century B.C., earned notoriety for his attacks on Homer in particular, which made his name proverbial for a carping critic. Similarly, Tigellius attacked Horace.

p. 71   *Cacus*: in Greek myth, Hercules killed Cacus in the course of his tenth labour. The heads of Hydra, the filth of the Augean stables, and the Stymphalian birds, feature in the second, fifth and sixth labours respectively.

p. 73   *Pausanias*: Greek geographer and writer of the 2nd century A.D., whose ten-book *Description of Greece* still survives. The remark in this paragraph concerning the Nauplians in Argos, to which Swift supplies one of his less informative side-notes, is from II, 38.

p. 73   *asses with horns*: Herodotus, *Histories* IV, 191.

p. 74   *Ctesias*: Greek physician of the 4th century B.C., author of a twenty-three-book history of Persia and of the first book devoted entirely to India. Some of our knowledge of his work, including the information reported here, comes second-hand via Photius (c. A.D. 810–c. 893), a patriarch of Byzantium whose records of his reading, often meticulous, are collected in a compendium known as his *Bibliotheca*, which in numerous cases provides all that is now known of the authors he describes.

p. 74   *so Herodotus tells us expressly in another place*: *Histories* IV, 129.

p. 74   *Diodorus*: Guthkelch and Nichol Smith suggest that this may be a slip on Swift's part, for Dicearchus.

p. 74   *Est etiam in magnis Heliconis...*: the footnote translation of the lines, from Lucretius VI, 786-7, is Creech's (cf. note to p. 47).

p. 75   *Terence*: Roman writer of comedy of the 2nd century B.C.

p. 76   *Themistocles*: Athenian statesman (c. 524–c. 459 B.C.)

p. 76   *the composition of a man*: Swift is alluding to the old adage, "nine tailors make a man".

p. 79   *his sovereign remedy for the worms*: "The worms here signify scruples and qualms of conscience on account of sins; alluding to Mark ix. 44, 46, 48..." (Swift's note, 1720.)

p. 80   *damage by fire*: "As the insurance offices, for a certain sum, insure houses from fire, &c., so in the Romish Church whoever pays for indulgences and pardons may be insured from scorching after he's dead. The things here mentioned seem either not to deserve, or not to stand in need of insurance; and that which is left out between *shadows* and *rivers*, seems to be something as little susceptible of fire as the first, and in as little danger of being hurt by it as the last; such as spirits, or immaterial beings." (Swift's note, 1720.)

p. 80   *universal pickle*: "The universal pickle is the holy water, to which superstitious people attribute so many virtues." (Swift's note, 1720.) "The consecration which makes the only difference between it and common water, is called by this author the powder of pimperlim pimp, a term used by jugglers." (Swift's additional note, 1734.)

p. 81   *spargefaction*: sprinkling.

p. 82   *varias inducere plumas ... atrum desinat in piscem*: that spreads plumage of various colours ... and tails off like an ugly fish. The phrases are from the opening of Horace's *Ars Poetica*.

p. 82   *fishes' tails*: throughout this passage, Swift does not distinguish between Papal Bulls and Papal Briefs. It was briefs, not bulls, that carried a wax seal showing St. Peter fishing. Cf. Guthkelch and Nichol Smith, pp. 111-2.

p. 82   *coil*: disturbance, tumult.

p. 82   *pulveris exigui jactu*: by flinging a handful of dust (C. Day Lewis's rendering). From Virgil's *Georgics*, IV, 87.

p. 88   *copia vera*: "This *copia vera*, it seems, has been lost, for the critics have been long disputing about the true readings: but to the great comfort of all critical believers, the learned and pious Dr. Bentley has now undertaken, with his usual modesty, to publish from his own elaborate conjectures, a more accurate and exact copy than ever has been known before or since the originals were lost." (Swift's note, 1720.)

p. 91   *Quemvis perferre laborem ...* : this persuades me to perform any labour and moves me to spend tranquil nights in vigilance. Lucretius I, 141-2.

p. 92   *utile ... dulce*: profit and pleasure, the two values of poetry identified by Horace in the *Ars Poetica*.

p. 92   *in balneo Mariæ*: i.e. in a bain-marie.

p. 93   *florilegias*: anthologies (literally, selections of flowers).

p. 93   *a complete body*: the quotation from Xenophon's *Convivium* (IV, 6) in the side-note means, "Homer comprehended everything pertaining to humanity in his poetry".

p. 93 *vix crederem ... ignis vocem*: I can hardly believe that the author has ever heard the voice of fire.

p. 100 *hardly a thread of the original coat to be seen*: "Ceremonys and innovations multiplied to such a degree, that there was no more of the ancient primitive Christianity to be seen." (Swift's note, 1720.)

p. 104 *Exchange women*: i.e. women who kept the shops in the galleries at the Royal Exchange.

p. 104 *mobile*: i.e. the mob, or *mobile vulgus*.

p. 104 *the fox's arguments*: in Aesop's fable of the fox without a tail, the moral of which is (in L'Estrange's translation), "When a man has any notable defect, or infirmity about him, whether by nature, or by chance, 'tis the best of his play, to try the humour, if he can turn it into a fashion."

p. 105 *Melleo contingens cuncta lepore*: I touch all with a honeyed charm. Lucretius I, 394.

p. 107 *the wise man's rule*: i.e. Solon's, in the *Histories* of Herodotus, I, 32.

p. 109 *sed quorum pudenda crassa, et ad talos usque pertingentia*: but whose genitals were thick and reached all the way to their ankles.

p. 109 *a custom*: described in Herodotus IV, 2.

p. 110 *the Grecian eloquence*: for the "feathers" in the country of the Scythians, cf. Herodotus IV, 7 and IV, 31.

p. 111 *Æolists*: "Spirit and wind are here made synonimous terms; so Æolists may signify all those that believe spiritual beings; or perhaps those that are called among the godly, spiritualisers or spiritually minded." (Swift's note, 1720.) "Spirit ... Beings, or all those that pretend to inspiration, or make any account of it." (Swift's additional note, 1734.)

p. 111 *Quod procul a nobis flectat Fortuna gubernans*: may ruling Fortune turn thus far from us. Lucretius V, 107.

p. 112 *a fourth ... the other three*: "The three *animas* bestow'd on Man by philosophers are the *vegetativa, sensitiva,* and *rationalis*, and the fourth bestow'd by the Æolists is the spiritualist." (Swift's note, 1720.)

p. 112 *hid under a bushel*: "Matt. v. 15." (Swift's note, 1720.)

p. 112 *belching*: "Belching, is in Latin called *eructatio*, a term used to express the action of the priests in the temples of the oracles when they delivered their prophecies or inspirations among the ancients." (Swift's note, 1720.)

p. 113 *learning puffeth men up*: "I Cor. viii. 1." (Swift's note, 1720.)

p. 113 *a terrible kind of relievo*: "This alludes to the grimaces and contorsions usual among inspired teachers, and their tone in speaking through the nose." (Swift's note, 1720.)

p. 113 *latria*: worship.

p. 113 *omnium deorum Boream maxime celebrant*: they venerate Boreas above all other gods. Pausanias (cf. note to p. 59) VIII, xxxvi, 6. The land of darkness presently referred to is Scotland.

p. 114 *a region of the like denomination*: "Our dissenters in England, who pretend to a much larger share of the spirit, than those of the establisht church, own the Kirk of Scotland for their mother church, where the Gospel shines in its greatest purity and lustre." (Swift's note, 1720.)

p. 114 *a contrivance for carrying and preserving winds*: cf. *The Odyssey*, X, 19ff.

p. 114 *Pancirolus*: Guido Panciroli (1523–99). The work Swift refers to in his footnote was published in the year of Panciroli's death.

p. 114 *barrels*: "Many dissenters, affecting extraordinary plainness and simplicity, have their pulpits of a figure not unlike a barrel or tub." (Swift's note, 1720.)

p. 114 *ex adytis et penetralibus*: out from the inmost recess. Virgil, *Aeneid* II, 297.

p. 116 *chameleon*: the meaning of this passage remains unclear. Cf. Guthkelch and Nichol Smith, pp. 159–60.

p. 120 *corpora quæque ... coire*: any other bodies (Lucretius IV, 1065); the body seeks that by which the mind has been wounded with love (Lucretius IV, 1048); he stretches toward that body from which the impulse has radiated, and desires to be sexually united with it (Lucretius IV, 1055).

p. 120 *Teterrima belli causa*: the most fearful cause of war. Horace, in his *Satires*, I, iii, 107, observes that before Helen's time there was many a woman who was the dismal cause of war. The word "cunnus" was excised from the quotation in the edition of 1710.

p. 120 *a mighty king*: "Lewis XIV." (Swift's note, 1720.)

p. 120 *page 160*: p. 112 in the present edition.

p. 121 *clinanima*: the word was used by Lucretius and Epicurus to mean the bias of atoms as they deviate from a straight line, and, by extension, the origins of free will.

p. 122 *Est quod gaudeas te in ista loca venisse, ubi aliquid sapere viderere*: it should please you to have come to the very place in which anyone may seem wise. Cicero, *Familiar Epistles*, VII, 10.

p. 123 *Jack of Leyden*: i.e. John of Leyden, or Jan Beuckelson or Bockhold (1509–36), the Dutch Anabaptist who in 1534 established a short-lived "kingdom of Zion" in Münster, with polygamy and common ownership of goods, but was tortured to death when the city was recaptured from the rebels the following year.

p. 127 *ingenium par negotiis*: a temper equal to public affairs. Swift slightly misquotes from the *Annals* of Tacitus, VI, 39 and XVI, 18.

p. 128 *Sir Edward Seymour ... John Howe*: leading Tory politicians of the day.

p. 128 *Bedlam*: originally a priory, St. Mary of Bethlehem by Bishopsgate in London, and in Swift's time at Moorfields (cf. p. 133), was a lunatic asylum. Swift's reference to "parts adjacent" is a glance at Grub Street and Gresham College (cf. note to p. 49), both of which were nearby.

p. 130 *the society of Warwick Lane*: the Royal College of Physicians was in Warwick Lane until 1825.

p. 135 *page 96*: p. 77 in the present edition.

p. 136 *seven ample commentaries on this comprehensive discourse*: "This alludes to the story of the seventy interpreters." (Swift's note, 1720.)

p. 137 *à cujus lacrymis ... mobilis*: from whose tears proceeds a moist substance, from whose laughter a lucid substance, from whose sorrow a solid substance, and from whose terror a movable substance.

p. 138 *page 96*: p. 77 in the present edition.

p. 140 *the universal medicine*: "This is a just banter on the superstitious veneration for the Bible, that most dissenters show on all occasions." (Swift's note, 1720.)

p. 140 *which seemed to forbid it*: "See Math. XV. 17, 18, 19 & Mark VII. 15. These or such like passages being foolishly applied, might give occasion to this banter." (Swift's note, 1734.)

p. 141 *It was ordained*: "Predestination, the favourite doctrine of most dissenters, is here exposed. Dr. Wotton calls this a direct profanation of the majesty of God." (Swift's note, 1720.)

p. 142 *an ancient temple of Gothic structure*: Stonehenge. "Gothic" here means barbarous. Theories of the origins of Stonehenge varied widely in Swift's time.

p. 143 *the Spanish accomplishment of braying*: cf. Cervantes' *Don Quixote*, II, 25 and 27.

p. 143 *feared no colours*: the phrase means "feared no enemy", but Swift punningly combines this with the meaning of a painter's colours.

p. 147 *Effugiet tamen hæc sceleratus vincula Proteus*: that slippery Proteus can't be tied down (Niall Rudd). Horace, *Satires*, II, iii, 71.

p. 148 *the six senses*: the sixth sense identified by Julius Caesar

Scaliger (1484–1558) in his *De Subtilitate* (1557), according to Burton in the *Anatomy of Melancholy*, was simply that of "titillation".

p. 149 *trepan*: dupe. A sponging-house was a place of preliminary detention for debtors.

p. 149 *a fair pair of heels*: "This alludes to K. James's dispensing with the penal laws against Papists and Protestant dissenters, & granting full liberty to both; which made the Church of England turn against him, & join with K. William; after which the Rom. Catholics were restrained again, but a toleration was granted to the Protestant dissenters, to the great regret & offence of many churchmen." (Swift's note, 1720.)

p. 152 *ut plenus vitæ conviva*: like a banqueter filled with life. Lucretius III, 938.

p. 153 *a very polite nation in Greece*: for this allusion, Swift draws on Pausanias II, 31, 5.

THE BATTLE OF THE BOOKS

p. 157 *of the same author*: i.e. by the same author as *A Tale of a Tub*.

p. 161 *Parnassus*: the Greek mountain sacred to Apollo and the Muses was often described as having two peaks, since the waters of the Castalian spring flowed between them, but in fact the true summit is hundreds of metres higher.

p. 164 *guardian of the regal library*: Bentley. Cf. note to p. 15.

p. 165 *Withers*: i.e. the poet George Wither (1588–1667).

p. 166 *the more ancient of the two*: in adding his side-note pointing to "the modern paradox", Swift had Wotton and Bentley in mind, but Guthkelch and Nichol Smith cite Fontenelle and Perrault in France, and in Britain Hobbes and Bacon, the latter (in *The Advancement of Learning*) to this effect: "These times are the ancient times, when the world is ancient, and not those which

248

we account ancient *ordine retrogrado*, by a computation backward from ourselves."

p. 171 *light-horse*: evidently the poets. The bowmen are
philosophers, the stinkpot-flingers chemists, the
dragoons medical scientists, the heavy-armed foot
historians, and the engineers mathematicians. For a
detailed account of the combatants, see Guthkelch and
Nichol Smith (pp. 235–8).

p. 174 *staid not for an answer*: cf. the opening of Bacon's
essay 'Of Truth': "What is Truth, said jesting Pilate, and
would not stay for an answer."

p. 178 *lady*: a hard part of a lobster's stomach.

p. 178 *Blackmore*: the poet and doctor Sir Richard Blackmore
(c. 1650–1729).

p. 179 *Ogleby*: John Ogleby (1600–76) produced translations
of Virgil and Homer described by Guthkelch and Nichol
Smith as "chiefly remarkable for their excellent printing
and paper and illustrations".

p. 179 *Oldham ... Afra the Amazon*: the satirist John Oldham
(1653–83) and novelist and dramatist Aphra Behn
(1640–89).

p. 180 *atramentous*: inky-black.

p. 181 *Scaliger*: here, presumably the father of Julius Caesar
Scaliger (cf. note to p. 148), Joseph Justus Scaliger
(1540–1609), widely considered the greatest scholar of
the Renaissance and the founder of historical criticism.

p. 182 *Aldrovandus*: Ulisse Aldrovandi (1522–1605), Italian
natural historian.

p. 182 *bull*: the brazen bull in which the victims of Phalaris
were roasted.

AN ARGUMENT [AGAINST ABOLISHING CHRISTIANITY]

p. 189 *the Union*: i.e. the Act of Union of 1707, which politically
united England and Scotland.

p. 190 *Horace*: cf. *Epodes* 16.

p. 191 *deorum offensa diis curæ*: an offence to the gods is the concern of the gods. Slightly misquoted from Tacitus, *Annals* I, 73.

p. 192 *Asgill, Tindall, Toland, Coward*: John Asgill, Matthew Tindall, John Toland and William Coward, theological writers who challenged Christian orthodoxy.

p. 192 *an old dormant statute or two*: the Test Acts designed to exclude Roman Catholics and Protestant non-conformists from public office. A number of acts passed in the period 1661 to 1681 were meant by the term; the Test Act of 1673 prescribed that all holders of civil and military office must be communicants of the Church of England.

p. 192 *Epsom and Dudley*: agents of Henry VII, notorious for reviving obsolete legislation in order to raise revenue.

p. 195 *heydukes*: in some parts of eastern Europe, brigands; in Poland, liveried personal attendants of noblemen.

p. 195 *patshaws*: properly *padishah*, a Persian title meaning "great king".

p. 195 *Margarita ... Mrs. Tofts ... Valentini*: fashionable singers of the day.

p. 199 *the sacramental test*: cf. note to p. 192.

p. 200 *author*: Matthew Tindall.

A MODEST PROPOSAL

p. 209 *Psalmanazar*: George Psalmanazar (?1679-1763), a literary impostor from France, author of a *Description of Formosa* (1704) and of memoirs.

p. 212 *the Jews ... the very moment their city was taken*: for faction and strife before the fall of Jerusalem, see Josephus, *The Jewish War*.

A TRUE AND FAITHFUL NARRATIVE

p. 217 *Mr. Whiston*: William Whiston (1667–1752), founder of a religious society (in 1717), lectured throughout Britain on the Second Coming, which he predicted for 1766.

p. 222 *Taylor's Holy Living and Dying*: *The Rule and Exercises of Holy Living* (1650) and *The Rule and Exercises of Holy Living* (1651) by Jeremy Taylor (1613–67) were often bound in a single volume under the title given by Swift.

p. 225 *Dr. Mandeville*: Bernard de Mandeville (1670–1733), physician and author, whose *The Fable of the Bees* (1714/1723) argued against optimistic views of society as an altruistic enterprise.